OFF
the
Air

OFF
the
Air

CHRISTINA ESTES

MINOTAUR BOOKS
NEW YORK

First published in the United States by Minotaur Books, an imprint of St. Martin's Publishing Group

OFF THE AIR. Copyright © 2024 by Christina Estes. All rights reserved. Printed in the United States of America. For information, address St. Martin's Publishing Group, 120 Broadway, New York, NY 10271.

www.minotaurbooks.com

Design by Meryl Sussman Levavi

Library of Congress Cataloging-in-Publication Data

Names: Estes, Christina, author.
Title: Off the air / Christina Estes.
Description: First edition. | New York : Minotaur Books, 2024.
Identifiers: LCCN 2023036542 | ISBN 9781250863850 (hardcover) ISBN 9781250863867 (ebook)
Subjects: LCGFT: Novels. | Detective and mystery fiction.
Classification: LCC PS3605.S7325 O34 2024 | DDC 813/.6— dc23/eng/20231004
LC record available at https://lccn.loc.gov/2023036542

Our books may be purchased in bulk for promotional, educational, or business use. Please contact your local bookseller or the Macmillan Corporate and Premium Sales Department at 1-800-221-7945, extension 5442, or by email at MacmillanSpecialMarkets@macmillan.com.

First Edition: 2024

10 9 8 7 6 5 4 3 2 1

DS and DE,

No matter how old you get, you'll forever
be my bedtime-story buddies.

I love you always, no matter what.

AUTHOR'S NOTE

Inspiration for this novel comes from my professional experience as a reporter and personal experience as a former foster parent. Both worlds bring joy and pain, which appear on these pages. The writing explores themes around neglect and abandonment. A content advisory can be found at the end of the book.

Social media plays a prominent role in many reporters' jobs. Keeping up with the latest platforms and features can be dizzying in real life and in fiction. As *Off the Air* entered final production stages, Twitter experienced changes. Rather than continuously edit the story until it went to press, with no guarantee it would be accurate at publication, I kept the original Twitter references. Thank you for understanding.

PHOENIX, ARIZONA

When most people think of Larry Lemmon, they remember the guy who called for a wall along the U.S.–Mexico border long before Donald Trump did. When I think of Larry Lemmon, I remember the guy who cut my lunch—and nearly my life—short.

Legally speaking, Larry turned out to be a victim. But not in everyone's eyes.

CHAPTER

1

"I'd like a cheeseburger with extra guacamole and—"

"Extra guac is a dollar," barks the man behind the counter.

"Sure, no problem." I force a smile, recalling one of the most valuable lessons I picked up waiting tables in college: never piss off the people who handle your food.

But the effort is wasted. The namesake behind Ben's Burgers never shifts his eyes from a grease-stained notepad.

"That all?"

It's more of a challenge than a question.

"Can I also get a large order of fries and a Pepsi?"

"No Pepsi. Coke."

And still no eye contact. My voice says, "That's fine," while my mind says, "Why am I giving money to this jerk?"

When Nate asks to change his order, Ben's gray hair shoots up like a pigeon. Eyes the color of mashed peas peer over clunky frames. He sighs so hard garlic smacks my face.

"You know what?" Nate says. "I'm good."

I marvel at the line stretching out the door. When it opened two months ago, a reviewer for the *Phoenix New Times* gave Ben kudos for using Arizona beef. That was enough to attract the "Buy local, eat local" crowd. Then, *Phoenix* magazine seduced old schoolers yearning for simpler times and young creatives craving a taste of *Seinfeld* by highlighting the differences between Ben and his downtown neighbors. Nestled between a vegan restaurant where orders are placed via iPads and a craft brewery where beer flights are paid by phone, you'll find Mr. Cash Only. No touchscreens, no sample-size drinks, and no gluten-free buns.

"Give it a chance," Nate says while squirting ketchup into a cup. "Everyone in the newsroom raves about the burgers."

"Can't be the service." I grab napkins and follow him to a crumb-coated table with wobbly legs and mismatched chairs. "Or the décor."

White walls, as frosty as the owner, provide a backdrop for posters of Central Park, the Empire State Building, and the Statue of Liberty. Across the menu board, a string of Yankees pennants hangs a safe distance from oil splatters. Maybe the New York vibe fills a void for some customers. Phoenix doesn't get as many East Coast transplants as it does Midwesterners and Canadians. For decades, Major League Baseball fans from Illinois, Wisconsin, Ohio, and Missouri have cheered on their teams at spring training games in Arizona, while their northern neighbors hosted the Great Canadian Picnic during the winter at South Mountain Park.

With October approaching, Arizonans will observe the end of triple-digit temperatures in their own ways. Some will return to hiking trails, others will unpack patio furniture, and the fashion-conscious will debate when it's acceptable to bring out boots. Everyone relishes the respite from air-conditioning bills. If you ever hear a Phoenician claim it's only hot in July and August, know you're dealing with someone who considers the teens hot—that's teens, plus a hundred degrees. Despite diverse weather interpretations—and demographics and political opinions—there's universal consensus this time of year that the worst is behind us.

Nate lines up his plastic utensils, napkins, and condiments as precisely as he does his tripod, lights, and camera. "What's the plan?"

"We can hit strip malls and get video of cars with out-of-state license plates. Then, play it by ear."

People who move to Arizona are often surprised by how much it costs to register their cars. Many states charge flat fees based on a vehicle's size, so someone with a ten-year old Camry pays the same as someone with a new Camry. Arizona's fee includes a tax based on a vehicle's assessed value, easily several hundred dollars for newer cars.

"How many snowbirds you think we'll find?" Nate asks.

"September's kinda early to flock here. I don't think it's even snowed yet in Canada."

"Isn't it always snowing somewhere in Canada?"

"Now you sound like New Yorkers who think it's always hot in Arizona."

"I think snowbirds—whether they're Canadians or Midwesterners—will be our best bet for the story."

To get around paying high registration fees, people can use out-of-state addresses. It's legal if they spend less than half the year in Arizona, but some scam the system. Nate Thompson and I are pursuing these "scofflaws," as the managers at our TV station have dubbed them.

"How about this? If we see someone with an out-of-state license plate I'll walk up, explain we're doing a story about car registration costs, and ask if they'll talk to us."

Nate cocks his head. "You think someone who lives here but doesn't register their car here and knowingly breaks the law will go on camera?"

"Come on, you know how it is. Everyone likes to complain about the government taking too much of their money. Get certain people talking and they don't stop."

I'm not ecstatic about the assignment, but it's the first in my hybrid role, which does excite me. I spend half the week as a general assignment reporter—covering anything from a dust storm during monsoon season to a newborn giraffe at the zoo— and the rest of the week on special projects, stories that take more time to research and produce and that get more air time. The switch away from full-time GA reporting came after my investigation into dangerous working conditions for Phoenix park rangers. I interviewed a ranger who tried to break up a trash-talking match during an adult softball game and ended up with a bloody nose. Another ranger quit after being ordered not to call the police on people using drugs in parks.

"My supervisor said I could request they quit using and then I was supposed to leave," he said. "I understand parks are public spaces, open to everyone, but children should be able to use the playground without stepping on needles. Sure, I can call the Human Services Department when there's drug activity, but the reality is they'll never respond the same day. The problem is too big and resources are too small."

Another ranger left after someone rammed a needle in her arm. She took a job in a small suburb where rangers are encouraged to call the police for help. After six months on the job, she hasn't had to. As a result of my story, Phoenix sent more behavioral health specialists offering services and treatment options to parks with the most complaints.

The story ignited intense comments from across the board: people appalled to learn about drug activity in parks to people concerned about criminalizing substance use disorders. After reading the emails and social media comments, my news director—who initially yawned when I pitched the story—perked up like someone had slipped him the winning lottery numbers. Attention is the drug of choice in local news.

A voice brimming with irritation erupts through an overhead speaker.

"Order forty-six, you're up! Forty-six!"

"Don't want to keep the king of customer service waiting." I leap up, knock the table's corner, and nearly topple our drinks. "Ope, sorry. Give me your receipt and I'll get your order."

I maneuver past a party of selfie photo takers and press through a pack of people circling the counter. A hefty heel smashes my foot and, for the thousandth time, I silently thank my grandma for passing along her sensible shoe trait. When I reach the front, Nate's food is also ready and, to demonstrate I can play by his rules, I present both receipts to Ben. He ignores them, shoves two trays at me, turns his back, and grumbles a number into a microphone.

Calling on another food service skill, I heft the trays, peek over my shoulder, and bellow, "Coming through!"

People split into two camps: ones trying too hard to fake interest and others reacting with "oohs" you hear at a fireworks display.

Nate paws a burger. "I'm starving."

But before we can take a bite, Alex Klotzman sends a text.

901-H. Need u 2 go.

Alex is our assignment editor and loves to talk and text in police code. I show Nate my phone. He nods and peels back foil, releasing a waft of bacon.

"A wise photographer once told me there's always time to eat." A toasted bun cradles his double patty showered in cheese. "A dead body's not moving right away. We can take five minutes to recharge so we can do our jobs."

My teeth scrape my lower lip.

"C'mon," Nate says. "Remember the last time they interrupted our lunch? Had to rush to the neighborhood fire."

It turned out to be kids lighting smoke bombs in an alley. I set the phone down and Nate tips his burger. "Bon appétit."

As I cram three fries into my mouth, a new text appears.

At KFRK. No ID yet.

I pound the table, point to my phone, and cover my mouth to avoid spraying partially chewed potatoes. "We gotta go! It's Larry Lemmon's station!"

Depending on how Nielsen ratings are dissected—and whether you believe his station's promotions—Larry Lemmon has the most popular radio show in the nation's fifth-largest city.

Nate swallows, holds up a finger, and inhales another bite.

"C'mon! You can have mine on the way."

I stack fries on my wrapped burger using condiment tubs as a buttress. Forgetting a key lesson from Restaurant 101, I whip around and slam into a guy slipping between tables. Ketchup splashes my favorite blue shirt.

Annoying. But that will soon be the least of my concerns.

CHAPTER

2

Nate and I cut through a clump of customers unaware of a potentially major story unfolding in their city.

Wiping ketchup off my shirt produces purple smears. "Can you work some photog magic on these stains?"

"No problem. I can make them disappear by framing your face extra close."

"Very funny but not what I had in mind."

We scramble out the door and what I see next stops me dead, every muscle freezing.

"It's okay, Jolene."

Nate's words are barely audible over the hammering of my heart.

"He can't touch you. He's tied to the post." Nate hooks an arm through mine and pulls me along. "Maybe you should talk to a professional. You really need to get over your fear."

"It's not all dogs." A backward glance reveals a dark mask around its eyes, drool dripping from a tongue the size of my hand. "Just the big ones, the ones that can rip you in half."

Now it's Nate's turn to brake. "Jolene, it's a Saint Bernard. They're known as gentle giants."

"Key word is 'giant.'"

At least we're riding in Live Seven. Or Lucky Seven, as Nate calls it, since it survived last summer without overheating or flipping over. Unlike Live Six, which blew a tire and careened on Interstate 10, almost crashing into a cable barrier. Or Live Eight, which nearly sent a crew to the hospital with heat exhaustion after the air conditioner conked out during record heat. Our station uses numbers to identify trucks with editing equipment and a microwave. The microwave isn't for popcorn—it's to send a signal to the station to establish a live shot. While the scent of popcorn occasionally drifts through the truck, it more often reeks of a rotten banana, stale French fries, or rancid salad left in an open trash bin.

After Nate checks the side mirror and pulls away from the curb, I flip the radio to KFRK. It's on the air but with no host and no commercials. Instead, the station is playing public service announcements. Stations run PSAs when they can't sell the time to advertisers—mainly weekends, holidays, and late nights.

A light-rail train passes us, its center section advertising KFRK as "Real talk for real Americans." As we head north on Central Avenue, I put Alex on speakerphone to fill us in.

"Initial scanner traffic referenced a 901-H at an office building. No mention of foul play, only someone collapsed and died. Then I hear, 'PIO en route,' so I check out the building. It houses KFRK."

"But you don't know if the body is at the station? It could be another business, right?"

"That's why we're sending you guys."

Nate and I exchange a look over background babble. We know what's coming before it's out of Alex's mouth.

"David says make sure you tweet."

As the newsroom's executive producer, David Matthew is responsible for content. He decides which stories will make air and which will not. Sometimes we call him "Sexy." Not because he's sexy, but because that's his favorite word. David's constantly asking if a story is sexy. He's never truly defined it, but it's guaranteed to make TMZ's website over a city council agenda.

"Tell Sexy I'll tweet as soon as I have information."

"Have you logged your interview with Larry Lemmon?"

"Not yet. There was no rush because the managers wanted to hold it while they worked with promotions to schedule an air date."

I interviewed the talk show host last week. He was the first in what the station plans to make an ongoing series called "Arizona Newsmakers."

Alex says he'll get someone to transcribe Larry's interview and email the notes. "If this turns out to be Larry Lemmon, you'll be the reporter who conducted his final interview."

A butterfly takes flight in my stomach, its wings flapping frantically.

"Every media outlet in the country will want your interview."

Calm down, butterfly. It could be anyone. But the butterfly's not listening.

"What's your ETA?" Alex asks.

"About ten minutes away."

Rubbing my stomach does nothing to quiet the butterfly as we head east on Camelback Road. It's named after the mountain that resembles a camel lying down, but today all I can see is an Emmy statuette. If it turns out Larry is dead, it could finally be my time to revel in the phrase, "And the Emmy goes to Jolene Garcia." Last year, I flinched hearing, "And the Emmy goes to Jessica 'JJ' Jackson." I tried a poker face, but my colleague's kick under the table indicated I had failed. My Emmy-nominated story featured neighbors showing up with balloons, party hats, and sparkling grape juice to commemorate the demolition of a former Omelet Manor. Four years earlier, the restaurant had closed, and when nothing replaced it, weeds grew, trash piled up, and people broke in. Someone set a fire in the dining area that destroyed half the building. After the owner snubbed notices to either clean up the property or tear it down, a judge gave the city approval to demolish it, and neighbors organized a watch party in the parking lot. The space is now home to a community garden and farmer's market. JJ's Emmy Award–winning story was about bubble wrap day at Chase Field, where the Arizona Diamondbacks play baseball. I'll never pop bubble wrap again.

Nate taps my shoulder, a signal to quit biting my fingernails. The taps are lighter and less frequent than when he started. Back then he spent half the day slugging me. It worked though. Instead of ripping nails off daily, I only munch on a thumbnail when highly stressed.

"Did you know Larry Lemmon spoke at my church about a year ago?"

My thumb comes out and my eyebrows go up. When it comes to Christianity, Nate plays for the progressive team.

"It was dubbed a community conversation about immigration. My church invited representatives from different groups to take part in a panel discussion. Larry was pretty intense about increasing security."

"When I interviewed him, he spoke fondly about starting the original 'Build the Wall' movement in southern Arizona. Even though there's been metal fencing in some areas longer than you and I've been alive, Larry pushed for a solid wall to run the entire length of the border. His listeners there loved it."

"Like they do here." Nate points to a pickup truck the color of bones.

An American flag decal covers the cab window of a Ford F-350. On the rear bumper, a sticker touts a lifelong National Rifle Association membership next to one that shouts, LET'S GO,

BRANDON. On the opposite side, a sticker proclaims, FREAKS LOVE LARRY.

The station's call letters, KFRK, became an easy target for critics who labeled listeners "Freaks." Larry jumped on it and claimed ownership. In a show of solidarity, he started calling his audience members freaks. It's grown into a badge of honor for loyal listeners and a steady revenue stream of buttons, hats, and shirts for Larry's station. As we pull into the parking lot at KFRK, we encounter another group of freaks: the media.

"Glad we're not the last ones here," Nate says.

Two English-language and two Spanish-language network affiliates beat us to the scene. That leaves one English TV station to show up. The thought of Jessica "JJ" Jackson forced to play catch-up makes me smile.

Nate cruises past a three-story building and eases into a spot next to Telemundo's truck. Not so close to the action we'll be asked to back up and not so far that we'll miss something. I wave to Mirna Esteban, who's sitting in the passenger seat of Telemundo's truck. She hops out with the ease and confidence of a male TV reporter. Mirna is the Hillary Clinton and Kamala Harris of Phoenix reporters, a long-standing member of the Pantsuit Nation. With a dozen more years of experience than most reporters in the market, Mirna doesn't feel the need to pose in trendy dresses on Instagram. But she admits a weakness for necklaces. They don't have to be expensive, she says, just have estilo. Today's centerpiece is a champagne bottle glistening with pink and gold beads.

"Hola," Mirna says. "It's been a while. How are you?"

"Bien. And you?"

"Muy bien. The public information officer isn't here yet and no one's talking, so we don't know if it was Larry Lemmon."

Nate grabs his camera and tripod and hands me the microphone, a trademark move that makes him a favorite among reporters. Not everyone understands audio can be as riveting as video—sometimes more. Paying attention to what's happening outside the viewfinder could be the deciding factor between an Emmy-nominated and Emmy-winning story. I turn on the mic, Nate pushes an earbud in, and nods for me to begin.

"Test, one, two, three, four, five."

"Sounds good," he says and hustles off.

I count fifteen people scattered across the parking lot, along with two marked police cars, an ambulance, and one local reporting legend. It's unusual for Scott Yang to respond to breaking news, but the never-ending flow of cutbacks keeps forcing reporters to take on extra assignments. Quantity, not quality, is the corporate mantra.

Scott is called the grandfather of Phoenix journalism. Some use it in a snarky way because he's in his sixties, not that into social media, and takes notes using paper and pen—never a phone. Others refer to Scott as the grandfather because of his market knowledge. No reporter knows the political movers and shakers in Arizona better than Scott. No one even comes close. Occasionally, the twenty-nine-year-old me takes the snarky view, but mostly the reporter in me respects Scott and wishes the industry viewed his experience as an asset, not a liability. Some days I wonder if local news will exist when I'm his age.

"There goes abuelo," Mirna says. "Will he be successful?"

We watch Scott approach two men who fit the radio mold. A middle-aged white guy wearing khakis who looks like he's hiding a pumpkin under his shirt. He yanks at orange fabric but the polo falls back over his belly. Standing next to Khakis is a guy half his age. Could be his first professional radio job, though you can't tell from the way he's dressed. Blue jeans and a black T-shirt with a neon-green image that, from my vantage point, could pass for vomit. Flip-flops on his feet might be a sign he's clinging to summer or believes casual Friday should be observed every day.

"It's not looking good," Mirna says.

Flip-Flops shakes his head when Scott tries to hand him a business card. Scott waves the card at Khakis, who then waves a finger in Scott's face. It's the index finger, but speaks like the middle finger. Scott's arms flutter like a tennis player challenging a line umpire's call before backing off in defeat.

When I started reporting in Phoenix, Nate offered priceless advice: "If you ever show up to a scene clueless or don't know who to talk to, just follow Scott. Do what he does." It's advice Mirna and I practice by joining Scott when he arrives at our self-designated media section. He removes eyeglasses, blows on the lenses, and slips them back on, the wire frames blending into bushy brows.

"Those guys were talking to cops, but they didn't want to talk to me. The PIO should be here anytime. You know what that means."

"You really think it's Larry Lemmon?" Mirna asks. "There must be a lot of people who work here."

"Massage franchise is on the first floor," Scott says. "Real estate agents on the second, and the radio station takes up the top floor. Actually, it houses three stations: what they call 'oldies'— for my generation—a hip-hop station, and KFRK. Quite the assortment, I'd say."

Mirna asks if anyone has seen a reporter from Larry's station and I shake my head. "They eliminated the local news department. Penny-pinchers at corporate figured when something serious happens locally, the show hosts will take care of it."

"But talk show hosts are paid to give their opinions," she says. "News reporting is supposed to be objective."

Scott makes a sound that's a little laugh, a lot of scorn. "Listen, I know you guys are younger than me, but you can't be that naïve. No one cares about covering issues that impact the community. It's just a memory for us old-timers to cherish. Now, it's all about posting cat videos or whatever the hell the digital department thinks will generate clicks."

I steer Scott back on track before he dives too deep into his frequent dissertation on why newsrooms should be run as non-profits and not part of a company's profit-making portfolio.

"You talk to anyone who works at the station?"

"See the woman in all black?" He points to someone performing exuberant hand gestures. "Talking to the redhead and the man in the suit? They work at the station. At least the woman in black does, based on this."

He draws a card from his back pocket. SHANA FORREST, KFRK PROGRAM DIRECTOR.

By far, she's the most animated. Redhead stays silent while the man's fingers graze her shoulder. Shana's hands collapse and she turns to watch the men who shooed Scott away. They're talking to an officer who's scribbling on a clipboard.

"What's the deal with the people Shana's talking to?"

"Don't know," Scott says. "She's the only one who opened her mouth. And that was just to tell me they're not talking."

Maybe they're not talking but I can listen. As Scott and Mirna vent their frustrations, I move away, check to make sure the mic is on, hide it behind a notepad, and alert Nate.

"Can you hear me? I'm going to try to talk to the station's program director."

He spins around and gives a thumbs-up.

"Thanks. Hold back unless it sounds like someone will do an interview."

Not going too fast or too slow, I aim for curious bystander, not vulture. But halfway there, my eyes lock on promising prey. A knot of four people fills a carless parking space. I smile at a woman holding a Harlow's Café bag.

"How was lunch?"

"Lunch was breakfast. Dinner will be too, courtesy of Eggs Maximilian."

"Way better than the handful of fries I scarfed down." I introduce myself and ask if they know what happened.

Egg woman says, "We came back from lunch and police asked us to wait outside. Said paramedics might have to bring someone out and they want to keep the route clear."

"What floor do you work on?"

"Second."

"All of you?"

"Yeah. Sounds like someone on the third floor's in bad shape. That's all we know."

I thank them and resume course, twisting my station badge to hide PRESS. With my phone clamped on an ear, I pretend to be engrossed in conversation, tilting the other ear toward Shana, who's saying she needs to get a host on the air.

"We're running a military tribute we've been saving for Veteran's Day. There's only twenty minutes left before we have dead air."

Redhead whimpers and buries her face in the man's chest.

"Ooh, sorry," Shana says. "Poor word choice."

The man wraps an arm around Redhead's shoulders and says, "I'm willing to help any way I can."

"Thank you, Darrell. I'll need you to fill in more than you have been."

My breath comes out in a thick whoosh. It must be Larry! This is going to be big. So big that I retreat and call the dreaded producer hotline. It's supposed to be more efficient because everyone can get on the same line at the same time and get the same information. But often the more people involved, the more comments.

"Everyone's here," Alex announces. "Go ahead, Jolene."

"Still waiting for the PIO to arrive, but I just overheard a conversation with the program director and sounds like it's Larry Lemmon."

"Then why haven't I seen any social media posts?" David asks. "And we need details to write the breaking news story for the website."

"You haven't seen anything because I haven't posted anything. We're talking about someone who died."

"But you have a sexy scene, right? Confused people locked out of their offices as first responders descend on a building where one of the country's most controversial talk show hosts has died—or may have died."

"Getting it right is more important than getting it first."

Shame sears my face as I repeat the admonition directed at me when I worked in Omaha. It was a horrible mistake. But it was avoidable. And it was all my fault. A dream job had opened in Minneapolis at a station that not only claimed to care about journalism but proved it with thoughtful reporting and resources. With an interview three days out, I was hyper-focused on setting myself apart from the other candidates. Showing up to a top-market newsroom and saying, "I just broke a major story," would do it.

When my station learned a renowned chef had been critically hurt in a car crash, I was assigned a hospital live shot. Ten minutes before the final evening newscast, a spokesperson told us no information would be released until morning. As reporters commiserated, I sought comfort at a vending machine. Like a trusted friend, the Pepsi logo beckoned me. The bottle stepped forward and toppled three rows to my welcoming hand. The cap was tighter than normal, its rough ridges fought my fingers, and I wrapped my shirt around it.

"Need some help?"

The voice behind me belonged to a guy in his thirties wearing a flannel shirt and smelling of Marlboro cigarettes. Or what I imagined Marlboros smelled like.

A psst sound escaped from the cap. "Got it."

"You're a reporter, right? Covering the crash?"

"Yes."

He introduced himself as the chef's brother and told me the king of Omaha barbecue had never regained consciousness and died an hour earlier. The brother didn't want to go on camera but accepted my card, said the family would talk the next day, and promised to be in touch. The Pepsi tasted extra sweet as I toasted my good fortune. Five minutes before the newscast, I tweeted the exclusive information and called the producer. He rewrote the script so the anchor announced the chef's death and tossed to me by asking what the family had shared. I finished the live shot saying we expected to hear more from the chef's brother soon.

I never heard from the chef's brother. Because the chef had no brother. But he had two sisters. Both noted my error by calling the station and using words not allowed on the air. Turns out the chef had suffered a mild concussion, bruised ribs, and a broken arm and would be going home in the morning. My station apologized and ran corrections on the air and social media sites. I did the same on Twitter, which triggered an avalanche of outrage from anyone who'd ever watched a local newscast. To this day, my screwup post has achieved the most impressions on my account, while my apology has garnered the highest engagement rate—light on likes, heavy on criticism. I spent hours scrolling comments and checking profiles to find the guy who duped me. Never did.

Sometimes I think I should've brushed aside journalistic ethics and simply deleted the tweets. By keeping them public and acknowledging the mistake (I know "mistake" is a soft word but that's what it was), the newsroom managers in Minneapolis were compelled to act. Which is what led the assistant news director to call and say they'd canceled my plane ticket and interview. She suggested I gain more experience before moving up. I will never repeat that blunder.

"David, I just called to give you guys a heads-up."

"At the very least you should tweet what you're seeing and post on Insta."

"I'm not on Instagram. Listen, we've been here less than fifteen minutes, Nate's shooting video, and I'm trying to talk to people, but we don't have official word on anything at this point."

"We can't wait for the official word. Other reporters are posting what's going on. Geez, do I have to send you step-by-step instructions?"

"Okay everyone, let's calm down," Alex says. "Jolene, we'll watch for updates through your texts, calls, tweets, or whatever you can handle. If it turns out to be Larry, we'll want you live in all the shows."

"Got it. And gotta run. The PIO's here."

CHAPTER

3

After I hang up with the producers, Nate meets me at the media staging area. Still no sign of JJ, thankfully. As everyone jostles for position, the PIO raises his hands like it's a stickup. "No rush, guys. I just got here. Give me a few minutes to get briefed and I'll be back."

Mirna points to the building's entrance. "Look."

Every camera and phone pivots ninety degrees to record paramedics emerging through double doors with a gurney. An empty gurney. When the male medic notices an audience, he slows his stroll and his female partner copies. Their relaxed pace provides us fifteen seconds of video before they stop to lower the gurney's legs. A wheeze erupts from the hydraulic system, silencing most conversations but not all communication. Cameras click and phones clack as medics slide the gurney into an ambulance, slam the doors, and take off.

As I compose a tweet that won't come back to haunt me, a demon appears.

"Hey, Jolene, what'd I miss?"

Ignoring the bleached blonde who sidled next to me is futile. When JJ arrives late to a scene, she does not accept rejection from other reporters. On the positive side, she's not bright enough to do a whole lot with whatever you give her, so it's usually best to play along and get her out of the way as fast as possible.

"Eww." JJ points a gold-colored fingernail at my chest. "What happened to your shirt?"

"It's nothing."

"Looks like blood." She sniffs. "Is that ketchup?" Her perfect nose wiggles. "And onions?"

I refuse to bite. "The PIO should have an update in a minute."

"That's what they always say and then they keep us waiting for hours." She flicks imaginary lint off her ruby dress. "You know, you have plenty of time to run to the station and get a clean shirt."

Weak, I think, even for JJ. "I'm staying until we find out who died."

Bright indigo eyes scan my boring brown ones. "My producers think it's Larry Lemmon. If it is, this story's going to explode and I'm going to be ready."

Being ready in JJ's mind means a fresh spray tan, full makeup, and a professional blow-dry. Growing up in Southern California, she appeared in commercials as a young child and, as a teenager, came close to landing a recurring spot on a daytime drama. After several years of falling short of regular roles—large or small—JJ's agent suggested she try TV news. In Los Angeles, there's often little distinction between acting and broadcast journalism.

In a move that would make David giddy, JJ opens a tote bag boasting initials I don't recognize, whips out a selfie stick, positions her phone, and presses a wireless remote.

"Hi, guys, it's JJ reporting live from Phoenix. See the building behind me? Inside are the studios for KFRK, where controversial talk show host Larry Lemmon works. But maybe no more. Why? We're hearing someone has died inside and I'm working to get answers. Keep following me for updates. Bye, for now."

A woman shuffles over to JJ. "Um, excuse me. What happened?"

"We don't know much right now, but see that officer coming our way? He should have answers for us. Be sure to follow me on Twitter, Insta, or Facebook."

Reporters stampede for spots nearest their photographers. There's some nudging as everyone huddles but no hard elbows. After six weeks in his role, the PIO is still figuring out who's who. But it didn't take long to learn the name of the reporter who strokes their egos the most.

"Hi, JJ, nice to see you again." He takes stock. "Everybody ready?"

Murmurs of agreement are drowned out by a plea. "Wait, please! ¡Un momento!"

Sergio Magaña, a reporter for Univision, is jogging while clutching a camera and hauling a tripod. "Hold on, por favor!"

He's covering this assignment solo, working as a multimedia journalist, or MMJ for short. In reality, we're all multimedia journalists because we tell stories through a combination of formats—video, audio, photos, and text—but somehow MMJ became code for stations to pay one person to do two jobs: reporting and writing and shooting and editing video. Part of the "do more with less" business model that took root like crabgrass during the Great Recession and can't be eradicated. As Sergio struggles to find space for his tripod, I can't help but sympathize. Not Mirna. She pinches her nose and waves a hand.

"El Fragrante wouldn't be late if he didn't spend so much time bathing in cologne."

To be fair, his affinity for Acqua Di Giò can induce nausea. Once Sergio's camera is set, the PIO begins.

"Okay, here's what I can tell you. Shortly before noon, a 911 call was made from this location. The caller reported a white male, approximately fifty years old, had collapsed and lost consciousness. Upon arrival, paramedics attempted to revive him. Their efforts were unsuccessful and they determined him to be clinically dead. We are currently waiting for the medical examiner's office to arrive and remove the body. That's all I have for now."

"Is it Larry Lemmon?" I ask.

"We are not releasing a name. Family members need to be notified first."

JJ cuts in. "Sources tell us it's Larry."

"I don't know who's telling you that. It's not the police department and we are the ones handling this investigation."

"Did it happen inside KFRK's studio?" I ask.

"I'm not going to reveal the location until family members have been notified."

"Can you say whether it happened on the third floor?" Scott asks.

"No."

"Do you mean no, it didn't happen on the third floor?"

"I mean no, I'm not going to say where the man collapsed."

"What kind of investigation is this exactly?" Mirna asks.

"We are treating this as a suspicious death."

"Suspicious like murder?"

"Suspicious like any other case where a death is unexpected and we don't know what caused it."

"We heard he collapsed during his show," JJ says. "Was he on the air at the time?"

"As I mentioned—"

"Was he talking about immigra—" Sergio asks.

"This is considered a suspicious death investigation because at this time we do not know the cause."

I lean into Nate and cup a hand around my mouth. "He didn't dispute the show reference. Must be Larry."

I point over the PIO's shoulder and ask about the two guys standing with the officer.

Without looking he says, "I don't know their names. I'm told they were in the area when the man collapsed."

"Can you find out? We'd like to talk to them."

"I'll ask, and if they're interested, I'll send them this way. All right, that's it, guys. You have all that's being released for now. I'll be back when I have more information."

As JJ reapplies lip gloss for her next social video, Nate asks if I'm ready for the onslaught of requests for my interview with Larry. Before I can respond, my phone trills.

Status? David wants posts ASAP.

I gather my long, flowy skirt, stuff it between my legs, and settle on the pavement. The sun's rays are like ice picks stabbing my eyes. Using the ground as a tripod and a hand to shade the camera lens, I find my go-to shot. It comes from viewing hours of Nate's raw video. Ninety percent of the time, he'll focus on an image and frame it off to the side. I fix on the police car, positioning it front and left with the building behind it. After tweeting the photo and basic details, I consider another angle of people waiting to get back into their offices. That's when I make out the woman who approached JJ before the briefing. Worn clothes, weathered skin, no makeup, and messy hair the color of dry dirt. Not the kind of mess some women spend time and money to achieve. Hers comes from a lack of grooming products and maintenance. I rise, prepared to find out her story. But the plan is thwarted by a man who cuts me off.

"I heard it was Larry Lemmon," he says.

"Where'd you hear that?"

"Receptionist on the third floor." He points to a woman standing with Flip-Flops and Khakis. "She was on her cell phone telling someone Larry collapsed during his show." He shakes his head. "It's tragic, man. He's one of the good guys."

"Do you know the people standing next to the receptionist?"

"No, but Darrell Arthur's over there." He motions to the man who's been comforting Redhead. "Darrell has a Saturday morning show and fills in for Larry when he's on vacation."

I thank him, conceal the mic between my chest and notepad, and whisper to Nate. "Be ready to move. Quietly."

I assess the competition. Scott's on the opposite side of the parking lot facing away from me, Mirna's gabbing on her phone, and Sergio's hanging out with photographers. Reporters from other stations are in their trucks—except for JJ. I nibble skin next to a thumbnail. Where is she? At the building's entrance, a door closes and a flash of red scatters like an alley cat. Did JJ get inside? A nub of flesh comes loose. What's she doing in there? Larry's co-workers are still by the squad car. But not the receptionist. Is that who JJ is talking to? No, no, no. She can't report Larry's death first. A thump on my shoulder brings me back.

"Hey, what's up?" Nate says. "Thought you were going to talk to someone."

"It's pointless now. JJ's interviewing the station's receptionist."

"No, she's not. She's across the street. At the coffee shop."

"Are you sure?"

"Go." His hand dismisses me. "I'll wait here."

"And distract JJ?"

"She's not here. Go. I'll be listening."

Rather than eavesdrop again, I apologize for interrupting the group's conversation and explain I'm seeking information.

"We all are," Darrell Arthur says. "Allow me to introduce you to—"

"Shana Forrest." She pounces, presents a firm handshake, and makes direct eye contact. "I'm program director. My pronouns are she/her."

What Shana doesn't say but conveys is she's the person who hires, fires, and makes deals.

"We're all in shock." She casts a sympathetic look at Redhead dabbing a tissue beneath swollen eyes. "It happened so fast. One minute Larry's doing what he does best. The next, he's on the floor."

I smother a whoop and raise the mic so Nate can catch the conversation. We need to get this on camera. No words will form until I clear my throat. "I'm sorry to hear that. Were you there?"

"No, I had an early lunch meeting." She waves behind me. "Ralph and Andy were with Larry when he collapsed. They're talking to the police."

"Did they tell you what happened?"

"Only that Larry seemed fine. He didn't get sick until shortly before he fell over and passed out."

Darrell acknowledges Redhead. "On more than one occasion Kelly and I suggested to Larry that he take better care of himself. Unfortunately, he smoked a pack of cigarettes a day and never exercised."

Redhead—aka Kelly—backs him up. "So sad. Larry loved his Whoppers and onion rings."

To prevent another crew catching me signaling for Nate, I remain still and try a telepathic message. To buy time and keep the group talking, I ask about Ralph's and Andy's roles. Shana says Ralph is Larry's producer and Andy runs the board. She reads the question in my eyes.

"The board operator makes sure the mics are on and off at the right times, commercials run when they're supposed to, and the music beds that play in and out of the breaks are smooth." She hikes a royal-blue Chanel bag over her shoulder. "If you'll excuse me, I've got to get back in there and make sure we stay on the air."

Before I can ask for an on-camera interview, Shana marches

away and a white Chevy cargo van arrives. Normally, it wouldn't attract attention, but this one has a Maricopa County seal on the side doors identifying the Office of Medical Examiner. It stops directly in front of the building. Nate and other photographers respond like kids to an ice cream truck. Hoisting cameras on shoulders, they abandon tripods and race to be first in line. From behind the wheel, a woman emerges keeping her head down. She meets the male passenger at the rear, where the buzz of cameras envelops them.

I excuse myself from Darrell and Kelly and speed walk to the van. I place my phone on a deserted tripod and start snapping. The gurney from the ME's office has no thick pad, just a black bag draped across an aluminum base. I crop a photo and compose a tweet based on advice my first news director jokingly dispensed. When faced with a deadline and uncertainty about a fact or figure, he said be either vaguely specific or specifically vague.

BREAKING: Source says #Phoenix talk show host Larry Lemmon collapsed at KFRK studio. Medical Examiner's Office on scene.

Twenty-five seconds later my phone rings.

"Way to go!" Alex says. "Who's your source?"

As I start to explain, others join the call. The four o'clock producer says an intern has finished logging my interview with Larry. "Check your email for the transcript."

Sexy wants me live in every show. "We're sending Gina to cover the nuts and bolts while you concentrate on your interview."

"Why can't I do both?"

"Because if this is Larry—"

"What do you mean 'if'? My tweet is accurate and attributed to a source."

David's displeasure rattles in my ears. "Hey, you're Ms. Let's Wait Until We Get Official Confirmation. Now, as I was saying, if it turns out Larry Lemmon is dead, we'll need team coverage. Your interview is the last one he gave. That puts us way ahead of the competition and we're going to stay there by maximizing our resources."

Another voice pipes up. It sounds like an adult attempting to reason with a toddler throwing a tantrum. "Hi, Jolene, it's Charlotte in the promotions department. We'd love you to shoot a stand-up tease and feed it back to the station to start airing ASAP. We'll also post to social. It'd be super if you could say something like, 'Hear Larry's Lemmon's last interview only on Channel 4 Eyewitness News.'"

"Things are very fluid here and I'd hate to miss something. You have the interview in-house. Can you pull something from there?"

She hesitates and loses the patient parent tone. "Don't most reporters who have exclusives like to promote them? I mean, that's been my experience."

Charlotte last worked at JJ's station, where the most dangerous place to find yourself is between a reporter and a camera. Especially JJ, who isn't afraid to use stilettos to empty a path. I've heard some reporters even place bets on how many times they can appear in a single story. No one's beaten JJ. In her world, stories are about JJ, not the person she's interviewing. She always shows up a minimum of three times in the edited story, and whenever possible, she surfaces in live intros and tags. If your favorite thing about TV news is being on TV, then JJ's station is where you want to work.

"Jolene, shoot the promo," David says. "It'll take you less than five minutes."

Pearl of wisdom from a manager who's never covered breaking news in the field. News flash: nothing takes less than five minutes when you really need it to. He also wants to stream the body removal live on our Facebook page.

"Isn't that kind of insensitive?"

"We've shown body bags plenty of times. Just because it's a local celebrity doesn't mean we shouldn't do it."

"Too late. I'm watching Nate shoot video of the body going into the van."

"Damn it, we should've been live!" David says. "And Jolene, you should've been tweeting pictures. We're not just reposting your stuff. We're compiling a timeline for the web. Come on, step it up! Let's plan on streaming the next media briefing live. Any idea when it's going to happen?"

"Looks like now."

"Son of a—"

"Gotta go. I'll be sure to tweet."

CHAPTER
4

Lugging Nate's tripod, I run back to the PIO where we form a horseshoe. Elbow jabs and shoulder bumps replace the earlier nudges. I write a tweet announcing Larry Lemmon's death so I'm one tap away from breaking it.

"As you have just seen, the Maricopa County Medical Examiner's Office has removed the body," the PIO says. "An autopsy will be performed to determine the cause of death."

A chorus clamors for confirmation it's Larry Lemmon.

"First, let me share the information I have. Then, I will address your questions. Everyone get that?"

He pauses until someone blurts, "Yes, go! We're on deadline!"

"I'm able to share the name of the deceased. He has been identified as Larry Lemmon, a fifty-one-year-old white male. He resides—excuse me, he resided in Phoenix."

As I hit the blue tweet button, Mirna whispers into her phone. I know muy poco español but make out "muerto"—it means dead. On my other side, Scott demands details. "You said he collapsed at work. Can you elaborate? Set the scene? What kind of work area are we talking about?"

"My understanding is that Mr. Lemmon was working in his

studio where he broadcasts his show. I have not been inside that studio so I can't describe it."

"Who was with him?" I ask. "And what are they saying?"

"I'm told there were two people nearby. The producer of Mr. Lemmon's show was with him in the studio and another employee who handled technical duties was in an adjacent room."

Not only do I have the last interview with Larry but I was the first to tweet he collapsed. Wish I could alert the newsroom managers in Minneapolis.

Sergio Magaña keeps pushing the immigration angle. "Was he shouting? Was he upset?"

"I am unaware of the subject matter being discussed at the time, but I'm told Mr. Lemmon collapsed during a commercial break."

"Back to the co-workers," I say. "What are they telling you?"

"The investigating officers have gathered a preliminary timeline that I will share. Let me stress this is very preliminary and based on information provided by others. This information may be subject to change." He reads from notes. "Mr. Lemmon arrived at eight thirty this morning, his normal time. His show started shortly after nine. He had cookies and coffee. No problems reported until almost three hours into his show when he complained about not feeling well. Then, around noon, he experienced difficulty breathing, collapsed, and never regained consciousness. By the time medics arrived, it was too late and they determined he was clinically deceased."

Behind me, someone asks if Larry suffered a heart attack.

"As I said, the medical examiner's office will perform an autopsy, which will include a physical examination and a toxicology screening that will check for a variety of things."

"What kind of things?" I ask.

"Prescription drugs, over-the-counter drugs, illegal drugs, possibly poison."

"Poison!" JJ pushes closer, her high heel grinding my pinkie toe. "What kind of poison?"

"Do you think it was in the cookies?" Scott asks.

"What kind of cookies were they?" I ask.

The PIO tenses like a burglar caught in the act.

"I don't know what kind of cookies. Let me be very clear about this: no one said it was poison. I said that might be—might be—one of several things they check for. It is very early in this investigation and nothing is being ruled out. That's all I have at this time. Thank you."

In his haste to unclip multiple microphones from his uniform, a windscreen cartwheels to the ground. I nab it and ask if we can talk to Larry's co-workers.

"You've already asked and they declined."

Yes, I want to say, but I have Larry's last interview and getting the last people with him when he died would make my story amazing. The network might even invite me on.

"Can you check again?"

"No. I'm not going to harass them. If you want to ask, go ahead. I can't tell you how to do your job." He thrusts the mics at me. "When we have something new to share, we'll issue a press release."

And with that, he turns his back on us.

"This is ultimate résumé reel material," JJ says, referring to a compilation video of a reporter's best work. "You know, perception is reality and sloppy is not a strong look." She blinks at my shirt. "But you still have time to change out of that."

If only she'd offer me the extra coffee in her hand, she'd get her own stain to worry about. Accidentally, of course.

Mirna gestures for me and Scott to follow her away from the herd. She suggests we approach Larry's co-workers together.

"Strength in numbers."

Scott thinks a group approach will scare them off, but I'm not willing to give him—or anyone else—the only shot at a critical interview.

"Nate, can you guys follow close behind? Keep your cameras down, but be ready to roll?"

"You got it."

Mirna's photographer argues that he should be up front, recording the entire time. I shake my head.

"No way. That could freak them out. If you just saw your co-worker die, would you want a bunch of cameras in your face?"

"I don't have to worry about that," Scott says. "But I do have an editor badgering me for quotes, so I'm going. You guys coming?"

Traveling shoulder to shoulder, we strive to convey compassionate humans, not competitive reporters. Yellow police tape sags like a full diaper, but it's Kryptonite to reporters. Cross it and risk arrest. Larry's co-workers are leaning against the car's trunk. Khakis, the older one, is talking on a phone, and Flip-Flops is texting.

We wave to catch their attention. No luck.

"Hello," I call out. "Over here!"

Flip-Flops's eyes take us in. He says something to Khakis, who glowers at us.

I wave again. "Hi there, we're reporters. Hoping to get a minute of your time."

Khakis walks away while Flip-Flops watches us.

I jiggle the tape. "We can't cross this. Would you mind coming closer?"

He moves like a tortoise—if a tortoise wore flip-flops. Scott mumbles something about lazy Millennials and I resist the urge to explain Gen Z. When Flip-Flops reaches us, I ask if he's Larry's producer.

"No, Ralph is." He nods to Khakis, who continues to shun us. "I'm the board op."

Scott cuts in. "And your name is?"

"Andy."

"Is that spelled A-N-D-Y?"

He nods.

"What's your last name, Andy?" Scott flips open a stenographer's notepad and draws a pen from his back pocket. "I need you to spell it for me."

Uncertainty spreads across his face. I bump Scott. His compulsion with the five W's—who, what, when, where, and why— could cost us the interview. We can fill in blanks later, including Andy's last name. The most important thing is to get him talking about Larry. And meeting our deadline.

"Andy, we're sorry for your loss. You don't have to give your last name if you don't want to." I ignore Scott's side eye. "We'd really like to hear from Larry's co-workers about what kind of man he was and what it was like working with him. Is that okay with you?"

"Is this going to be on TV?"

"Yes." I give him my best "Isn't this fabulous?" smile.

"And in the *Arizona Republic* and azcentral.com," Scott says, inserting his outlets. "You could become famous, kid."

Interest tops uncertainty as visions of social media saturate his head.

"Okay, then. My last name is Symson. Spelled S-Y-M-S-O-N."

Scott elbows my ribs while scratching on a notepad. Mirna's photographer plows between us and Nate does the same. In order to get the best shot, they shove Scott out of Andy's direct line of sight. Scott employs print reporter payback by peppering Andy with questions. Andy will look at Scott to answer, forcing the photographers to adjust positions to avoid shooting Andy's profile. No station wants video where the person is obviously talking to a competitor.

"Where were you when Larry collapsed? Did you see it? And what did you do?"

Andy's mouth opens and closes before he says, "I thought you wanted me to talk about working with Larry. You know, what he's like."

"Yeah, yeah, we'll get to that," Scott says. "But first tell us what happened. Did you see Larry collapse?"

For all his experience, Scott's out of his element. Andy is a young employee, not a seasoned politician. And this is a death scene, not an impeachment trial.

"Um, I'm not sure I should be doing this. Let me check with Ralph."

"Please, Andy, it'll only take a minute," I say. "You don't have to talk about what happened today. Can you just share a memory of working with Larry? Please?"

But the only response is the fading sound of flip-flops. We've lost him. Even worse, JJ has Ralph. Standing along the side of the building, JJ hands him a coffee as her photographer joins them. Nate, Scott, Mirna, and her photographer chase after them. My brain says I should follow, but my ego handcuffs my feet. The only thing more humiliating than not getting the interview is attempting to latch onto JJ like a flunky. Three minutes later, they're back. Turns out I saved energy and protected my pride.

"He shut us out," Scott says. "Told us he's only talking to JJ."

Mirna's fingers knead her bottle necklace, as if it'll grant a wish. "This stinks. I'm supposed to be live in an hour and all I have is sound from the PIO."

JJ may have an exclusive with Ralph, but I still have the last interview with Larry Lemmon.

Plus, I have Jim Miranda.

CHAPTER

5

Jim and I met less than two years ago, when he was a PIO for the police department. He's forty-something, tall (to me, but average height to others), and handsome (unanimous opinion). Jim could be cast as the lead detective in a Hallmark mystery movie. Except he would never tolerate an amateur sleuth bungling the investigation. Jim's famous, often repeated, line to the media was, "We don't solve crimes based on your deadlines." With his penchant for bluntness and lack of patience for perceived incompetence, Jim didn't last long as a PIO. Now he oversees the Special Investigations Unit, known as SIU.

"It stands for 'Someone Is Unhappy,'" he once told me. "And that someone is usually high up the food chain at city hall."

The unit was formed to handle cold cases and those deemed "high profile" through internal channels. In the past, "high profile" has applied to a domestic violence charge against a city council member, sexual assault allegations against high school football players in hazing situations, and a drunk driving case against a reality TV star.

As Nate leaves to update our colleagues on what we know, I unlock the live truck, toss my bag on the floorboard, and heave myself up. After two rings, Jim answers with a "Hold on," and I reach for my laptop.

"If you're calling for kimchi, you're too late," he says. "I already had lunch."

Jim introduced me to Korean barbecue and kimchi, a traditional side dish of fermented cabbage. It's our favorite meal on the rare occasions we talk face-to-face.

"You think I would trust a half-Filipino with kimchi?"

"You think I would trust a half-Mexican who can't habla Español?"

I laugh. "Let's keep it civil. You know why I'm calling, right?"

"Yes, that's why I stepped out of a meeting. My unit is not officially involved and I'd like to keep it that way. We've got enough on our plates."

"You must have some information."

"I was copied on an email. Stand by while I find it."

I open a Word document to take notes.

"Okay, here it is. Larry's on-air shift ran from nine a.m. to one p.m. He arrived around eight thirty. The cookies had already been delivered."

"The cookies were delivered? By who?"

"No name. Says a couple minutes after eight o'clock a woman dropped off two heart-shaped tins of cookies for Larry. She left them with the receptionist, who'd just unlocked the door and was turning on her computer. Receptionist called someone named Andy Symson to let him know—hey, I hear typing. You can't attribute this to me. We're still operating under our deal, right?"

I work with Jim differently than any other source. When we talk about a case, everything is considered off the record. Then, after he's spilled all he knows, we talk about what I can use publicly. Purists' heads would burst because it goes against the traditional rules of journalism. In college, I was taught both parties should agree up front to what areas will and will not be on the record before any conversation takes place. But this way works better for us. It's quicker for me and Jim doesn't have to worry about saying too much and getting into trouble. He can let it all out and then we negotiate. He knows that, unlike other reporters, I won't burn him. And he won't get busted for being my source because he uses a personal cell phone when we text and talk.

"Of course our deal stands."

"Okay. Around eight fifteen, Andy picked up the cookies and dropped them off in the studio. Around eight forty-five Larry and his producer—a guy named Ralph Flemski—went into the studio with their coffee and notes. Larry ate a cookie before the show started."

"What kind of cookie?"

"Chocolate chip. Says here the other tin had almond cookies. The show started at nine-oh-five, right after the national news-cast ended. Larry commented on the air about how good the cookies were, thanked the listener who dropped them off. Says there was a note with the cookies. Computer printed, not signed. It said, 'Never surrender.' With an exclamation point. Followed by 'Freaks love Larry.' With two exclamation points."

Larry coined "Never surrender" as his signature slogan, calling on listeners to never surrender to terrorists, liberals, the "lamestream" media, or anyone with an opposing view.

"Wait. You're saying they didn't know where the cookies came from and they ate them?"

"Jolene, think about what you said. We both know how the media operate. You guys will eat anything."

"Point taken. Please continue."

"There was another news break at ten o'clock. The producer, Ralph, went to the restroom. Returned to find Larry eating an-other cookie—before you ask, it was probably chocolate chip. But Ralph can't be a hundred percent sure, he said. During the eleven o'clock newscast he left to get fresh coffee. During a commercial break—around eleven forty-five—Larry had another cookie—almond, per Ralph—and shortly before noon Larry started complaining his head hurt and he wasn't feeling—quote—'so hot.' Right around noon he started groaning and gasping. Then he collapsed, appeared to have a seizure, and lost consciousness."

"Who called 911?"

"Andy did. Ralph thought Larry was choking and rolled him onto his side. Told medics there was no pulse, no breathing. Larry never regained consciousness. You know the rest."

I ask about the woman who delivered the cookies.

"Not a good description. The receptionist covers calls for three stations. Said she had two lines ringing when the woman showed up. Described her as white or Hispanic, in her thirties or forties, maybe around five-four or five-five. Not fat, not thin. Brown hair. Not long, not short. Maybe shoulder length. Unknown eye color."

"Could she be less clear?"

"That's the way it goes sometimes. Heck, she could've felt under pressure and made it all up. Wouldn't be surprised if she was Asian, in her teens, six feet tall, with blond hair and glasses."

"Did the woman say anything when she dropped them off?"

"Only that she had a delivery for Larry Lemmon. The receptionist took the tins and the woman left."

"What about security video?"

"There's a camera in the reception area. Maybe others covering the main entrance and parking lot. Couldn't tell you what kind of quality or coverage. You know some places install decoy cameras that don't even record. Why are you asking about video?"

"Seems logical to nail down the woman who delivered the cookies since the PIO suggested the toxicology screening will include poison."

Jim groans. "He said that?"

"In his defense, he didn't lead with poison. It just kinda came out. Anything else I should know?"

Silence.

"Jim? Anything else?"

"I wish you hadn't asked."

My hands hover above the keyboard. "I'm waiting."

"One medic suspects cyanide poisoning."

What a scoop! My first instinct is to ask Jim if anyone else knows about the cyanide. My second instinct is to get an interview with the medic. But I don't want to spook Jim. Appearing too eager could make him skittish and clam up.

"Why does the medic suspect cyanide?"

"The odor. Cyanide is sometimes described as having a bitter, almond smell, but not everyone can detect it. The other medic didn't."

I make an effort to steady my voice. "Sounds like a possible big deal."

"Hey, don't get too worked up. Remember one of the tins contained almond cookies."

"You're saying it was the cookies that smelled? Not cyanide?"

"I'm not saying either because we don't yet know. But the ME is going to test for cyanide."

"Just because of the smell?"

"The smell and other things. Lemmon got really sick, really fast. His symptoms mesh with cyanide poisoning. He had trouble breathing, collapsed, suffered a seizure, and lost consciousness. When medics arrived, his face was pink—that can happen when oxygen stays in the blood instead of moving into the cells. That's what cyanide does—stops the cells from being able to use oxygen."

"Where would someone get cyanide?"

"Jewelry-supply companies sell it. Cyanide is used to clean metal. Some research labs use it, too."

"Can anyone buy it or order online?"

"It's not supposed to be that easy but it happens. Before you worked in Phoenix, there was a defendant who swallowed cyanide pills in the courtroom after a guilty verdict was read. Guy collapsed and died right on the floor in front of jurors and the judge."

"For real? Tell me about it."

"He was a former investment banker convicted of setting fire to his mansion after he reportedly couldn't keep up with mortgage payments. Investigators found a canister of cyanide he'd ordered from a chemical supplier in another state. And then there's Jonestown. Mass suicide—or mass murder—depending on your point of view. That was way before your time. Google it. I gotta run."

"Wait, wait. What can I report about the cyanide?"

"Whatever you can get from someone else."

"C'mon, Jim."

"Can't use me."

"When will you know if it was cyanide?"

"You'll have to ask the ME's office. I don't know if it'll be requested as a separate test or combined with a full workup. You know a complete tox report can take four to six weeks."

"I can't wait that long. How about the woman who delivered the cookies? Can I get the surveillance video?"

"Sure, no problem."

"Seriously? When?"

"No, not seriously. You can't have the video. We need time to track her down—if we even need to track her down. We can't have an overly ambitious reporter blasting her picture all over the place. Come on, I thought you were one of the smart ones."

While Jim and I occasionally butted heads during his PIO tenure, we've always respected each other and he's become irreplaceable. Like me, Jim has a love-hate relationship with his profession. There's much to be proud of when you're providing a community service. And then there's the reality of egos and assholes. Not just sleazeballs we sometimes encounter doing our jobs but co-workers who have no business being cops or reporters. Bad apples that can destroy public trust.

Negotiations begin. I want to report the suspicious cookies and the woman who delivered them, but Jim says no way, not unless the PIO releases it.

"But that could be huge."

"You got that right, and if it is, investigators will need to find and talk to her, so let's not frighten her. I can count on one hand the number of people who have this information. If you ever want more from me, you better stick with our deal. And keep in mind the guy's been dead for what, three, four hours? Let's figure out how he died first. For all we know it was a heart attack. He was an overweight fifty-one-year-old. Could've had clogged arteries or a hundred other medical conditions."

"I hear you. But promise you'll let me know immediately when I can run with the delivery woman or when you have new stuff."

"Agreed."

"You know if it turns out to be poison this is going to make national, maybe international news."

"I hope not, for the PIO's sake. And mine."

After Jim hangs up, I replay our conversation. In all likelihood, one of the most loved and hated radio hosts in America has been poisoned. How can I get to the medic who reported the smell of cyanide? And how can I get my hands on surveillance video of the mystery woman delivering the cookies? A thump against the truck startles me and my laptop falls to the floorboard. The side doors whip open and Nate leaps inside.

"Everything okay?"

"You mean other than you almost scared me to death?" I reach for the laptop. "Did you have to bang so hard?"

"I barely touched it. I wanted to give a heads-up so you wouldn't freak out when the doors opened."

"Didn't work."

Nate unhooks a bungee cord, and a chair slithers out from under the editing station. He begins a performance of flipping switches, pressing buttons, and beaming signals. Showtime is imminent. The medic and mystery woman must simmer on the back burner so I can address looming deadlines. David answers my call to the producer hotline and lives up to our nickname for him.

"We hit the sexy story jackpot! Here's the plan: we're working on a special open for all the shows that will include a clip of your interview with Larry, then we'll go live to Gina. She'll explain what we know at this time. She'll use PIO sound and any other information gathered from the scene. Is she there yet? We sent her with Mike."

"Yes, Nate already briefed them."

"Awesome. After their live shot, we'll toss to you."

"Hey Jolene, it's Lou. Congratulations!"

Oh, no. Lou is the general manager. He supervises all station operations: local news, programming, production, and sales. Emphasis on sales. His job is to make corporate happy and corporate is happy when the shareholders are happy and guess what makes them happy?

"Your interview is exactly what we need, a celebrity whose mouth sometimes got him into trouble. It's sure to go viral."

The official title for our newscasts is "Eyewitness News," but among reporters and photographers it's "What Matters to Lou." Some people think advertisers control news content but that's never been my experience. It's more likely to be the GM or GM's spouse who influences coverage. Once, after a manicure, Lou's wife got an infection and I had to visit dozens of salons until I convinced ten to provide samples of liquids they use on acrylic nails.

We tested them for a cheap adhesive called methyl methacrylate monomer. The Food and Drug Administration says it shouldn't be used on nails, but two samples we tested contained high levels. It touched off the most comments on the station's Facebook page that month, which caused a frenzy among managers for more salon stories and fierce nail biting for me. Twenty-four hours later, a forest fire north of Phoenix grew out of control and manicure mania vanished. Fingers crossed it's permanently gone.

Before Lou can get under my skin, Alex interjects. "We know it's a hectic scene, so we'll let you get back to work. The full log of your interview should be in your inbox. Let us know what clips you plan to use."

"For sure something about immigration."

"There's also good sound when you asked about his critics," the four o'clock producer says. "It's your story, your call, but the 'Never surrender' response was classic Lemmon. I'm pulling it now so if you don't want to use it, let me know and we'll find another place for it."

"Okay. And FYI, even though we're on private property, all the stations are staying put. There's not enough space on the street."

"If KFRK management has any influence, I guarantee you'll be reporting from there as long as you want. Your presence will help their ratings," Alex says. "As a reminder, we have Gina doing quick hits for Facebook and the web."

"And remember to post," David says. "This is a prime example of why tonight's meeting is so important."

"What meeting?" I ask.

"To discuss our new social media strategy."

I shudder at the memory of Bob's email announcing the return of Shelley Munro Hammett, a consultant the station brings in every year or two to improve our content and ratings. Allegedly. We call it SMH time.

The lie spurts out effortlessly. "Oh yeah, sorry I'll miss it."

"You won't. The meeting is mandatory."

"David, this story's blowing up. I gotta keep working it."

"Of course you do. And you will. But when the news director requires everyone's attendance, you must make time."

He hangs up before I can argue, leaving me to scroll emails for the transcript of Larry's interview. As the social media meeting sinks from my thoughts, the medic and mystery woman resurface. Since Jim won't share the surveillance video or let me report the medic's suspicion about cyanide, where else can I get it?

The answer comes as I squirm, knocking my notepad off the seat. My eyes flash to the information copied from the business card Scott showed me. Checking the time, I fire off an email to Shana Forrest, the program director, expressing condolences and asking if she can direct me to the appropriate contact for surveillance video. I end with appreciation and a request to keep in touch about the station's plans to remember Larry.

As for the medic, I could go the formal route and request an interview through the fire department's PIO, but given the high profile, the department would strongly encourage the medic to decline. So, I text a firefighter I went out with a couple times. No sparks but we remain friendly. Meaning he tolerates occasional texts asking for help with stories.

Hey, it's Jolene. Covering Larry Lemmon's death. Can you find out who responded?

Since a watched phone never rings, I cover my bases and shoot a request to the fire department. The swoosh of email is followed by the ding of a new text.

They're under orders not to talk.

That was quick. Too quick. Either word has spread faster than fire at a paper plant or he knows them.

What did they tell you?
Nice try. Not talking.
Please give my name and number in case they change their mind.
K. Don't hold ur breath.

"Ready to go," Nate says. "I have your raw interview cued up. Let me know when the clips are ready to feed to the station. I'm going to start setting up the live shot."

I swing around to view the monitor. The four, five, and six o'clock producers expect two sound bites each. Since illegal immigration launched his radio career, I choose this clip to run in all three newscasts:

"I am not a racist. I am a patriot who cares about my country, a country based on laws. When we allow people to break the law by entering our country illegally, we are saying to the world, 'Laws don't matter. Do what you want.' If the bleeding-heart liberals get their way, our nation will be overrun, our welfare system drained, our economy weakened, and our position as a world leader diminished. We cannot allow that to happen. I will not allow that to happen."

It runs twenty-three seconds, about double the normal time. A manager's approval is usually necessary to run clips longer than fifteen seconds, but I make the executive decision on my own. If someone wants to argue, we can do it after the newscasts.

I choose the "Never surrender" sound bite for the four o'clock producer. Larry calls on his "Freaks" to keep fighting for their faith, families, and future. The five o'clock producer will get Larry saying there's no such thing as man-made climate change, only God is responsible for the weather, and liberals are lying because they want everyone to ride bikes. And the six o'clock producer will get Larry's interpretation of the Second Amendment to mean people are allowed to carry concealed weapons of any kind, anywhere.

Gina's knuckles brush against the driver's window and I unlock the door. Too bad Nate missed a learning moment.

"Mike is editing our story and I thought I'd check on you. Need anything?"

"How about a way to get out of tonight's meeting?"

"Considering your story could make national news, that should be a valid excuse."

"Not in Sexy's view. He said I have to be there."

Gina makes a tsking sound. "Sorry I can't help with that." She nods toward my shirt. "But that I can help with."

"You have an extra shirt?"

"No shirt." She opens a burgundy tote. "But let me see what else I have."

As Gina Robinson, fashion extraordinaire, digs through her bag of beauty tricks, I recall our awkward introduction. It was my first day at Channel 4 fumbling around with the newsroom computer system. Gina came in around one thirty to report for the late newscast. Chatting on a cell phone, she smiled and waved before settling into a desk next to mine. Gina was stunning. With no makeup on. Every feature seemed to be her best. And flawless skin. As someone who uses maximum-strength Clearasil, I was mesmerized. And the way she carried herself and sat with a straight back, as if it was the most natural, comfortable posture, captivated me.

"Please hold a moment," she told the person on the phone

while turning her perfectly proportioned face toward me. "Is something wrong? Or have you never seen a Black person before?"

I bumbled my way through an apology, saying something about zoning out, before finally spitting out my name.

"You are the first Jolene I've met."

"Family name," I lied.

It wasn't a total lie. My mother did name me Jolene. But it was after Dolly Parton's song, a song where Dolly begs Jolene not to steal her man. My grandma didn't mind the name Jolene, but hated my mom giving me my dad's surname. Only Grandma didn't call him my dad. She used an ethnic slur. I remember being confused, not understanding why she used that word or what it meant. But I didn't ask because her tone was clear: the topic was off-limits.

"How about this?" Like a magician pulling a rabbit out of a hat, Gina presents an ivory scarf.

"You're the best. Well, you'll be the best when you show me how to wear it."

Gina continues her magic act by looping the smooth fabric around my neck, covering the purple smear, and tying delicate knots.

"It's so soft. Is this silk?"

"No, it's viscose. I would never endanger silk in the field."

I pull down the visor and check the mirror. "It's lovely. Thank you."

"Let's keep it that way." She whips out a package of facial tissues. "Use as many as you need to cover the scarf while you put on makeup. I'll see you later."

I manage to get through our first live shot without staining Gina's scarf or anything else. Within fifteen minutes of our broadcast, a parade of people begins dropping off flowers and cards. One woman sets a poster board near the entrance. It reads,

RIP, LARRY. THE FREAKS WILL ALWAYS LOVE YOU. A man and a boy, around six years old, hold miniature American flags.

"Dad, where should I put it?"

"Wherever you want, son. And remember to say a prayer."

I tweet of photo of them and check my notifications. Whoa. Close to two hundred people have liked the station's tweet promoting my interview with Larry and forty-nine have retweeted. I tap the screen and smile when it changes to fifty.

CHAPTER

6

Navigating a live location gets trickier at five o'clock when everyone leads with the same story. In this kind of situation, most of us know how to play together in the sandbox. And then there's Sergio, who thinks it's okay to walk behind other reporters during their live shots, apparently unaware he's wearing a microphone. Why else would he shout during his live shots? Other reporters' microphones pick up his voice so if you're watching another station, you can hear him in the background. Maybe even pick up his scent. Mirna swears El Fragrante's cologne seeps through the screen, creating "smellavision."

Off to the side, Gina and Mike stake out a spot where they can show flowers and read messages without colliding into other crews. Even JJ's staying in her lane. Nate and I escape the congestion because we're farther away. He only needs to frame the shot to show the building and activity behind me. No one asked me to cut the sound bites and things are going exceptionally well. Until I get a text from David.

JJ reported cookie delivery. Why didn't you?

Shit.

Nate checks Facebook while I check Twitter. Both have links to JJ's interview with Larry's producer, Ralph.

JJ's story opens with cell phone video of Larry Lemmon wearing a KFRK cap and holding a gun. Ralph's voice plays over video of Larry firing at a paper target.

"Before moving to Phoenix, I worked for Larry at his gun range in Douglas. All kinds of people came from all over southern Arizona to practice. There were ranchers along the border and good ol' boys who liked target shooting in the desert. There were single females looking to protect themselves at home. And hunters. Larry had pronghorn and elk head mounts on the walls and pictures of him with animals after the kills. Yeah, the hunters enjoyed trading stories with him—the real ones and the ones who fancied themselves hunters."

JJ leans in, confident her "I'm a serious journalist" face will make it into the story. "I need to ask a difficult question. Do you think Larry was poisoned?"

"Well, now, I don't want to say the cookies made Larry sick, but we are concerned about where they came from because there was no name on the note."

JJ performs a dramatic nod, encouraging him to continue.

"I guess anything's possible," he says.

JJ regards the camera, speaking directly to viewers. "Anything's possible. That's what police are saying, too."

I text Jim, alerting him to JJ's story and asking if I can report the delivery details.

Get it from another source. Can't be me.

As I consider the best curse-free response, my phone rings. I show Nate the caller ID.

"I know you don't want to answer it, but it's better to get it over with."

Before I can finish saying "Hello," David wants to know if I've seen his text.

"Yes."

"Are you getting Larry's producer?"

"He only wanted to talk to JJ. We all tried."

"So, that means we won't have anything new to report for ten o'clock."

And that's how I go from being a newsroom hero to a zero.

"I'll keep trying."

Maybe Ralph or Andy will respond to another Facebook request. My money's on Andy since he initially liked the idea of being on TV.

"If you can't get anything solid lined up before the meeting, we'll just have to go with what we have."

"That's only thirty minutes."

"Yes, I'm aware of the time, Jolene. Tick tock."

A half hour later, I join a newsroom full of mostly skeptics. We know major stuff's coming. And it's not raises. The quality of pizza ordered for newsroom meetings reveals a whiff of what's ahead. Quick, cheap pies from big chains generally indicate mundane announcements like corporate benefits and policies. The more expensive pizzas from local places are reserved for election nights. Or bad news. No polling sites are open and Alex is carrying boxes from Oregano's, an Arizona-based chain that doesn't do deep discounts.

Gina refuses to sit by me because she claims I whisper too loud and she can only fake cough and sneeze so many times. She's by the producers' pod while my other desk mate, Elena Ramirez, is collecting pepperoni off her plate and plunking them on mine. As a fellow snarky commenter, Elena tops the list of people to sit next to during meetings. The extra pepperoni is a bonus.

"Thank you for all coming," Lou says.

"Like we had a choice," Elena mutters.

Lou's standing in front of the assignment desk, an elevated platform that extends twenty feet. He faces the newsroom like a college professor in a lecture hall. Standing on either side are the consultant and my news director. They mimic a saguaro cactus with Lou as its tallest, oldest arm.

"As you know, I don't like to get involved in newsroom operations." Lou's hand clinches Bob's shoulder. "Bob runs the show here and that means he's running this meeting. But I want to show my support and make sure everyone understands this plan is key to the station's success. Everyone plays an important role." He pats Bob's shoulder. "Without further ado, I'll step aside and let him explain."

Bob Wilson started out as a reporter so he understands what it's like to work in the field. Sometimes he serves as a buffer between unreasonable demands from people who only leave the building for lunch and reality. Bob also cares about quality journalism. As much as he can these days.

"Thank you, Lou." He takes two steps forward. "And thank you all for your hard work and dedication." He pauses to take in the stragglers. "What we do matters. I am proud of what we accomplish day in and day out under tight deadlines and often less than ideal circumstances. We've had ratings challenges lately. As most of you know, if the network has a popular show leading into our newscast, it can increase our ratings considerably. And the reverse is true with unpopular shows. Regrettably, that's what we're facing with the network's current lineup."

I catch a glimpse of Gina. She's listening and chewing along with everyone else, the premium pizza keeping their attention. And so does Bob's next line.

"While our traditional newscasts have been suffering, our digital side is growing and that's where we will increase our efforts. From this day forward I want you to stop thinking of yourselves as TV reporters or photographers. Everyone here is a multi-media journalist."

A wave of grousing sounds threatens to squelch Bob's speech.

"Hold on." His hands rise. "Before anyone gets worked up, let me tell you what that does not mean in our newsroom. An MMJ does not mean one person going out alone all the time to shoot and edit video and to write and report. I'll be honest, there may be occasions when that will happen. But it will not be the norm. We care about quality and, most importantly, we care about your safety. We've seen journalists become the targets of taunts, insults, even physical assaults. There is safety in numbers and we'll do everything we can to avoid sending anyone alone to a questionable situation where there are no other media members. Is that clear?"

Reactions range from visibly annoyed reporters who will be most affected to exaggerated head bobs from anchors and producers who will never be asked to shoot, edit, and report.

"Now, let's talk about what it does mean to be an MMJ in this newsroom. It means you will produce stories in various ways using video, still photos, text, and graphics. You'll need to put more attention into web stories. I want to see photo galleries, slide shows, and graphics. Our digital team can create engaging images. You just need to ask. Going forward, we are not a TV news organization. We are a digital news organization. And we must all think digital first."

He surveys the newsroom. "What exactly does that mean? That's where our guest comes in. Many of you know Shelley Munro Hammett."

"SMH," Elena hums while dropping crust on my plate.

"Shelley is a widely respected social media guru. You'll hear from her in a moment, but first, I want to acknowledge David's work. He's been instrumental in expanding our digital reach and he's responsible for our successful text alert campaign."

Sexy makes a feeble attempt at humility. His "Aw, shucks"

routine fools no one. "It's a privilege to be part of such a strong team of journalists." His smile is as phony as mine. "Rather, I should say, multimedia journalists."

Elena beats me to the eye roll.

"You all know how successful our text alerts have become, especially for traffic updates and breaking news. We dominate the market in subscribers. We're going to keep growing those numbers and use texts to not only push people to our website but promote our social media platforms. That's the impetus of this meeting, as Bob will share."

David bows out of the spotlight and Bob kicks off the sales pitch.

"Every month, Facebook has about three billion active users. That's roughly ten times the population of the United States. Instagram has two billion and Twitter has more than three hundred million. Social media is where our audience is and that's where we've got to be."

And that's when Shelley takes center stage to perform her memorized lines.

"Change can be scary. But you know what? Change can also be exciting, a chance to try new things."

Does she really think she's going to win over reporters by treating us like kindergartners on the first day of school?

"The evolving media landscape provides revolutionary opportunities to reach a wider audience. How do we do that? By making the audience feel like they're our friends. We do that by inviting them to watch, listen, learn, and—here's the key—provide their input. Who doesn't like to share their opinions?"

Hand over mouth, I lean toward Elena. "I'd like to share mine right now."

"When a story goes viral, it spreads like a virus and 'infects' people. The infection triggers people to share and talk about it. The content can be packaged and delivered in a variety of ways, but the goal is always the same: to move people to think, to talk, to share—to infect them, if you will."

"Eww," Elena says. "Keep your infection to yourself."

Bob resumes the lead. "Starting tomorrow, in every newscast, we will highlight a minimum of three comments from our Facebook page. And, of course, we'll invite people to participate and watch for comments on all our sites and newscasts. Depending on the news of the day, we may feature three comments from a single story or one or two comments from several. The final call will be made by each show producer in consultation with David."

This sparks another lackluster attempt at modesty by Sexy.

"In addition to Facebook, we want to build other followers. I'm not saying we're going to reach Barack Obama or Justin Bieber Twitter status, but we've set a reasonable goal and you're going to help us reach it through more frequent posts. When you arrive to a breaking news story, you should share—on Twitter, Instagram, whatever platform you like—and then work on your web and TV versions. Think continuous updates with photos and video. Remember, you are multimedia journalists. Digital first. Questions?"

"What about non-breaking news?" the five o'clock producer asks.

"I still want people posting. Let's say you're going to interview a business owner about a proposed hike in the minimum wage. When you get there, you can take a photo of the business and post where you are and why. After interviewing the business owner, maybe post a line about what they said and tease the full story coming up in the newscasts. You should repeat the process at your shoots throughout the day."

"Do we have to tweet our bathroom breaks?" I murmur to Elena.

"Jolene, do you have something to add?"

Bob's challenge scorches my cheeks. But I've experienced enough live shots with technical glitches to ad-lib pretty well.

"Aren't most people on Twitter politicians, celebrities, and the media? That's not really our audience, is it?"

"Why wouldn't they be our audience? We don't discriminate. To put it bluntly, our audience is anyone with a pulse. Especially anyone with a pulse who can repost our content."

Shelley's peppy laugh is guaranteed to land her an all-expenses-paid return trip next year.

"We saw the power of Twitter during the Trump presidency. It was his primary source for public communication," Bob says. "It can only help the station's brand to be in as many places as feasible."

Lou's muzzle flies off. "Excuse me, I'd like to add something. While we're talking about reaching more people through different platforms, we're going to be consistent in how we refer to them. We will call them friends. They are not followers, users, viewers, or visitors. They are our friends."

"That segues into our social media center," Bob says. "It will provide an opportunity for anchors and reporters to interact with our friends by inviting them to share their thoughts and read their comments on the air. It's also another way to handle breaking news and showcase our work. For example, if we'd had it today, we could've promoted our sites and encouraged people to post their reactions to Larry Lemmon's death."

"How long is this social media segment supposed to be?" the six o'clock producer asks.

"It will vary, just like every story does. Depends on what's happening that day and what kind of resources we have. The only guarantee is that we will feature the social media center in every newscast. And that transitions nicely to another new element."

He motions for an anchor, Rick, who nearly trips over his feet rushing to join station management.

"At the end of our late newscast Rick will provide commentary on a timely topic."

That bombshell throws off my drinking aim and the straw rams my lip. As I massage it, Bob says commentaries will be sixty seconds long and serve as the "last word" of the newscast before the anchors sign off. Practicing immense restraint through this nonsense is no longer an option.

"Excuse me, isn't that unethical? Journalists are supposed to present the facts and other people's opinions. Not our own opinions."

"A few years ago, I would've agreed with you a hundred percent, but times change. The most profitable—excuse me—the most popular media outlets are those with newsmakers who express opinions. People tune in to hear what they have to say. The audience has come to accept and frankly expect journalists to include their personal opinions. We are simply doing it in a controlled and transparent way."

"It doesn't seem right."

"That's the way it is. Between Facebook, Twitter, Instagram, TikTok, and countless other channels, everyone's sharing personal opinions and details."

"Not everyone."

"No one's asking you to do commentaries, Jolene. You can keep your thoughts to yourself."

If you walked into the newsroom, you'd know something was wrong. Everyone has given up eating free pizza to eyeball me. A charge in the air gags any more dissent.

"I understand this is a lot to digest," Bob says. "Keep in mind this is about our future. We adapt or we die. Any other questions?"

A chair squeaks, but no one speaks until Lou swoops in.

"Can I just say how promising this is? My wife adores the ideas, and we all know how important female viewers—oops, almost messed up there." Lou laughs like he's auditioning for the role of shopping mall Santa. "We all know how important our female friends are. Research shows, more often than not, they control the household budget. Advertisers want to reach them, especially ones with strong social media platforms. My wife's already telling her friends to visit the station's Facebook page and comment every day. And she's toying with the idea of creating an Instagram account for our dog and calling it Channel 4 Newshound."

He delivers another phony "Ho, ho, ho." No way he'd get the Santa job.

After the newsroom meeting ends, agitated reporters gather to rehash and complain that no one stood up for them. Really? No one spoke up? I'm done. I pilfer a pizza box with three slices and leave.

CHAPTER
7

On the dive home, I turn on KFRK. Since the last locally pro-
duced show ended an hour earlier, there's nothing about Larry.
The guy currently broadcasting lives in Idaho and buys air
time to rail against the government covering up the truth about
UFOs. I punch it off. Wish I could do the same to the thoughts
churning in my head.

My attention shifts gears as I arrive home. There's no escaping Norma. She straddles the line between neighborly and nosy.
Based on her enthusiastic wave, I brace for nosy and pull into
the carport we share. When I moved to Phoenix, getting covered parking close to my apartment was a must. Mistakenly, I
thought a double-spaced carport between our homes would provide an adequate barrier. Tonight, I'd give anything to zip into a
garage, close the door, and enter my place undisturbed.

"Hi, Jolene!" Norma touches what could pass for an eggplant
on her head. "What do you think?"

She changes hair color more than I change contact lenses.

"It's called fairy-tale plum."

It screams purple. Prince would have loved it.

"It matches your lavender tracksuit."

"Thank you!" Norma is fiercely loyal to the Puma brand. She

jokes it's because she fancies herself a cougar. In reality, she's a sixty-something widow who misses her husband of thirty-nine years. "And did you notice the baby's matching bow?"

Norma's baby is a ten-pound shih tzu named Tuffy who is not fond of humans beyond Norma. Fine with me. I appreciate the distance. We have a silent understanding to occasionally feign interest in each other for Norma's benefit.

"It's a cute bow."

She shakes a paw. "Tuffy says thanks." She dips an ear. "What's that, Tuffy? You want to know if Jolene has met the new guy yet?"

My muscles tighten, preparing for fight or flight. "Norma, what are you talking about?"

"Oliver. Don't you remember I mentioned him? He's from Minnesota. You know how pleasant people from Minnesota are. Perhaps because they're so close to Canada, eh."

She places Tuffy on the ground and he tugs the leash toward their apartment.

"Norma, it's not a good time."

"He's on the other side of the pool. In the Greers' unit, the one closest to the clubhouse. Oliver is their son. His mom's having back surgery so they're not traveling this winter. Oliver can work from anywhere. Isn't that something? They asked him to make sure everything's okay here and he's going to stay through October—maybe longer." Her left eye twitches. "Maybe all winter if he likes it." Another twitch.

"You okay? Is something in your eye?"

"Oh, dear, I'm fine. I was winking." She gives the leash a gentle pull and Tuffy gives her a hard stare. "Oliver's been asking about you."

"Why would he ask about me?"

"I saw him at the mailboxes, and you know me, I'm the friendly type, so I introduced myself."

"And?"

"He's single and I mentioned you're single."

My fingers squeeze the apartment key.

"He seemed interested so I told him about you."

Norma may not hear when someone says they're busy, but she can read a face filled with frustration. She picks up Tuffy and takes a step back. "But only a teensy bit."

"What did you tell him?"

"That you work for Channel 4 News. Boy, that really piqued his interest. He had lots of questions."

Questions he never would have asked if you hadn't volunteered my business.

"Like what?" I ask through gritted teeth.

"Let's see, he wanted to know when you were on TV, what you look like, and when he could meet you. But don't worry, I didn't tell him where you live. I only said you work a lot and you're on TV at all different times."

"Norma, I would appreciate it if you didn't talk about me to strangers. You've watched enough news. How many times have you heard people describe the serial killer who lived next door as a normal guy?"

"Oh, sweetie, he's not a serial killer. Besides, I think you two will hit it off. When you have a chance, I can introduce you."

To say I have zero desire for Norma to play matchmaker is an understatement.

"I'm going to be incredibly busy with work."

"Ooh, are you covering Larry Lemmon's death? I saw JJ interview his co-worker and he was talking about poisonous cookies."

My eye twitches in offense. "It hasn't been determined the cookies were poisoned. They have to run tests."

"Any idea who sent them?"

"Not yet." I pretend to yawn. "Please excuse me. I'm tired."

"Sure thing." She lifts a paw. "Tuffy says sleep well."

"Good night, Tuffy."

A minute later, I greet another boy—I think. Oscar lives in a bowl on the kitchen counter between a paper towel holder and a fruit basket that's only held mail, keys, and Reese's. Since I don't cook there's no chance of spilling anything on Oscar. And since he's in my sight daily, I can't forget to feed him. Though there are plenty of times I'm late. Oscar may be a goldfish but he's got a memory like an elephant. And he doesn't forgive.

"Sorry, buddy, it's been a long day. How about a special treat?"

As the freeze-dried blood worm splashes water, Oscar channels his inner piranha.

Before calling it a night, I call on Pat Sajak and Vanna White to ease my irritation. It's not necessarily the *Wheel of Fortune* game itself that brings peace, it's the memories from watching the TV show with my grandma.

My parents split up when I was around two years old. I have no memories of my father and fuzzy recollections of my mother. After he left, my mom supposedly started drinking more and using drugs. Neighbors called police after spotting me in the front yard, alone, crying, wearing only underwear in a freezing downpour. Cops found my mom inside on the couch passed out. A hair follicle test came back positive for amphetamines and methamphetamines, and at the age of four, I was sent to a foster home. About a year later, my mom got clean and got me back.

But not for long.

When my first-grade teacher reported me stealing other kids' lunches and not wearing a coat in the winter, I was put in foster care again. When the couple got tired of being foster parents, I was shipped to another home. That's where I stayed until I moved to my grandma's house in Omaha at the age of twelve. It wasn't until my last year of high school—when my grandma died—that I learned how I ended up in the child welfare system. In the back of a dresser drawer, under Grandma's socks, my fingers found a folder from the Illinois Department of Children and Family Services documenting my mother's parenting failures. The final entry before my grandma took custody said, "Whereabouts of biological parents are unknown."

Grandma addressed my mother's poor choices only once, the week I moved in. She framed it as "your mother," not "my daughter."

"If your mother decides to act like a sensible adult, she knows where to find us."

From that point on, my grandma emphasized personal responsibility and not counting on anyone else. Lessons I like to think I've mastered.

While some families share hugs and kisses, my grandma and I shared an affection for consonants and vowels. We easily watched hundreds of hours of *Wheel* together. The opening theme song's da, da, da, da, da, da was Grandma's version of "I love you." It would've been nice to hear the words. I'm sure she felt something beyond obligation. Pretty sure. Sometimes. Her sacrifice saved me from spending my teenage years in a group home, saved me from dropping out of school, saved me from becoming a statistic slapped on too many kids in foster care. *Wheel* became my North Star, a constant source of solace.

Except tonight.

In the bonus round, the contestant has ten seconds to solve the puzzle. It's a phrase.

R _ _ SE _ O _ R G _ ME

He can't come up with a response before the buzzer sounds. But I do.

Raise your game.

Message received. I'll work harder on Larry Lemmon's case.

CHAPTER
8

On my way to work the next morning, I listen to Darrell Arthur hosting what had been Larry's show twenty-four hours earlier. Darrell's cadence is slower and his voice is softer than other KFRK hosts.

"He was one of kind. No one can ever fill Larry Lemmon's shoes. And I would never try. What I will do is try my best to honor his legacy by talking about his contributions and inviting you to share your memories. Please give us a call or post your thoughts on our Facebook page."

KFRK is only three miles out of my way and I swing by. Crews from four stations, including mine, are wrapping up live shots. Someone planted a United States flag in the ground flanked by poster boards that read, NEVER SURRENDER!, RIP LARRY, and FREAKS LOVE LEMMON.

On the air, a state legislator is paying tribute. "We may have disagreed, but Larry's intent was sincere—to do what he believed was best for Arizona and our country."

This is the same politician who frequently referred to the former host as "Lucifer Lemmon."

As my Honda Civic heads south on Seventh Street I'm

grateful for missing what locals call the suicide lanes. Officially, they're labeled reverse lanes. During rush hour, they change from allowing left-turn lanes in either direction to mostly one-way traffic. If it sounds confusing, it is. Commutes can trigger road rage and panic attacks from near head-on collisions.

After enduring the humiliation of JJ reporting the cookie delivery and her exclusive interview with Larry's producer, I'm in no rush to return to the newsroom. I pull into a Circle K, counting on a forty-four-ounce Pepsi to drown my disgrace. Instead, my shame surges when a woman approaches, bony arms swinging like weak branches in the wind. A dingy white tank top skims belt loops on too-tight jeans. They must be child size. She can't weigh more than ninety pounds. Her eyes blink like fluorescent lights on the fritz.

"Can you spare a couple bucks?"

"No."

"For bus fare."

A map of lines laminate her face. She could be twenty-five or forty-five. I keep moving.

"It's not for drugs," she says.

"No, sorry."

The guilt used to haunt me. Now it angers me. And the anger often descends into sadness. Not just for the person panhandling but all the others. And maybe my mom. Then, the anger comes roaring back until I squash it and lock it away.

Shake it off, I tell myself while pulling into the parking garage. The first level is for the station's trucks and vehicles belonging to newsroom employees: mostly Kias, Hyundais, and Toyotas, mixed with fewer Fords and Chevys. Heading up the ramp is like entering North Scottsdale. It's where the general manager and sales staff park. I pass a BMW, Mercedes, and Porsche. I back into a space next to a Nissan sedan (must be the GM's administrative assistant) and walk by a black Jaguar in a spot reserved for employee of the month. I've never known a newsroom colleague to park there.

Taking the stairs requires going past the sales department and GM's office so I opt for the elevator. Entering the newsroom, I'm drawn to the assignment desk, the hive of activity. Alex has a phone jammed between his shoulder and ear, another clasped in both hands, thumbs flying. Elena bustles nearby preparing to unveil her latest creation.

While Gina is the best-dressed person in the newsroom, Elena is the best baker. She makes the most intricate cakes. For Dr. Martin Luther King, Jr.'s birthday, she baked a sheet cake with icing that outlined King's statue in Washington, D.C. Her Veteran's Day cake was shaped like the United States and adorned with seven straws serving as poles for flags representing the U.S., POW/MIA, Army, Navy, Air Force, Marines, and Coast Guard. She even positioned plastic military figures around the cake to symbolize protecting our country.

"Jolene, come here!"

Edging closer, I shoot Alex a questioning look. He responds with a "Who knows?" gesture. It's too late for Labor Day and too early for Halloween.

"Ta-da!" Elena presents a cake shaped like an ice cream cone.

"What's the occasion?"

"It's for you!"

"It's not my birthday."

"I know, silly. It's because of your interview with Larry. You scooped the competition. Get it? It's a scoop of ice cream."

Alex's snort makes me wish he'd been drinking chocolate milk and wearing an expensive tie. Elena doesn't know I was out-scooped.

"I didn't have much time and had to keep it simple."

"It's beautiful. Thank you so much."

"Want to cut it now?"

"Maybe after lunch?"

Her mouth crumples. "But if I put it in the break room, it'll never last."

"Alex, we can trust you with it, right?"

"Affirmative."

Elena eyes a half-mauled doughnut in Alex's hand and frowns like I'm asking her to leave a baby with a tiger.

"Here." I pluck a Magic 8 Ball and Kung Fu Panda off the desk. "If you put it next to Alex's most prized possession, safety will be guaranteed."

"Whoa," he says. "Not so close."

To the uneducated, a chunk of cracked concrete the size of a shoebox could be mistaken for junk. But to Alex, the black "M" outlined in white paint is a jewel rescued from the rubble, a reminder of Metrocenter Mall's glory days. As a young child, he ice-skated inside Arizona's first two-story mall. As a teenager, he spent weekends cruising its eighty-acre perimeter. And then, along came *Bill & Ted's Excellent Adventure*, a film I'd never heard of until Alex quoted a line from the movie: "Strange things are afoot at the Circle K." My obvious confusion led to Alex's master class on Metrocenter's role in the cult classic starring Keanu Reeves and Alex Winter. Released in 1989, the science-fiction comedy features several scenes shot in Phoenix, including historical figures being chased through the mall. Thirty-four years later, the city organized a final farewell and Harkins Theatres showed *Bill & Ted's Excellent Adventure* one last time before the iconic mall was demolished.

Alex's hand guards the chipped block that once welcomed shoppers to the food court. "Let's not chance frosting on my 'M.' Your cake will be safe enough next to the doughnuts."

"You swear?" Elena says.

"Roger that."

We make our way into the "Haboob Room," named after dust storms. One of Arizona's largest reached five thousand feet in height and stretched a hundred miles wide. Airing storm video in Phoenix is like airing police chases in L.A.: practically everyone drops what they're doing to watch. A vast wall of dust rolling across entire cities can be breathtaking—and dangerous. Visibility plummets to zero, fifty-mile-per-hour winds hurl objects in all directions, and a blanket of dirt coats everything in its path. Anticipating a dust storm always whips up newsroom managers. We usually know the hour it will strike so crews can coordinate, but Mother Nature can be a prankster and not every storm lives up to the forecasted hype.

During the editorial meeting, Sexy reminds everyone about JJ's interview with Larry's producer before turning to me. "Do you think you can talk to him?"

I want to respond with, "Do you think you can stop being a jackass?" But I surprise myself and keep it classy. "I'm working on it."

From the head of the table, Bob taps a pen to gain attention. "We need to continue promoting Larry's interview. There's plenty of sound we haven't run yet. That's something no one else has and we need to capitalize on it." He fiddles with the pen. "Jolene, what can we do about the poison angle today?"

"Toxicology tests usually take about a month, but I'll connect with a source to see if I can get anything."

Bob nods and knocks the pen on the table three times.

"Listen up," he says. "Going forward, all news conferences involving this story will be streamed live online. We need to push social media and our website hard. Ideally, we should be posting updates at least every four hours. Jolene will get us a new angle today, but I expect more than one story in every newscast, whether that's Gina back at the memorial outside the building or an element that an anchor can front in the studio. We'll meet at noon to plot out the shows. And let me be clear, everyone: we will own this story."

As I head to my desk, I text Jim to call ASAP. Shoving aside a stack of *Arizona Republic* newspapers, I log onto my computer and send another interview request to Larry's producer, Ralph, via Facebook. Then do the same for Andy, the board operator who called 911. As much as I dislike Facebook personally, it can be a treasure trove professionally. Andy's page is typical for a twenty-four-year-old. Lots of photos with friends and former classmates at Arizona State University. Ralph's page reveals two interests: a megachurch where he records videos of Sunday sermons for its YouTube channel and a no-kill shelter he built to care for dogs. A timeline of the shelter called Max's Place includes several photos with Larry and Ralph. There's a group shot with six men, titled "Grand Opening." Besides Ralph and Larry, the only person I recognize is Darrell, the host now covering Larry's former time slot. Another picture, titled "Max and Us," shows a large dog sitting between Ralph and Larry. Dozens of pictures show dogs of distinct sizes and colors, but Max is the star. He could be part rottweiler, part German shepherd. Definitely fully ferocious.

My mouth goes as dry as the desert and I'm seven years old again. At the park. He looks so sweet lying in the grass. His fur, the color of a brownie, blends into the tree trunk. His body unwinds, begging to be pet. I hop off the swing, determined to make a new friend. When I bend down to pat his head, he jerks awake, clamps my wrist, and knocks me back. The stench of garbage spews from his mouth. Where his eyes should be white, I see red. Trying to yank free only brings more pain. My flailing feet find his body and his fangs loosen a fraction. I kick so hard I fear my legs will rip off. Teeth slice into my thigh.

The pain didn't let up after the dog let go. Because the wounds were deep and no one could track down the dog, I underwent a series of rabies shots. And since I was in foster care, the state had to foot the bill. Plus, my foster family was investigated for possible neglect. That's what the other foster child in the house—a thirteen-year-old-girl—told me. I don't know what happened to the girl, the foster parents, or the dog. Out of all three, the dog most often invades my thoughts. I take a greedy slurp of Pepsi and, when my pulse stops pounding, move on to Larry's ex-wife.

During our interview, Larry mentioned they married young, had a son, and divorced after he moved to Phoenix. On Facebook, Annabelle Lemmon lists the suburb of Mesa for her home and bank loan officer as her profession. After sending a private message, I head to the assignment desk where Alex uses a palm to play traffic cop.

"Stand by. Monitoring a 10–32."

He ignores a ringing phone and watches frequency numbers streak across the scanner's digital display. A smooth voice flows out of the black box.

"Single, adult male, unresponsive in the bathtub."

"Probably a 3–90," Alex says. "Maybe a 9–0–1-O."

"What's that?"

"A 3–90 is drunk. And 9–0–1-O is fatal overdose. Either way, don't care. What can I do for you?"

In addition to being the master of police codes, Alex is the king of online searches. He has access to more databases than the rest of us. And he's a whiz at sifting through enormous pieces of information to pull out the most useful nuggets.

"You can get more details on Larry Lemmon's co-workers and ex-wife, please." I hand him a sheet of paper. "I don't have much. I wanted to check court records for current and past cases, but need to prioritize my time. And talking to a source takes rank."

"No problem. You do your thing, I'll do mine."

As I walk away, my phone rings. It's Jim.

CHAPTER
9

"Hey, thanks for calling, Jim. Anything new on the Larry Lemmon case?"

"Nothing I've heard."

"How about helping me match names with faces? I know the guys who worked on Larry's show, and I met Shana, the program director, but she was with a woman I don't know. She's thin and short. Stereotypical Scottsdale look."

Scottsdale, sometimes called Snobbsdale or Snottsdale, is a wealthy suburb of Phoenix known for celebrity sightings.

"I'm gonna assume you mean Botox, implants, and bleached hair," Jim says.

"She's a redhead."

"Must have been Kelly Lemmon. Larry's ex."

"Wait, I thought his ex-wife was Annabelle."

"She's his first. Kelly was his second wife. Used to work in sales at KFRK. That's where they met. She was at lunch with Shana when they got the news about Larry."

"That's her. How's it—?"

"K-E-L-L-Y."

Thank you, Jim for unofficially confirming your unit is involved in the investigation.

"Listen, everyone's reporting the poison angle and JJ beat me with the cookie delivery info. I could really use something new."

"All I know is detectives are reviewing the surveillance video in case we need it."

"Can I get a look at it?"

"No."

I consider calling in my chip. Months ago, I got a tip that cops were investigating a state lawmaker suspected of shoplifting. A steady visitor to McClain's department store near the capitol complex, she would spend lunch hours browsing the racks. That's what everyone thought until a new employee noticed her slip a skirt into a shopping bag. The employee told his manager, who scolded him, said the woman was a powerful politician with more than enough money to buy whatever she wanted. But when the same employee saw the lawmaker walk out the door with a shirtsleeve dangling from her Louis Vuitton bag, he clicked a photo and showed his boss. The next time the lawmaker visited the store, the manager mentioned what the employee saw. The lawmaker called the employee a liar and threatened a defamation lawsuit, which freaked out the manager, who called corporate. The company's lawyers instructed him to call the police and file a report. That's when I heard about it. I wanted to pursue it, but Jim asked me to hold off.

"Store security wants to watch and try to catch her in the act," he told me. "I'll keep you posted."

Nine days went by before the lawmaker returned. Security approached her outside the exit and recovered a necklace and socks. But I didn't hear about it from Jim. Another shopper recognized the politician, snapped photos of her being arrested after allegedly taking a swing at a cop. When the shopper posted the photo to Instagram, she tagged JJ. Rather than getting the promised exclusive, I lost it to Phoenix's most mediocre reporter.

"C'mon, you won't give me the video. You won't let me report the paramedic's suspicion. Just throw me a bone, okay?"

No response.

"You still there?"

"Anyone ever tell you that you can be annoying?"

"Me? Never."

Jim grunts. "Yeah, right. Listen, you can say we're looking for the woman who delivered the cookies. But she is not to be identified as a suspect. Just say we'd like to talk to her. She is not a suspect, hear me?"

"Got it. Not a suspect."

"You can attribute it to a source only. Now I really have to go."

"Thanks, Jim. Just one more thing. Do you have a contact at the ME's office? I left voice and email messages but haven't heard back."

"I do have a contact."

"Mind sharing?"

"Yes, I do mind."

"I'm not going to bug them. I just want to make sure my messages are getting to the right person. I really need to get an idea of when we'll know the result of the cyanide test. To help plan our content."

"Jolene, I'm not your personal assistant. Like you, I need to protect my sources. I'm not giving it out."

This is the hardest Jim has ever pushed back. But it's understandable. A year and a half ago, his career was almost destroyed after working with a reporter. Jim was disgusted with a dirty cop who'd managed to fly under the public's radar for years. He racked up complaints about unprofessional and even criminal conduct. In one case, a woman claimed he pulled her over for a suspected DUI and offered to let her go if she had sex with him. When the woman and her attorney showed up at police headquarters to file a complaint, the cop said he'd never met her and an internal investigation turned up no evidence of a traffic stop. A restaurant manager driving home after a late shift reported seeing a woman who matched her description standing next to a light-colored sedan that matched her car. He saw her talking to a uniformed officer, but with the flashing lights from the cop's car, there was no way he could ID either one. Citing a lack of evidence, the county attorney's office declined to pursue a case. Nine months later, a court-ordered paternity test identified the cop as her baby's father. The city quietly settled a $2.5 million lawsuit and the cop, who ultimately claimed it was consensual sex while on duty, was suspended for thirty days without pay. He ended up quitting and took a job with another law enforcement agency in Arizona.

One could argue Jim's punishment was much worse. He tipped off a reporter with the understanding his name would never be mentioned. And it wasn't. Not directly. But the reporter revealed enough specifics about his confidential source that it took less than five seconds for everyone in the police department to identify Jim. He was booted from the public information office and sent back to patrol where he worked overnights for fourteen months. Then, a new police chief arrived and met with him. Jim never told anyone what was said—at least not anyone who repeated it to a reporter—and a month later the chief named him commander of the Special Investigations Unit.

"Let me know ASAP when you have more. I'll do some cyanide research so I'm ready."

"I don't want to burst your bubble, but remember we're talking about an overweight, middle-aged guy who smoked for years and didn't exercise. It's more probable he suffered a heart attack than was the target of a conspiracy."

"Conspiracy, huh? What are you hearing?"

"Right now, I'm hearing a reporter grasping at straws. Don't let your quest for a good story get you into trouble, Jolene. Bye."

After a few minutes grazing on my thumbnail and racking

my brain, I'm no closer to finding a way into the ME's office. Recalling Jim's previous reference to Jonestown, I start googling—and questioning humanity. Before September 11, 2001, it was considered the largest single loss of American life in a deliberate act. Jonestown refers to the Peoples Temple Agricultural Project organized by Jim Jones, a former preacher from Indianapolis who created a settlement in Guyana. In 1978, it was the scene of a mass murder-suicide. More than nine hundred people, including babies, drank or were forced to ingest a powdered drink laced with cyanide. The phrase "drinking the Kool-Aid" was coined after Jonestown.

"Hey, what are you working on?"

Snatching the mouse, I close the browser. "Nothing."

"Jonestown, huh?" Alex says over my shoulder. "Do cops think Lemmon was poisoned by cyanide?"

"No, no, just doing research."

"Whatever. I know you, Jolene. And how much you respect your sources so I'm not going to push it."

"I'll push you then. What do you have for me?"

"I don't know what happened to Larry Lemmon, but I'm pretty sure I know who didn't want him to die."

Alex pauses for drama. I signal him to hurry up.

"Okay, I have info on Lemmon's two ex-wives."

"Wait. I just learned he had two exes. Seriously, like five minutes ago. How did you find out?"

"If I told you, I'd have to kill you."

He says Larry married Annabelle in his early twenties, after he left the army. They had a son named Travis who's now in his mid-twenties living in the D.C. area and working for the federal government.

"I couldn't nail down his exact job title but he's with the Internal Revenue Service."

"IRS? Larry must have hated that."

"Larry might not have known. He divorced Annabelle when Travis was eight years old."

"When I interviewed Larry, we didn't talk a lot about family, but he did mention a son. Said he worked in financial services."

"That's one way to describe the IRS." Alex holds out my notes. "I added his first wife's phone number and address if you're interested."

"Of course I am. Thanks. Was she getting alimony?"

"No, she got nothing beyond child support and that ended when their son turned eighteen. Now, ex number two is a different story."

"Kelly Lemmon?"

"You know her name. I'm impressed."

"Yeah, we reporters can still learn things by talking to people, not computers. I was told Kelly met Larry when she worked in sales at KFRK."

"And she has the most to lose from his death," Alex says. "As part of their divorce, Larry was paying twenty-five hundred a month. Supposed to keep paying for ten years."

"Sounds like a good deal for her."

"A three-hundred-thousand-dollar deal to be precise. Of course, she might end up with a lot more if this turns out to be a repeat of her first marriage."

"What do you mean?"

"Before Kelly moved to Phoenix, she lived in Buffalo, where she was married to a guy who owned a snowplow company. Considering Buffalo can get as much snow as we get sunshine, he had a solid business. Presumably, she got it all."

"How'd he die?"

"D-R. Accidental."

"English, please."

"Accidental drowning. That's the official word."

"You don't buy it?"

"No judgment. I ran out of time and couldn't dig anymore."

"What you found is incredibly helpful. I'm going to call someone who might have insight into ex number two's background. Thanks for everything, Alex."

"10–4."

After two rings, I get Shana Forrest's voice mail. As KFRK's program director, she would have worked closely with Larry. And since she was having lunch with Kelly the day he died, their relationship could be more than professional. I explain I'm following up on Larry's memorial service and ask her to call.

Kelly doesn't answer either, and I leave a message, offering condolences and requesting a call back. Ex number one answers and agrees to talk on camera, giving me time to review more of my interview with Larry.

In addition to immigration and climate change, Larry had a history of criticizing one of Arizona's most beloved politicians, the late U.S. senator and former GOP presidential candidate John McCain. He frequently called McCain, who endured more than five years as a prisoner of war in North Vietnam, a warmonger obsessed with Russia. During our interview, Larry described McCain's daughter Meghan as a RINO, Republican In Name Only, and accused her of cashing in on Daddy's legacy. Larry even attacked former President Donald Trump for being soft on people known as Dreamers, undocumented immigrants brought to the United States as children. He expressed disgust that Trump didn't immediately end a program put in place by his predecessor to shield Dreamers from deportation.

"Meeting in five minutes," Bob's voice booms across the newsroom. "And heads up, Jolene. We'll have guests arriving soon who could use your help."

CHAPTER

10

My news director's announcement has me biting the inside of my cheek. How can he expect me to help someone else when I'm the one in need?

"Hey, chica." Elena drops into a chair, rolls toward my desk, and rests her face in her hands. "Don't take this the wrong way, but you're giving off negative vibes. What's going on?"

"Thought I was going to kick ass on this story. Now I'm playing catch-up—the worst kind."

"Trailing JJ, huh? Did her thigh-high boots strike again?"

"She got an exclusive interview with Larry Lemmon's producer. Plus, she reported something a source gave me first, but it was off the record."

"That sucks. But hey, you still have Larry's interview."

"You know how it is. No one cares what you did yesterday. They want to know what you have today."

She rolls back to log onto her computer. "If it's any consolation, I have an idiotic story lined up."

"What?"

"A woman complaining a TSA officer tested her five-year-old daughter's hands for explosive residue."

"How'd we hear about it?"

She gave me the look.

Ah, Facebook. The modern newsroom's source for story ideas. So many wasted days hunting down posts that have slim to no chance of being accurate all because some manager thinks it could go viral.

"Cue sound of an angry mom, show video of people waiting in lines, and wrap it up by saying TSA could not comment on the specific case." She throws up her hands. "What's the point?"

"The point is simple—it will fill ninety seconds of your local newscast."

"I don't like taking off my shoes or having to throw away my shampoo bottle, but it's not the employees' fault. If Americans don't like it, they need to make Congress change things. We shouldn't be picking on frontline workers who are following orders. Did you know forty percent of TSA employees are veterans?"

"No."

"My cousin is. He's only been there three months and he's ready to leave. Some of the same people who would thank him for his military service totally disrespect him when he's wearing his TSA uniform. Name another job where you're responsible for preventing a terrorist attack and yet people call you names and curse you out while you're trying to keep them safe. And they're supposed to stay quiet and take it? I couldn't do it."

"Me either." I pick up a notepad. "And I don't know if I can handle the editorial meeting, but I have no choice. Good luck with your story."

"You, too."

"I could've used some luck," Gina says, breezing by us. "Crash on the Piestewa Freeway. Took forty minutes to move two miles."

"You did have luck," Elena says.

Gina's bag lands on her desk with a clunk. "Do tell."

"You weren't involved in the accident."

"Hey, ray of sunshine, why don't you fill Gina in on your up-lifting assignment?"

Elena sticks out her tongue as Gina rummages through a pile of legal pads on my desk. "We know you hoard office supplies. Don't you have a clean one?"

I open a drawer and do my best Vanna White gesture. "White or yellow?"

Gina holds out a hand. "Yellow. You ready for more Larry?"

I hand her a pad. "Are you?"

"Let's find out."

Bob has traded his pen for a red marker. On a whiteboard, he's drawn columns designated by first names. The marker screeches as he writes "Larry interview" under my name. "Okay, what do you have?"

I want to tell him about the medic's suspicion, but I've been in newsrooms long enough to know you can't trust everyone to keep their mouths shut. Sometimes the information is unintentionally repeated. Sometimes it's not. Either way I won't risk burning—and losing—my source.

"I've contacted both ex-wives. His most recent, Kelly Lemmon, used to work in sales at KFRK. She hasn't gotten back yet but I have an interview with his first wife, Annabelle, this afternoon."

More squeaking as Bob adds, "Ex number one interview."

"I'm still working to get his producer and I'd like to research poisons."

"They think the cookies were poisoned?"

"It's too early to say, but, as we've reported, they'll likely test for poisons. When a full battery of toxicology is run, it can include things like cyanide and strychnine. I have a source that will give me more details, but nothing I can report yet."

"When can you?"

"I don't know. I'm pushing, but everyone's being cautious because this is considered high profile."

"I'm glad you mentioned that." Bob's eyes swoop over the group of reporters and producers. There's a range of ages but no technology gap between generations. Everyone's gripping phones. Scrolling. Texting. Deleting.

"Hey." Bob whacks the marker against the board. "Up here."

Faces swing up, but no phones go down.

"A high-profile case means more interest and more potential to reach a wider audience. We need to keep that front of mind. As I've said before, we will own this story. Understood?"

As the nods and mumbles fade, Bob asks what else I have.

"On the delivery angle, we can say police are looking for the woman who dropped off the cookies. She is not considered a suspect, just someone they want to talk to."

David dives in. "What about surveillance video? That would be sexy."

"I'm told there's video. Not the best quality and we can't get it yet. They don't want to scare her off. We need to clearly state that she is not a suspect. As you know, that can change in the future, but my source is adamant we can only say she's someone police want to talk to."

The marker yelps out "Delivery woman" under my name, along with "Poison." Bob asks if I have anything else.

"That's it for now."

"Okay, since the memorial outside the radio station is growing, we'll have Gina reporting there live again."

He swaps the red for a sky-blue marker that glides across the board. "We'll have an anchor front the latest on the investigation, mention the search for the cookie delivery woman, and also what kind of poisons could be in the toxicology report."

As Bob plots how to make an anchor look brilliant, my teeth chomp on a thumbnail and my knee bounces under the table.

The anchors have done nada to gather information. Letting them present my work when their only field experience is emceeing charity events and reading to preschoolers is unfair.

My teeth release the nail. "I can handle the investigation and the interview with his ex."

"I appreciate your offer," Bob says. "But there's too much to limit to one person or a single report. Since you have Larry's interview, you might want to pull new sound from that and combine it with whatever you get from his ex. Or, you can do the latest on the investigation and let someone else interview his ex. What's your preference?"

It's a bullshit choice. But I get it. Team coverage is all about emphasizing that we are the station of authority.

"It's my interview. I'm doing it."

"Fair enough. David can work up details on the investigation for an anchor. Then we'll toss to you with the ex's interview and we'll end with Gina at the memorial. Questions?"

"I just want to remind everyone about the importance of social media," David says. "We need to champion this story on Facebook, Twitter, anywhere you can think of. Oh, and Jolene, if you need help just let me know."

You can help by not irritating me, Sexy.

Bob looks through the glass wall into the newsroom. "It appears our guests have arrived."

What I see makes me groan.

"As Jolene mentioned, this is a high-profile case and the network has sent a crew to cover it," Bob says. "As always, we'll share what we have and help them however we can. Jolene, they'll want your interview with Larry."

"Are you kidding? That's my exclusive."

"Yes, and the station will be credited every time our network and any affiliates run it. It'll be outstanding exposure for us."

He's delusional. Once we give up control of my interview,

it becomes everyone's interview. Just because our station's call letters will be displayed for three seconds doesn't mean the audience is going to notice the puny font or care who did the interview. But it's yet another battle I'll never win.

"Reporters, you can go," Bob says. "Producers, you stay. Let's talk specifics for each show."

As I trudge out the door, Gina joins me and says, "Here come the big dogs thinking they can show us local yokels how it's done."

I recognize the photographer with the network crew clustered around the assignment desk. He used to work for another Phoenix station before he got fed up chasing car crashes and fires and started freelancing full-time. Now he shoots corporate videos, runs a camera at Arizona Diamondbacks games, and picks up lucrative gigs with networks. Next to him are two women. One must be a producer who will help with research, arrange interviews for the reporter, and coordinate with the network people in New York. The other may be a freelancer to handle audio. The networks seem to be the only broadcast entities left where someone still has one primary job title. Nailing the reporter is easy. He spends more time on his hair than the other three combined. Based on his age, he's a network rookie. That means the decision makers think the story is big enough to send a crew but not big enough to send one of their biggest names.

Alex sprouts from his seat. "Hey, Jolene, got a minute?"

"Godspeed," Gina says as we split up.

Alex begins introductions, but he's not going fast enough for the reporter who claws my hand. "I'm Jeffrey Cooper. You can call me Jeff."

No, I'm calling you Network.

"We just got here and could use your help. We have the transcript of your interview with Larry Lemmon. Do you have other notes or information?"

I motion to the conference room. "When that meeting breaks up, you'll want to talk to David Matthew. He's the executive producer and he's—"

"Yeah, yeah, I know who he is," Network says. "I want something new."

"David is handling the latest on the investigation."

"How long's that meeting going to last? We've got to get going."

Network is oblivious to his inconvenient request and annoying presence.

"Don't know but I sure hear you about needing to get going."

I start to turn away and Network's producer steps in front of me.

"Hey Jolene, congratulations on getting the last interview with Larry Lemmon." She flashes a mouth full of spiky teeth. "We really appreciate you sharing it. We hear you have an interview scheduled with his ex-wife and we'd like to join you."

That's network code for "We want to show up when you do so we can take over and set up lights and seating to give the impression she's only talking to us. Even better, we might convince her to talk to us first and leave you out in the cold."

I give her a toothless smile. "I don't think so."

Network's head bobs up from his phone. An eyebrow shoots up. Yes, one brow, like The Rock. Except it works for The Rock. Network looks ridiculous.

The producer, who no doubt has been told we'll share everything we have, isn't sure how to respond and goes with, "Excuse me?"

"Listen, I've worked hard to get this. You guys can talk to her right after I'm done."

"Maybe you don't understand," Network says. "We're on East Coast time. That's three hours ahead of you. Our deadline is very tight."

"So's mine. Happy to connect you with her after our interview. Just let me know."

Out of the corner of my eye, I see Alex shaking his head. As I scurry away, the producer barrels toward the conference room.

CHAPTER

11

I need to find Nate and get out of here now. I sling a bag over my shoulder and dash out of the newsroom, across the hall, and into the greenroom. Thanks to a couch and overstuffed chairs, it feels like a living room. Thanks to a gigantic bowl of potpourri, it smells like a Cinnabon. The room was designed for guests of a morning talk show supposedly tailored to the Phoenix lifestyle. It lasted less than a year.

"Oh, it was a terrible time slot, just terrible," Lou said during a staff meeting. "I always knew an afternoon show would be better, but, as you know, that's when the network airs syndicated programming we are contractually obligated to run."

The show's failure had more to do with management's interpretation of the Phoenix lifestyle, a metro area with more than five million people representing numerous countries and states, with multiple languages, skin tones, ages, religions, and income levels. Just like America. But in Lou's mind, one voice out of five million matters most: his wife's. While some may find that endearing, it can be maddening for the newsroom. The spouse of a general manager who makes hundreds of thousands of dollars a year should not be considered the "average" Phoenician. And yet, Lou relied heavily on his wife's social circle for show input.

In all fairness, it did highlight Phoenix essentials: hiking trails, magnificent sunsets, and Sonoran-style Mexican food. But it catered to stay-at-home moms from high-income households. Segments on kid-friendly events bypassed free programs at public libraries, while promoting five-hundred-dollar weekend camps for kids to run drills with Arizona Cardinals and Phoenix Suns players. And the producer couldn't get enough "best of" lists: best caviar facial, best couples' massages, best spas for mommy-daughter pedicures. Surprising only to Lou and his wife, the show didn't connect with most people who call Arizona home.

Now Gina, Elena, and I call the greenroom home, a place we can talk privately or escape the newsroom nuttiness. Currently, it's my hideout. I close the door and call Alex.

"Hey, Nate and I need to leave ASAP."

"Nate's daughter is sick. He's not coming in today."

"Oh man, I have to go."

"You can take William. He's loading up in Live Eleven."

"Is there anyone else?"

"Negative."

William Slater is known as "Woman Hater" among female reporters. Ten months after his wife left him for her personal trainer, William hasn't moved on, he's only become bitter.

"You still there?"

"Can you let him know we're going to interview Larry Lemmon's ex? I'll meet him at the truck in two minutes."

"Where are you?"

"Not near the newsroom. No way am I risking an appearance."

"Smart call. As we speak, the network producer is talking to Bob. And he does not look pleased."

"If anyone asks, we already left."

"Copy that."

I push the door open six inches. The newsroom hums in the background. Peeks in both directions reveal a clear getaway. The trade-off for dodging the news director's wrath is suffering William Slater's fury. Google says the thirty-two-mile trip will take forty-four minutes, but no mapping service can calculate the amount of discomfort. I'm fairly certain Woman Hater suspects reporters don't like working with him. Sometimes I take pity on him but generally it rockets out the window as soon as we hit the road. Like now.

"I bet this woman doesn't work and collects a fat alimony check every month."

Can't let him get to me this soon.

"She's probably never worked a day in her life."

I stare out the window and follow a geometric pattern of landscaping rock.

"Or maybe she went to college to get her MRS."

I consider pitching a story about artwork along Arizona freeways.

"You know what that is, right?"

I bet people would like to know how lizards, coyotes, and Gila monsters become part of their commutes.

"MRS is a Mrs. degree."

But first, I must deal with a snake in the truck. "All I know is she and Larry married young, had one son, and they divorced around the time he moved to Phoenix."

Woman Hater grunts. "So, she didn't want to support her husband's career."

My phone rings and I treat Charlotte from the promotions department like she's calling to offer me a network job.

Her voice dribbles with suspicion. "Were you expecting someone else?"

"No, not all. What's going on?"

"I know you're busy so I'll be quick."

"No need to rush. What can I do for you?"

"I want to run a tease by you. Ready?"

"All ears."

"Here it is: 'She promised to love him till death do us part. Now, Larry Lemmon's former wife is talking about life without him. Only on Eyewitness News, hear what she thinks happened to the controversial talk show host.'"

"Hmm. Kinda sounds like they were close. They haven't been married for many years."

"Remember, this is a tease." She's using her "trying to talk sense to a toddler" voice again. "We want to catch people's interest, get them to tune in. We can't tell the whole story in ten seconds."

"Okay, but you may have to drop 'Only on Eyewitness News.'"

"Why?"

"The network crew is hot on our trail."

Her voice switches from patient to peeved faster than a viewer can change channels. "Lose 'em, will you?"

For the next twenty minutes, it's like I'm sitting midcourt at a tennis match. My eyes dart to the side mirror. No one on our bumper. Check for our exit. Back to the side mirror. SUVs dominate six lanes of traffic on the Loop 202. The network crew could be in any of them. An overhead sign says we're two exits away. Could Network and his pals have made it this far already? My eyes shift to the side mirror. There's a sedan behind us and what might be an SUV farther back. Of course, there's no guarantee they would be in our lane. Or that they would follow the speed limit. Unlike us, they're not traveling in a marked truck, so they can be less than courteous to other drivers.

The next exit leads to the Orange Patch, where a since-retired photographer taught my first economic lesson about Arizona's five C's: copper, cattle, cotton, citrus, and climate. In the early years of statehood, copper mining, along with beef, cotton, and citrus production, created untold jobs, while abundant sunshine and varied topography attracted new residents and tourists. You could argue Arizona needs a sixth "C" for chips. The world's leading semiconductor manufacturers keep expanding chip fabrication plants here. Still, smaller operations, like the Orange Patch, remain important contributors. As urban sprawl swallowed acres of citrus groves, the family-owned store remained standing like a stubborn bulldog. Freeways replaced many trees behind the store, but if you're young enough—or your imagination is strong enough—it can almost feel like being in the middle of a grove while peeling an orange or sipping freshly squeezed grapefruit juice.

The exit after the Orange Patch takes us to Tranquil Meadows, a manufactured home and RV park for people fifty-five and older. Less than half the homes are occupied, but come October, water, electric, and internet providers will cheer the first flight of snowbirds.

Woman Hater slows for a speed hump and says, "If I ever end up in one of these places just shoot me."

GPS voice navigation directs us to a right turn, over a speed hump, a left turn, over two more speed humps, and a final right turn before we reach Annabelle's home. It's not unusual to find flags hanging in retirement communities, but Annabelle's choice of display is impressive. A custom-built flagpole climbs twenty feet high. From the top, an American flag proudly waves to us. Below are two smaller flags: the red, yellow, and blue Arizona state flag, and the black and white POW/MIA flag. Lights are positioned at the bottom for illumination at night.

"I hope she knows to take them down when it rains," Woman Hater says.

"I'm sure someone who cares enough to have a display like this is aware of flag protocol."

While Annabelle's home is a double-wide, her driveway is not. A silver Dodge Ram pickup and brown trash bin eat up the space. Steam is seeping out of Woman Hater's ears.

"Exactly where am I supposed to park?"

"You can pull right in front of her driveway and still leave plenty of room for passing cars." I look around. The only movement outside comes from the flags. "This is no major thoroughfare. Or a minor one. Probably we're the first to use it today."

Woman Hater puts the truck in reverse, setting off a high-pitched blare meant to warn passersby. In this case, it alerts a woman across the street to unexpected activity in her neighborhood. A head covered in pink foam rollers pokes out a front door.

"What's going on?"

I wave. "Just visiting your neighbor."

"You can't park on the street."

"Old biddy, mind your own business," Woman Hater says under his breath.

"We won't be long!" I add a smile to the wave. "Thanks!"

While Woman Hater checks his camera battery, I press the tripod to my chest, prepared to wedge myself through Annabelle's carport. But it's a short excursion. There's no way Woman Hater can get through. To make room, I haul the trash bin to the end of the driveway.

"Hey!" Pink roller woman shouts. "You can't put that there. It's only allowed on pickup day."

I offer another wave and smile.

"You have to move it."

"We'll be gone before you know it," I call out.

"I'm going to report you to the park."

As she patters back inside, I hurry to a windowless door and press a bell that sets off the opening notes to "The Star-Spangled Banner." When Annabelle Lemmon opens the door, it's obvious she's been crying.

She raises a finger. "Ex-ex-cu—"

A sneeze sends curly hair into her eyes. Annabelle blots a wadded-up tissue across her nose and pushes back tawny strands.

"Sorry. Allergies. Please come in."

In her stocking feet, Annabelle is about four inches taller and forty pounds heavier than me. Or it could be the oversized shirt makes her look bigger. That's the fashion knowledge I've absorbed from Gina. Also, to avoid horizontal stripes.

"Where's your cameraman?' she asks.

"Getting his gear. He'll be here in a minute."

"I just had a manicure. What do you think?" She flaunts fingers in my face. "The color's called cherry tomatoes."

"Very pretty."

Annabelle leads me through a closet-like space that holds a washer and dryer before opening bifold doors that lead into a kitchen.

"Is this okay? I thought we could sit at the table."

"This should work. Why don't you take a seat facing the window so William can take advantage of the natural light?"

As Woman Hater sets up his camera, a yapping sound overpowers our small talk. Are those claws raking a door?

Woman Hater lifts his head from the viewfinder and widens his stance. "That's going to be a problem. Can you do something about the dog?"

For once, I agree with him.

"Oh, that's just Diego. He doesn't like to miss the action. But don't worry, he's in a back bedroom with the door closed. He'll quiet down in a minute."

"He better," Woman Hater mutters.

Annabelle places a forefinger near her earlobe. "Excuse me?"

Before this turns ugly, I express sympathy for her loss.

"Loss?" She huffs. "More like good riddance."

Sounds like we'll have a promo-worthy interview with the

woman who once promised to love, honor, and cherish Larry. I glance at Woman Hater who nods, signaling he's ready to roll. I ask Annabelle to explain how she and Larry met.

"I'm an army brat. During my sophomore year of high school, my father was stationed at Fort Huachuca. Know where that is? Southeast Arizona?"

"Near Sierra Vista?"

She nods. "Fifteen miles from the border. After I graduated, Dad retired and that's where we stayed."

"Did you and Larry meet in school?"

She shakes her head. "Before my family moved here, Larry'd already dropped out and joined the army. I was a manager at the Dairy Queen and he came in all the time. After Larry put in his four years, we got married."

"How old were you?"

"Twenty, Larry was twenty-one."

"What did he do after the army?"

"What didn't he do is more like it. Larry wanted to be a police officer, but he lied during the interview about smoking marijuana. Funny thing is if he hadn't lied, he would've been hired. At the very least, he would've continued through the process. Did you know you can have a history of using cocaine, meth—heck, even heroin—and still get hired by some agencies? You can't be a recent user. And you can't lie about having tried it. My dad said there used to be a time when using marijuana—even once as a kid—was enough to keep you off the force. Now they're okay with what they call 'experimentation.' Unless cops catch other people experimenting, then it's a crime—or used to be. Guess anything goes now that marijuana is legal here. Times change. And not always for the better."

I guide her back on topic by asking what Larry did next.

"He was a security guard at an office complex for a few years. Too Barney Fife–ish though. Ended up losing his job."

"Barney Fife–ish?"

She sucks her teeth. "You are a young one, aren't you? Barney Fife was a by-the-book deputy on *The Andy Griffith Show*. You know Andy, right?"

"I think I've heard of him."

Another irked headshake. "That show's an oldie but a goodie. Even though it aired before my time, I caught reruns. This was back in the day before everyone spent their lives on their phones. Did you know we watched shows on a TV set back then? Sometimes even in black-and-white like Andy Griffith's show. Anyway, Barney was hilarious. There was this one episode where he was writing everyone tickets for petty things and Gomer got mad and tried to arrest Barney. He called it a citizen's arrest. Ran around hollering, 'Citizen's arrest! Citizen's arrest!'" She says it like, "Sit-zen's uh-rest." "Ol' by-the-book Barney nearly lost his mind."

"Mmm, maybe I can find that episode online. Back to Larry, why would he lose his job for going by the book?"

She shrugs. "You know, he never really told me. I got the sense he was too aggressive with some bigwig who didn't appreciate being questioned by a rent-a-cop. Anyway, Larry got a job at Walmart." She snickers. "Working undercover is what he called it. That just meant he wore regular clothes instead of the company's blue vest and roamed the aisles for shoplifters. Larry always liked to make his jobs sound more important and dangerous than they were."

"When did he open the shooting range?"

"After watching all the guns and ammo fly off the shelves at Walmart." She dabs her nose with the tissue. "Larry knew the guy who was selling the range. He convinced me we should take out a second mortgage on the house to cover the down payment. I ran the office and kept the books as best I could. Travis was three years old when we took it over. A very active three-year-old, could never sit still. Maybe that's why he's been on the go since graduating college."

"How old is Travis?"

"Twenty-six." Her lips curl but the smile doesn't reach her cheeks. "He graduated from the University of Arizona and moved to Washington, D.C. Sure do miss my baby. Talk to him just about every Sunday but he doesn't make it back here very often."

She sniffs and wipes her nose. This time, it has nothing to do with allergies. I study my notepad to give her a moment.

"Is it fair to say you handled business finances while Larry was the figurehead?"

"That's a charitable way of putting it. He was more like a wild turkey strutting around all the time. So full of himself." A red nail cuts through the twisted tissue. "People liked him though. Encouraged him to run for city council and mayor."

When I interviewed Larry, he said losing the city council race by sixty votes inspired him to run for mayor two years later. After losing that race by fewer than fifty votes, he started a podcast to give his supporters a voice he said the mainstream media dismissed. Larry became a frequent guest on the cable news circuit, mostly commenting on immigration. His show caught the ear of KFRK's program director.

"What happened when he was offered the talk show in Phoenix?"

"I told Travis we were moving. Showed him a map and explained Phoenix was the state capital. But Larry said, 'Honey, it's just me now.' Did you know he only had Travis visit for one week during the summer? Even that ended up being too much after a few years. By the time Travis started high school, they didn't hardly talk anymore."

She picks at the cuticle on her left ring finger. I keep my mouth closed and silently count seconds the way Grandma did:

OFF THE AIR 101

one Mississippi, two Mississippi, three Mississippi, four Mississippi. By the time I get to five, Annabelle's eyes meet mine. I expect tears but see flames.

"For years, I stood by him as he shuffled from job to job. Listened to him drone on and on about foreigners invading our country, the liberal media, the attack on gun rights, blah, blah, blah. In the end, the guy who claimed to be a family man was a selfish prick who abandoned his family in search of fame."

William is rubbing a boot against his Wrangler jeans. He claims it keeps them polished and, while that may be true, I've noticed the shining coincides with his urge to blurt out something inappropriate. Time to wrap this up.

"One last question, Annabelle. As you know, we're waiting to hear the official cause of death. I'm sorry to have to ask this, but do you think someone could have killed Larry?"

"You bet I do. And if someone did kill him, I say give him a medal."

Woman Hater clucks his tongue.

"Is there anything else you'd like to say? Any heartwarming memories you'd like to share?"

"Nope. Like I said earlier, good riddance."

CHAPTER

12

As we pull away from Annabelle's home, Woman Hater lets loose. "Damn. She was negative, huh?"

I choke on my Pepsi, which causes a coughing fit but doesn't slow Woman Hater.

"I mean she couldn't think of anything positive to say about Larry? Not a single thing? That's what's wrong with women. Always knocking us. Don't how to support their men."

A text to call the producer line saves me—and Woman Hater—from saying things that would land us in the HR director's office. Alex answers on the first ring.

"Before the others get on, you should know the network crew was beyond mad you left them."

"I never promised they could tag along. It was my interview."

"Hey, don't shoot the messenger. Just letting you know so if Bob calls you into his office, you're not caught off guard. Okay, stand by. David's joining us."

"Jolene, how'd it go? Get some sexy sound bites?"

"She's not a member of the Freaks Love Larry fan club. And she didn't hide her feelings."

"Excellent! We'll want the strongest sound ASAP so we can promote it on air and social media."

"I'll tweet a tease as soon as we hang up."

"Glad to hear you being proactive."

You better remember my team effort when I need reinforcements against Network.

Alex asks our ETA and I say we're going to KFRK, where we'll feed video to the station before our live shots. I tell him it'll be more efficient, which is true. It's also true it'll buy me time before I have to face my news director. Maybe if I avoid Bob until tomorrow, he'll forget the network snub.

When we pull into KFRK's parking lot, Woman Hater resumes griping. "Prepare for foolishness. Hollywood has arrived."

The memorial outside the building hasn't grown much, but the number of media vehicles has tripled. In addition to Phoenix TV and radio stations, FOX News and MSNBC sent reporters from their Los Angeles bureaus. CNN sent Anderson Cooper. And there are crews from the syndicated shows *Entertainment Tonight* and *Inside Edition*. Probably TMZ has someone here, too. Then again, with their reputation for paying for sensational content, they don't need an employee on the ground.

"I'm going to run across the street for coffee," Woman Hater says. "You want anything?"

Did he just demonstrate common courtesy to a woman? It's a good thing the armrest was down on my seat or I would've fallen over.

"No, thanks. I'm going to start writing."

But first I watch JJ run around like a kid in a candy store. An inappropriately dressed kid searching for the sweet taste of a new job. She strokes the arm of a guy standing next to a tripod, and when he moves to check the camera shot, the *Access Hollywood* logo on his jacket comes into view. After a finger wave, JJ struts to the next camera.

There's not much time before our live shot so I keep the writing simple, telling Annabelle's story chronologically. I record my audio tracks and tell Woman Hater I'm going to touch base with Gina while he edits.

"Text if you need me," I say.

He replies with a grunt.

Outside the truck, I accidentally make eye contact with Network. He smirks and gives a knowing nod. Uh-oh. Big League must have complained big-time to Bob. Thank goodness we skipped the newsroom. I pass a small riser set up for CNN with director's chairs—one for Anderson Cooper, the other for the person he'll interview. A camera with a teleprompter is parked in front of the chairs and a second camera is set up for an aerial shot to show the flowers, flags, and signs outside the building. A woman wearing a CNN shirt tells a man holding a clipboard to find a way to crop the other crews out of the shot. Adjacent to the riser, CNN has set up a barstool and table littered with makeup, brushes, and hair products. Lots of hair products. There's no riser for *Entertainment Tonight*'s reporter, but there's a king-sized mirror secured to a step stool. A thick container rests on the top step. It reminds me of the attaché case that travels with the president in doomsday movies. A man clacks open the lock and pulls out a drawer loaded with shadows, blushes, and lipsticks.

Nearby, JJ is sucking up to someone she hopes can lead her out of the Sonoran Desert and into the Hollywood Hills. "I really miss L.A., you know? The whole industry mood."

"You're not too far away," says a man wearing a Dodgers cap. "Our flight took less than ninety minutes."

"But it's like a totally different world here." She catches me listening. "It's so Midwest—you know, hearty eaters and passé dressers. Total Walmart crowd."

The guy laughs. "I do feel more in shape here than in L.A."

Tickled to have an audience, JJ raises her voice. "And don't get me started on the restaurant scene. I can't find a decent brunch in the entire city."

Someone calls my name, but as I circle around, no one acknowledges me.

"Look down, Jolene. Over here!"

Gina is huddled on a cement block at the front of a parking space. No teleprompter, no field producer, no makeup artist.

"Now that's true talent," I say.

"What is?"

"Putting on lipstick without a mirror."

"Years of practice." Gina smears her lower lip. "Know what my other talent is?"

"What?"

She stands. "I can hold my bladder for hours."

"Yes, we are the superheroes of holding pee. If only there were a way to make money off our unique skills. How's your day been?"

"Nothing to complain about. You?"

"I'm with Woman Hater so he complains enough for both of us."

"Speaking of complaining, did you catch Elena's story?"

"Yeah, the dumb TSA assignment."

"Oh, she's not covering that. Something better came along."

"According to . . . ?"

"Sexy. Who else? Someone posted video on the station's Facebook page of FedEx leaving a package at a front door. Then, a minute later, a woman sneaks up and takes it. Supposedly, contained a child's birthday gift."

"People steal packages every day. How is it better?"

"TSA story only had a picture the mom took. FedEx story has video."

"Oh, the tough journalistic calls that separate managers from reporters. I'm heading back to the truck. Need anything?"

"No, I'm good." She gives me a quick once-over. "Want to borrow a scarf?"

I inspect my shirt. "Please don't tell me I have a stain."

"No, you're fine. Just thought you might like a pop of color."

She opens her bag and pulls out a pink paisley fabric that might be a scarf or something more complicated.

"Gina, I appreciate the offer, but the fewer accessories I have, the better."

"Okay. See you on TV then."

Woman Hater doesn't grumble during our live shots because he's crushing on the reporter from *Entertainment Tonight*. Turns out to be a perk for me. In his quest to impress, William provides an extra light to the *ET* crew and sets up two lights for me. Unheard of. For him, setting up one is a monumental undertaking. Lighting is everything. Done correctly, it can fool an average-looking reporter into thinking she's almost pretty. No one else has talked to Annabelle, and as we wrap up our live shot, I'm savoring the moment. Then I get a text from David.

Why didn't you report cyanide?

Shit. That explains Network's smirk. An online search confirms it. Network got the scoop. It happens sometimes when local cops want to rub shoulders with national reporters. Doesn't make it any easier to accept.

"I'm putting a nightside reporter on the cyanide angle," David says.

"No, let me do it."

"You had your chance."

"I'm sorry, but I couldn't burn a source. Now that it's out there I'm sure I can produce something fresh for ten o'clock."

"How sure?"

"Come on. This is my story."

"Fine. But don't let me down."

Now I have to deliver. Before contacting Jim, I watch Network's story. Standing outside Phoenix Police Headquarters, he swaggers toward the camera.

"A source close to the investigation tells me Larry Lemmon was poisoned by cyanide, a substance so powerful it can kill a person in a matter of minutes. And it only takes a miniscule amount to do the deadly deed."

The video cuts to a close-up of a coin in Network's hand. "This nickel is small. Now think much, much smaller. Experts say a fatal dose of cyanide can equal one-twenty-fifth the weight of a nickel."

The story goes into an edited interview with a toxicologist who taught criminal poisoning classes at the FBI Academy. The interview was clearly conducted by someone outside Phoenix because the toxicologist is wearing a coat and standing next to a holly tree in front of a colonial-style house. She describes potassium cyanide as resembling sugar, able to quickly dissolve in liquid, and easily added to foods without detection.

"Food like cookies." Network is back on camera. "That's why detectives want to speak to the woman who delivered what appeared to be homemade cookies to Larry Lemmon's station shortly before he died. Lemmon's producer told a local reporter the controversial talk show host had two, possibly three, cookies before he collapsed."

No time to play text tag with Jim, so I call.

"What's up?" he says.

"That's what I was going to ask you. Our network just reported the cyanide and ran a clip from a toxicologist talking about how easy it is to put in food."

"Who gave them cyanide info?"

"No name. Just ID'd as someone close to the investigation."

"Ah, yes. The ambiguous, overused line of reporters."

I shrug off the dig. "You okay with me reporting cyanide was in the cookies? I can attribute the information to a police source."

"Who's your source?"

"Duh. You."

"No can do."

"C'mon, Jim. First, JJ gets the exclusive with the producer who reveals the cookies were delivered by a mystery woman. Then, Mr. Network—who has never stepped foot in Phoenix before today—swoops in and, in five hours, manages to kick my ass on a story where I had the last interview with the victim. Do you know how bad I look?"

"Sorry. Too few people know the details. I haven't even seen a tox report. If I'm caught as the source, you'll not only lose information on this case but anything else in the future."

"Please. I've got to have something new."

"Then find someone else."

"Let me ask you this: who do you think was the network's law enforcement source?"

"No idea. You know how it goes. Some guys get starstruck, some like to feed reporters info just to watch them chase it down."

"Jim, I really, really need something."

"Try the ME's office."

"I have. No one's responding."

"If you want to continue our relationship you better leave me out of it."

This is ludicrous. He can't expect me to quietly accept getting beat again and again.

"You know, technically you owe me."

"For what?"

"Sitting on a story about a lawmaker caught shoplifting. Remember that?"

A garbled curse is followed by silence.

"Jim?"

"Just hang in there. I'll get you something as soon as I can."

Yeah, but when?

Turns out not soon enough for our late newscast. Tracking down an expert after six o'clock who's willing to talk on camera about poisoning someone is impossible, so I'm forced to use Network's interview. Plus, I have to credit him for the cyanide scoop. At least I can attribute the search for the delivery woman to my source, and even though my report isn't groundbreaking, I'm able to turn a story that most viewers accept as semi-fresh.

Still, Bob's not impressed. He texts me to report to his office first thing in the morning.

CHAPTER

13

My night doesn't get any better. Norma is walking Tuffy, a stroll I suspect is timed to coincide with my return home. As soon as my feet hit the ground, Norma's voice hits my ears.

"What a news day, huh?"

Like my grandma, Norma gets most of her news from TV. But while Grandma spoke respectfully about legendary *CBS Evening News* anchor Walter Cronkite, Norma admires the morning show anchors at JJ's station for showing off their dance moves.

"I can't believe someone poisoned Larry Lemmon. How scary!"

"Norma, that hasn't been officially announced."

"But JJ says police suspect someone put poison in the cookies and then delivered them to the station."

"As shocking as it may sound, JJ is not the detective investigating the case. Just because she reports something doesn't mean it's accurate."

Tuffy gives me the evil eye, but Norma's not fazed.

"If I'd been there, I would have warned Larry." Her eggplant head sways. "You never eat anything unless you know how it was prepared. I've seen too many disgusting things over the years. Did I ever tell you about the seafood buffet in Chandler?

That place was awful, let me tell you. Had to shut it down right in the middle of lunch. Boy, that was a mess. People demanding their money back. One guy asked for a 'to-go' plate. Can you believe that?"

Someday we should do a story about Norma's experiences as a former health department inspector. But tonight, I just want to wallow in self-pity and go to sleep. As I exaggerate a yawn and prepare to excuse myself, Norma leans in, as if to share a secret.

"You know I don't like to speak ill of the dead, but Larry Lemmon didn't come across as very kind. What do you think?"

"His political and social views could upset people."

"I'm not talking about politics. He just didn't seem to be a nice person. When my Thomas was alive, we saw him one morning at Moon Valley Park. Thomas sometimes listened to Larry and wanted to say hello. Tuffy wanted to say hi, too. You know how affectionate he can be."

Norma's address is next door, but sometimes she lives on another planet. Tuffy is not affectionate. The closest he's ventured has been my shoes. Mercifully, he didn't like what he smelled and backed off.

"Anyway, Larry practically bit my head off. Told me to keep Tuffy away from his pants. Poor Thomas was almost as upset as me. He used to talk about how much Larry liked dogs and supported an animal shelter, but after that, he didn't listen to Larry much."

"Norma, I need to get going. I haven't eaten yet."

"Poor thing, you must be famished. Would you like some chicken pot pie? I can warm you up a plate."

"Thank you for the offer, but I'm fine."

"Are you sure? I don't think I've ever seen you with groceries. I bet you could use some home cooking."

What I could use is solitude.

"I have plenty of food, Norma. Good night."

As I turn my back, she asks Tuffy if he'd like a snack. A white envelope sticks out from my doorjamb. Thanks for the menu suggestions, Norma, but it'll have to wait while I play chef for Oscar.

"Sorry. I know it's late. I'm hungry, too."

He gobbles the flakes and retreats. The grocery fairy skipped my place again. Still, there's enough in the refrigerator for what I call brinner—a combination of breakfast and dinner—on the days it's my only meal. Crack three eggs in a bowl, stir, and microwave for ninety seconds. Cover with shredded cheddar cheese and drizzle sriracha on top. Brinner of champions.

My limited domestic skills extend into the living room where the décor cries, "Presidents' Day Sale." The three-piece collection features a glass-top table and black faux leather couch with matching chair. The fifty-six-inch flat-screen TV in the corner completes the conventional bachelor pad look.

Clicking the remote control takes me to CNN, where coverage of the latest partisan fight in Washington ends in a draw. Then, a map highlighting Phoenix fills the screen, the image large enough to include California to provide context for people in the middle of the country and the East Coast. The anchor runs through a speedy summary before introducing three guests to "discuss and debate" Larry's death. What they're debating I don't know and don't care to find out. I hit the scheduled recordings on my DVR and watch JJ's station. She manages to spend three minutes reporting nothing new while appearing on camera more times than I can count. Honestly, I could keep counting but stop at four and turn it off.

I return to the kitchen for the second course and make a mental note to replenish my dwindling stock of Food City tortilla chips. I manage to pry open a plastic container without slopping salsa fresca on my shirt, but Norma's envelope isn't spared. After dabbing the red splashes with a paper towel, I slide a fingernail under the corner and remove a card. There's a catfish on the cover. Or maybe it's a bass. Something grayish-green. A playful touch by Norma to share seafood suggestions. But there are no recipes inside.

> ROSES ARE RED,
> VIOLETS ARE BLUE,
> I TRULY ENJOY
> WATCHING YOU.

I drop the card and rush to the front door. Dead bolt is secure. Double-check the door connecting the kitchen to the carport. As I grab my phone and punch the number nine, I waste no energy trying to convince myself I'm overreacting. TV news has taught me vigilance can make the difference between being safe and becoming a victim. I press the number one and flip on the hallway light. Holding my breath, I strain to make out anyone else's. All quiet. Until I sneak into the bathroom and the screech, screech, screech of violins attacks my ears. I rip back the shower curtain and my heart bangs in relief. No Norman Bates.

One room to go. I refresh my phone, making sure the numbers nine and one are still entered before smacking a light switch on the wall. Was that box poking out from under the bed when I left this morning? Patio apartments—all ground level—make up this complex. I like not having noise above me and appreciate the quiet from a place that caters to older residents. But in case of emergency, I worry whether anyone would hear me scream. Getting on hands and knees to investigate could prove lethal. Or not. My choice is to check or fret all night. I kick the box.

"I already called 911." No movement. "Cops are on the way." No response.

I place my phone within reach and kneel next to the bed. Palms and knuckles grind into knotty carpet. As my body lowers, my heart rate rises. Stale air clogs my nostrils and two boxes of books mock me. Resting on my heels, trying to control my breathing, I consider this the catalyst to finally vacuum under the bed and donate to Friends of the Phoenix Public Library. And to test my physical endurance. I vow to get up early and run.

Back in the kitchen, as I snap the lid back on the salsa, a glob hits the poem's last line, slashing the "YOU." Wiping off salsa leaves bloody smears. I consider throwing the card away, but my reporter's instinct is to save it. Getting anonymous notes at work isn't unprecedented, but I've never received anything at home. Retracing my steps, I turn all the lights back on and contemplate calling Norma, the self-appointed Neighborhood Watch captain. She might have seen whoever left the card. But what could I say that wouldn't lead to a lengthy conversation—or worse, an in-person visit? I put the card back in the envelope and toss it in the fruit bowl next to Oscar.

"Don't suppose you know who's behind this?"

He ignores me, so I turn to the duo who never let me down— Pat and Vanna. The puzzle for *Wheel of Fortune*'s bonus round is a phrase.

_SK_NG _OR TRO_ _ LE

As soon as the clock starts, the contestant calls out the correct answer.

Asking for trouble.

CHAPTER
14

The next morning, there's going to be no run. Not even a walk. Usually, the deal I make with myself goes like this: give it ten minutes and then you can stop. Almost always, at the ten-minute mark I'm starting to warm up or deluding myself into believing endorphins are right around the corner. Either way it's easy to accept ten more minutes.

But not today.

There's not enough Visine on Target's shelves to get the red out of my eyes. My contact lenses want to stay in their beds, too. Circling the storage case, my finger struggles to get ahold of a lens. Three attempts later, it sticks to my right eyeball. Takes four tries for the left eye. After a night of flipping side to side, yanking covers off and on, and staring at the clock, my body now demands sleep. Thank you, wretched dreams. One jolted me awake to administer an oral exam. First, I ran my tongue across my teeth. All there. Then, I pushed on molars in the back to incisors in the front. Still firm. An online search divulges what I could have deduced if I wasn't so sleepy. Dreaming about teeth falling out means you're stressed out.

I shuffle into the kitchen where the envelope spent a restful night, its crisp exterior soaking in the morning sun. Lack of rest impairs my judgment and I text Norma to ask if she saw anyone around my place.

> **No, dear. Is anything wrong?**
>> **No. Someone left a card with no name.**

Watching bubbles on the screen as Norma composes a reply nearly makes me doze off.

> **I'm on it!**

And I'm too exhausted to ask what she means. I pull a Pepsi out of the fridge, text Jim to call, and boost the TV's volume so I can hear it while getting ready for work.

"Hands down, it's Rock Springs Café. No one can touch their apple bourbon pie."

"Is that the place off Interstate 17 on the way to Flagstaff?"

The news anchors and meteorologist are discussing their favorite pies and encouraging viewers—or friends—to share their favorites on the station's Facebook page. Before I can change the channel, my phone rings. The caller ID appears as "unavailable," a common ID for law enforcement agencies. Jim must be using a work line.

"Hey, thanks for calling so fast."

"You media scum."

It's not Jim.

"You all act like you're holier than thou, but you don't care about real people or real issues. All you care about is exploiting tragedies."

"Who is this?"

"A patriot." His words crack like a baseball bat. "Just like Larry Lemmon. He spoke the truth. The truth you media elites refuse to accept. You better wake up before it's too late."

Click.

My pulse ticks up as I mull over the call, comparing his message to the anonymous poem left at my door. No way it's the same person. The call annoys more than unnerves me. I'm used to posts on social media criticizing my appearance and emails complaining about story coverage. We can respond to those, but callers like Mr. Patriot are not interested in conversations that could lead to a deeper understanding of issues and other people. On a positive note, at least someone's watching my stories. JJ hasn't captivated every single viewer in Phoenix. It just feels like it.

The phone rings again and the ID comes up as "unknown."

"What do you want, asshole?"

"Whoa. You're the one who asked me to call."

"Sorry, Jim. Thought you were someone else."

"Glad I'm not them."

"Your number didn't come up. Why?"

"My personal cell is charging, I'm using a desk phone, so let's make this quick. What's up?"

"Any chance we'll get the official cause or manner of death today?"

"Same odds as me winning the lottery. And I don't play."

"How long will it take? Can't you rush it?"

"No one's rushing anything. We don't want to be accused of playing favorites. Lemmon's body is at the medical examiner's office where it'll wait in line with the others."

"That's not completely accurate. There's already been a test for cyanide."

"Have you independently confirmed that?"

"Not yet, but I will. After the network reported cyanide poisoning, every other outlet repeated it. There's no way the ME can keep quiet now."

"Maybe. Not my call though. Everyone involved in this case is being extra careful. It's like the whole country is watching."

"So you understand the pressure I'm under, right?"

"What I understand is that no one wants to say something that could end up being wrong."

"What do you mean?"

"The cause of death is just what it sounds like: what caused a person to medically die. Sometimes it's an underlying issue like heart disease. Sometimes it's from blunt force trauma, like a car crash. And sometimes it's poison from drugs, alcohol, or a toxic substance."

"Toxic like cyanide?"

"Sure."

"If the cause is from a toxic substance like cyanide then the manner would be murder, right?"

"No," Jim says. "A medical examiner never labels a death as murder. The closest it comes is homicide—that means death was caused by another person. That could be a car crash where an impaired driver killed someone. Murder is a judicial term, not a medical one. It's up to the court, not the medical examiner, to classify a death as murder."

"So, if someone is poisoned, their death is labeled a homicide?"

"Not necessarily. If someone accidentally ingested poison then the ME would label the death an accident. If someone intentionally ingested poison, the ME might label it a suicide. If there's no way to determine how the poison got into someone's system the ME might label it undetermined."

Undetermined would be the worst.

"How about giving me something I can go with today? Or would you rather I sink into a deeper depression as the networks scoop me in my own backyard? I'm like the local cop who gets screwed over when the feds come to town."

That's a feeling Jim can relate to. Five minutes later, he calls from his phone with a list of people cops will talk to if turns out Larry Lemmon was poisoned.

OFF THE AIR 121
OFF THE AIR 121
OFF THE AIR 121
OFF THE AIR 121
OFF THE AIR 121
OFF THE AIR 121
OFF THE AIR 121
OFF THE AIR 121
OFF THE AIR 121
OFF THE AIR 121
OFF THE AIR 121
OFF THE AIR 121
OFF THE AIR 121
OFF THE AIR 121
OFF THE AIR 121
OFF THE AIR 121
OFF THE AIR 121
OFF THE AIR 121
OFF THE AIR 121
OFF THE AIR 121
OFF THE AIR 121
OFF THE AIR 121
OFF THE AIR 121
OFF THE AIR 121
OFF THE AIR 121
OFF THE AIR 121

OFF THE AIR 121
OFF THE AIR 121
OFF THE AIR 121
OFF THE AIR 121
OFF THE AIR 121
OFF THE AIR 121
OFF THE AIR 121
OFF THE AIR 121
OFF THE AIR 121
OFF THE AIR 121
OFF THE AIR 121
OFF THE AIR 121
OFF THE AIR 121
OFF THE AIR 121
OFF THE AIR 121
OFF THE AIR 121
OFF THE AIR 121
OFF THE AIR 121

"This is a suspect list?" I open a Word doc.

"Not suspects. Persons of interest. People we'd want to talk to for information, not necessarily because they were involved in a crime."

"Okay, go."

"You already interviewed one—his first ex-wife. You can add his second ex to your list. And before you ask, we don't have any reason to suspect either of them of wrongdoing. It's standard procedure to evaluate spouses, lovers, all the people closest to Lemmon if he turns out to be a victim."

"Who else?"

"His show producer and board operator."

"Got them. What about the guy who's been filling in during Lemmon's show time?"

"Yes, Darrell Arthur is on the list."

"Any bad blood between them?"

"Not that we know of. Darrell's on the list because he works at the station."

"And he benefits professionally with Lemmon off the air."

"That might be the view of a cynical reporter."

"More like a realistic reporter. Any other station employees?"

"Shana Forrest. She's the program director you talked to."

"I can't imagine she'd want to kill her cash cow. What about other exes?"

There are no other exes, Jim says, but there's a guy who got upset because Larry dated his wife while they were separated. And a woman the station had to threaten with a restraining order to prevent her from calling. She was a longtime listener who reportedly went too far when it came to illegal immigration— even for Larry. Supposedly, she advocated violence, encouraged Arizona property owners along the border to shoot trespassers first and ask questions later. The station's legal team demanded she no longer be allowed to spout her views on the air.

"But the Constitution protects stations under freedom of speech and freedom of the press," I say. "The FCC isn't allowed to dictate points of view."

"I'm a cop, not a First Amendment attorney."

I tally the names. "Eight people's not much for a man who built a career on controversial comments."

"I'm not done. Two more made the short list—community activists who publicly clashed with Lemmon."

"Give me all you have on them."

"Phillip Ellys. Two 'Ls' in both names. Last name pronounced like Ellis Island, but spelled with a 'Y.' Environmentalist, I guess you'd call him. One of those guys who thinks cars and climate change are gonna kill us all. He and Lemmon had some heated exchanges on the air. Same with Ignacio Cortez—nickname Nacho."

"I know Cortez. He's outspoken on immigration issues. Likes to use one of Larry's catchphrases at protests and news conferences. Gets supporters to chant, 'Take back our country.'"

While Lemmon made a name for himself pushing for a border wall, Cortez did the same pushing for the border to be redrawn back to when Arizona was part of Mexico. Scanning the names, I ask Jim if anyone stands out.

"They all do, that's why they're on the list."

"How much of this can I use on the air?"

"No names. You can say we have a list and give some general information, but do not get specific. I don't want people to be able to identify anyone. And I bet your station's lawyers don't either. Unless you want to be sued for libel."

"Actually, libel refers to defamatory statements in writing. It's slander when spoken. But I'm not calling anyone a suspect so it doesn't matter legally. Besides, people have seen enough cop shows to know you'll investigate exes and the guys who were with him when he died. How about I go with that—stressing that no one who worked with or was married to him is a suspect—that it's simply standard procedure to talk to them? And I'll mention two community activists and a listener who had verbal run-ins with him. No names for them. Sound okay?"

Jim doesn't respond.

"Hello? You there?"

"Yeah, I'm just curious why you're skipping the jealous husband and the guy covering Larry's show."

"Because they sound the least promising right now. And because I want to impress you by demonstrating how reasonable I can be."

"More like keeping their names in your pocket in case you need something new."

"Good detecting, Commander Miranda. Since you're being so generous, how about contact info on these guys? Preferably cell phone numbers."

"Try Facebook."

"Now you sound like a TV news manager. I prefer the old-fashioned phone and email if you have it."

"Can't give you that."

"Pretty please?"

"No can do. I've already given you more than I should."

"And I appreciate it."

"Promise me I won't be sorry."

"You won't. Promise me no one else has this list?"

"As far as I know, you're the only one. Gotta go now."

I text Alex to run background checks on the community activists. Their run-ins with Larry place them within the realm of possibility for murder. So does wanting the premier time slot for a talk show. I text Alex to do a similar check on the fill-in host.

Closing my laptop, I turn to Oscar. "What do you think? This could be the start of more exclusives."

He ignores me, but I don't mind.

CHAPTER
15

The rush from getting names to check out is crushed by reality. While I have important information to track down, I also have a news director unimpressed with my performance. I creep along the assignment desk, shoulders hunched, face down.

"Not gonna work," Alex says. "Bob's 10–8. Ready to talk."

"More like yell. You sure there's no breaking news to send me on?"

He crams a doughnut into his mouth and shakes his head.

"There's gotta be something on the scanners. Maybe a 9–61 or 9–62?"

Alex flips a notepad to a clean page, removes the doughnut, sets it on the paper, and slides the back of a hand across his mouth. "Car accidents the only codes you know?"

"Uh-uh. I know 9–9-9 means officer needs help right away."

"Bravo." He slow claps three times. "Now, if you don't mind, I'm 10–6."

"Hungry?"

"Yes, but 10–6 means busy. If you want background on those names, you better vamoose."

The scent of sugar is replaced by the smell of onions. It's lunchtime for the morning show staff. Not easy to find places serving pasta, pizza, and burgers on their schedule, so by nine o'clock the newsroom exudes a fragrant bouquet of leftovers. Most of the early crew share a corner I rarely visit, but since I'm taking the long route, I observe their smorgasbord. An anchor slurps soup, a producer plops sour cream on enchiladas, and a photographer inhales fried rice. Occasionally, a morning staffer will say hello and ask about newsroom life during what they call "banker's hours," but no one's interested in chatting today. Except Bob.

Gina cuts across the newsroom, gently pulls my thumbnail out from clenched teeth, and hugs me. "I'm rooting for you."

Her embrace is an unwelcome reminder that the rumor mill is stronger than my reporting.

After tapping twice on Bob's doorframe, I dip my foot inside, testing the temperature. "Is this going to be a closed-door meeting?"

"It's up to you. I just want to understand what's going on."

Closed door, it is. I slog across the room and sink into a chair. The bags under his eyes are puffier—like bruised orange slices.

"Jolene, it's not like you to get beat on a story, especially when you started so far ahead of everyone else by having Lemmon's interview."

"No one feels worse than me. You know how hard I work, but there's nothing I can do if other reporters get lucky."

"You're right. We can't control if others get lucky."

My shoulders loosen and I lean back. It's about time someone feels my pain. "Too bad other people don't understand that."

"Here's what you need to understand, Jolene: you must stay focused on what you can control. Work your sources harder."

My mouth opens and Bob's eyes tell me to shut it.

"This is a golden opportunity for us to reinforce the relevancy of local news. And higher ratings would be helpful, too."

"I do have a new angle, a list of persons of interest to pursue when we get official word Lemmon was poisoned. I can't go public with names, but Alex is running background checks so we'll be ready. I'm not sitting around though. I'm going to contact those people. Now."

Bob stays quiet so long I fill the silence with a promise. "This is my story. I will not be chasing other reporters."

"That's what I want to hear. And if you need help, speak up. I know you see this as your story, but it's bigger than you. Station before self, you know? This is our chance to win the war."

I imagine military members would not appreciate equating local news to war. Then again, I'm not leading the newsroom troops. I'm just a reporter who keeps losing battles.

"While you continue working the Lemmon story, I have another assignment for you. A consumer investigation."

Sounds okay.

"We want to test dry cleaners to determine which ones are best at getting stains out."

Uh, not okay.

"Alex will assign an intern to help you get undercover video. If the story does well—and I'm sure it will—we'll do more and brand them as 'News you can use.'"

"Don't you mean, 'News Lou's wife can use'?"

Bob's expression signals I've crossed the line and to underscore the point he says, "Get over it, Jolene. I understand you're under pressure. I'm under pressure, too. You can keep working the Lemmon story—we expect you to come up with something new—but in the meantime you need to produce other content."

"And you're telling me, as a station, we think covering the suspicious death of a high-profile talk show host is on the same level as figuring out which dry cleaner can get spaghetti stains out? That's absurd."

"It's not up for discussion. We may live in a democracy, but a TV station is a dictatorship run by a general manager who answers to corporate who reports to shareholders who expect returns on their investments. As the news director with a mortgage and four kids, I need to deliver. Just like you do, Jolene. You can go now."

Bob trumpets an open-door policy and I claim a minor victory by closing it. As I near the reporters' pod, I can almost see a cartoon bubble above Gina's head asking what happened. I want to pop it.

"Jolene, I have something for you."

Hussein Aden may have just saved my friendship with Gina. He hands me a padded envelope, five by seven inches.

"It came yesterday when you were gone."

Hussein works as a combination mail sorter / security guard for the station, a job he could've never imagined in a country he never planned to live in. Born in Somalia, Hussein witnessed family members murdered at the hands of government forces. After fleeing civil war, Hussein spent his teenage years and young adulthood living in a refugee camp in Kenya. There, he met and married Mumina and they had two children. After undergoing extensive background checks, Hussein's family was invited to Phoenix. Over the past forty years, Arizona has welcomed more than ninety thousand refugees from Afghanistan to Zimbabwe, and a hundred countries in between. Ten years after they arrived, Hussein and Mumina were allowed to apply for citizenship, and after completing a comprehensive process, they swore an oath of allegiance to the United States. To support his family, which has grown to five children, Hussein also works weekends cleaning rental cars at Phoenix Sky Harbor International Airport.

"I didn't want to leave it on your desk in case something happens to it."

"Thank you, Hussein."

No return address. Postmarked Phoenix. Heavy black ink just like the card left at my apartment. Or is it? I should take it home to compare.

"Nothing bad inside," Hussein says. "It goes through the scanner, no problem."

He's talking about a machine that, at first glance, could be mistaken for a desktop printer. It's stored in a portable office away from the building. That's where mail is delivered and examined. Like an X-ray scanner, the machine can detect weapons and explosives, but it can also catch anthrax, ricin, and other pathogens. The precautions were a result of what the FBI dubbed "Amerithrax," the worst biological attacks in U.S. history. Following the terrorist attacks of September 11, 2001, someone mailed letters containing powdered anthrax spores to media outlets and two U.S. senators. The bacterial disease killed two people and made seventeen sick. In 2008, federal prosecutors announced a breakthrough in the case and planned to charge a biologist at the U.S. Army Medical Research Institute of Infectious Diseases. The suspect killed himself before charges could be filed. Three years later, an investigation by ProPublica, PBS, and McClatchy raised new questions about some of the evidence, but the government has made no attempt to reopen the case.

"Thanks for checking the envelope. How's your family?"

"Everyone is doing good. Mumina is healthy, the children all healthy. Even Ibrahim."

Ibrahim was a year old when they arrived in Phoenix and he missed the only food he'd ever known: porridge and nutrient-enriched flour served at refugee camps. Ibrahim wouldn't eat cereal, oatmeal, or much of anything else. He refused to take supplements prescribed by the doctor and Mumina had to give him daily injections for years. Today, Ibrahim is a healthy thirteen-year-old who loves pizza and tacos as much as his mother's rice and goat dishes.

"Please say hello to everyone and thank Mumina again for her delicious sambusas."

When Hussein brought sambusas to the station, they reminded me of empanadas. But Elena pointed out empanadas are semicircles while sambusas are shaped like triangles. Mumina stuffs the fried dough with minced meat and vegetables and makes a meatless version with potatoes.

"Everyone loved them."

"I'll tell her. See you later, Jolene."

I grab scissors, cut the envelope's top, flip it over, and shake. A thumb drive plops onto my desk. I peer inside the envelope and pull out a single piece of white paper. In large, bold type it reads:

UR CLOSER TO LARRY'S KILLER THAN U KNOW.

I'm about to violate corporate's guidelines on cybersecurity, rules we're required to read and pledge to follow.

Please don't screw me, mystery mailer.

I press the power button on my desktop computer and plug in the thumb drive. There's no video, no photos, only audio clips. All labeled *Larry Lemmon Show* followed by the numbers one through three. I put on headphones, turn up the volume, and click the first clip. Lemmon's voice roars.

"The problem with you people is you don't know how to take a joke. How can you not laugh at this commercial? It's first-rate advertising."

Larry described a Taco Bell commercial from the late '90s featuring a talking Chihuahua before he played the tagline that became a pop-culture punch line: "Yo quiero Taco Bell," which translates into "I want Taco Bell."

"How can you not love this? It's a textbook example of American creativity and capitalism. A bilingual advertising slogan that crosses cultures. You could argue it's more genius than 'Where's the beef?' Remember that line from the eighties? The old lady—I think her name was Sara or Clara—always asking, 'Where's the beef?' She turned Wendy's into a household name."

The next voice is slower and deeper.

"As you'll recall, Larry, the Wendy's commercial did not reinforce cultural stereotypes or demean people. By using a dog to symbolize an entire ethnic group, Taco Bell's ad degraded us. And it encouraged Americans to look down on Mexicans."

"C'mon, Nacho! That's nuts!"

"My name is Ignacio." Any softness from his voice has evaporated. "Only my friends and family call me Nacho."

"Oh, now we're not friends?"

"Never mistake a cordial conversation for friendship."

"And never forget that this is my show. I control who shares the airwaves with me. And guess what, Nacho? It's time to say adios to you!"

"Larry—"

But Ignacio doesn't get another word in because "El Jarabe Tapatío," the Mexican Hat Dance song, fills the air. In the background, Larry's laughter sounds like a pig's squeal.

The second clip starts with a different voice.

"If you were honestly as God-fearing as you claim to be, then you would care more about Mother Earth."

"Oh, Phillip, Phillip, Phillip. You tree huggers just don't get it. Global warming is a farce. Haven't you seen the blizzard hitting Colorado? It's September, for Pete's sake! What kind of warming is that?"

"One snowstorm does not negate the scientific evidence which unequivocally shows—"

"Yeah, let's talk about your so-called evidence. It's put together by extremists in their ivory towers at liberal institutions where they use our tax dollars to conduct so-called research. Research that's used to issue reports that benefit their cronies. These are the same institutions that brainwash young people into believing their so-called scientific reports are more important than the word of God. I bet they've never even read the Bible."

"I have, Larry. And I must say you sound like a hypocrite. You claim to follow the teachings of Jesus Christ, but your actions contradict everything he stood for. What do you think Jesus would say about the way we're treating Mother Earth? We're polluting our air, land, and water with no regard for—"

"Here we go again! A wacko liberal lecturing me about Christianity. Maybe when you get a clue we can talk, Phillip. Until then I'm going to finish this coffee, toss my Styrofoam cup in the trash, hop in my Range Rover, and take the long way home. All while enjoying the freedom to burn as much gas as I want. God bless America!"

The final clip also addresses the environment and Phillip riles up Larry instantly.

"Climate change is real," Phillip says. "The scientific community has spoken and ninety-eight percent of experts agree that—"

"Oh, the all-knowing scientific community has spoken! But they don't want to talk about the unproven computer models they rely on to scare the public. If they're so confident about the gloomy future they've painted for us then why can't they provide more accurate weather forecasts? I mean, c'mon, how are we supposed to believe someone who says the earth's going to burn up in a hundred years when they can't tell me with any certainty whether it's going to rain this weekend?"

"Weather and climate are different and the level of predictability is different. Listen, Larry, even the oil companies acknowledge the emission of greenhouse gases is responsible for contributing to climate change. You're not going to argue with your beloved oil companies, are you?"

"I'm not going to argue with an environazi anymore."

"Larry, one of these days you're going to regret thinking this way."

"I'll tell you what I regret today: talking to you. See ya, wouldn't want to be ya!"

Three show clips add up to one confused reporter. I try to decipher the note. What does it mean that I'm closer to Larry's killer than I know? Did Phillip and Ignacio work together?

There's no way I can sit on this. For the second time in an hour, I find myself in the news director's office. A meeting with three managers prompts three reactions. The executive producer, David, wants to go on the air pronto with both the note and audio. Alex, the assignment editor, cautions it could all be a hoax, and my news director, Bob, reminds me—unnecessarily—that we need to report something new.

"Last night's ratings were up slightly," he says. "The most notable growth continues to be from our social media platforms. Engagement has exploded and we can't lose that momentum."

"That's why we need to push the audio now," David says. "It's sexy."

"I haven't even talked to cops. Let me see what they think. And I should try to interview Ignacio and Phillip. Plus, I have other names I need to follow up on."

"Let me guess," David says. "You can't go on the air with any details."

"My source gave me the names with the understanding I would not publicly release them."

"Yeah? Other reporters have sources, too. Maybe one of them will go on the air and we'll lose our lead on this story."

Better to lose a lead than lose my reputation. No way can it survive another hit.

"Remember journalism school, David? The famous print motto: Get it first, but first get it right. I know it's more than a hundred years old but some things shouldn't change."

"News flash, Jolene. We're not in the heyday of newspapers. We live in the Twitterverse where no one is loyal to any media outlet and TMZ beats everyone."

"If we want to pay people to call us when a celebrity overdoses, has a fender bender, or files for divorce, then maybe we can give TMZ a run for their money."

"That's enough," Bob says. "Jolene, call your source and let us know what he says about the audio and note."

"I want to be clear that I have never identified my source's gender."

David's eyes roll like marbles and Bob says, "Fine. Them. Call them. Anyone else have anything new?"

"I found something," Alex says. "About four years ago, the state attorney general's office investigated Lemmon's shooting range in Phoenix. A group of women filed discrimination complaints claiming they could go into his shop to buy weapons and ammunition but weren't allowed on the shooting range."

"What happened?" Bob asks.

"Lemmon argued that, because he charged a five-dollar annual membership fee, the club was private and the state had no right to tell him who he could or could not invite in. There was a lot of back and forth. In the end, Lemmon agreed to open the range to everyone."

"Bet he was furious," I say.

"The opposite. There was a national newspaper article about the deal he reached with the AG's office and Lemmon was quoted as saying all the controversy had improved business at the range and increased his talk show ratings."

"We could go with that if Jolene can't come up with anything," David says.

"It's interesting," Bob says. "But I prefer a new story that relates to his death, not an old story about his shooting range. Let's go find something. Right, Jolene?"

I present my phone. "Going to make the call now."

Unlike my managers, Jim is not pumped up.

"There are a lot of haters out there," he says. "I'll send a detective to pick up the note. Try not to touch it anymore."

All I've done for the last thirty minutes is touch it.

"I have to make a copy, but I'll try to keep my fingers on the corners."

"Why do you need a copy? Please tell me you are not going on the air with it. You know this could be potential evidence."

"You just told me not to get excited."

"Yes, but we also have to check it out. I need you to hold off on running anything about the note."

"I don't know if I can."

"Do you want to get flooded with emails and calls? That's what'll happen. Every nutcase will contact media across the city, maybe the country, spewing their ideology. We don't have the manpower to chase 'em down."

I release a breath and collapse in my chair. "I hear you, Jim, but I can't keep getting my butt kicked. You know, if you give me something else, I might get the managers to hold off on the note."

Now it's his turn to sigh. "I'll give you contact information for our persons of interest. In exchange, no reporting on the note until I say otherwise. Deal?"

I swivel toward the news director's office. Empty. I should run the offer by him first, but can't risk losing it.

"Deal," I say. "Let's start with Ignacio and Phillip."

CHAPTER
16

After Jim supplies contact information, I leave messages for Ignacio Cortez and Phillip Ellys by text, voice mail, email, and Facebook. Then, I move on to Rosie Rangel, who went from being a welcomed caller to banned from the show. As the phone rings, I expect it to be answered by someone holding a grudge. That's not what I get.

"You know my nickname, right?"

"I do not."

"Larry called me Rosie 'Run 'Em Out' Rangel." She cackles. "He loved having a Mexican like me on his show. I don't go for that politically correct bull like calling people 'undocumented.' They broke the law, they need to leave, and get in line like everyone else."

"I understand there was a situation that created a problem between you and Larry. Can you tell me what happened?"

"Oh, it wasn't really a problem with me and Larry. It was more like Larry had a problem with all the attention Donald Trump got. When Trump said Mexico was sending rapists and drug dealers to the U.S., I backed him up. I mean, they are, right? Look at fentanyl. The cartels are making rainbow-colored pills, smuggling them over here, killing our kids, and destroying families. You can't tell me every single person comin' across that border is an angel. We need someone on the national stage speaking the truth—even if it hurts the liberals' feelings."

"Sounded like Trump and Larry were on the same page. What was the problem?"

"Larry didn't like me supporting Trump again for president. Wanted me to tone it down. But how could I? Not after the 2020 election was stolen."

I could point out many Republicans who oversaw state elections, reviewed results, and investigated complaints found no widespread irregularities or fraud. But then the conversation would go off track and I don't have time for that.

"I was told the station's lawyers questioned some of the things you said. Things that may have been perceived as calling for violence."

"Idiot lawyers. All I did was advocate to secure our border and protect our country. It's no different than a burglar breaking into your house. You have the right to protect your property by using walls and weapons. That's why the poor ranchers carry firearms. They have to be armed to defend themselves against the smugglers. You know, the ones that take people's money and promise to get them to America and end up raping and abandoning the women in the desert? Or they hold people for ransom in a shoddy house with no food or water. Damn right Americans along the border should be ready to fight."

"Weren't you upset Larry wouldn't put you on the air anymore?"

"Honey, he would have eventually gotten over it. Besides, I've been busy helping save America. Got a little free time now, I can do an interview. Would you like me to come to your station? I can talk about President Trump, illegal immigration, border security, whatever. Or I can talk about Larry and what a magnificent man he was. Hey, do you guys ever have guests come on and do those uh . . . oh, shoot, what do you call them?" Fingers snap in the background. "You know, like the newspaper used to do when people gave their opinions. Maybe I could come in and try out?"

"We don't do commentaries during—"

Two days ago, I could have finished that sentence, but after the preposterous plan to empower an anchor to give his opinions, it requires editing.

"Rosie, right now, I'm just reaching out to people who knew Larry. Thanks for your time."

"I'm here to help. I can be at your station in an hour. Or anytime. Just give me a call. I know the score. You need someone to get worked up, I can do it. Or you want someone to get sentimental and cry about Larry, I can do that, too. Just let me know what you need."

Her offer is unethical. I'd never ask someone to act a certain way during an interview, but I don't have the energy to explain that either.

"I'll keep that in mind, Rosie."

I can't see her sending poisonous cookies. She wants to be part of the scene too much and Larry was her way in. I leave a message for the man who reportedly threatened Larry for dating his wife while they were separated. That gets me thinking about Larry's most recent wife. Maybe the way to her is through the program director, Shana, since they had lunch together the day he died.

Over the phone, Shana tells me they're working on a memorial service to be held Monday morning. "I don't have any details to release yet, but I'll send a media advisory once things are finalized."

"Thanks very much. I'm sure you've heard police are searching for the woman who delivered the cookies. Any chance you

can point me in the direction of whoever handles your surveillance video?"

"The station doesn't have anything to do with it. We don't
own the building, we're tenants. You'd have to contact property
management. It's through a company called Bentley Enterprises.
I don't have their number handy, but should be easy to find.
They're in Phoenix."

"Okay. Hey, while I have you on the phone can I get your
take on something?"

"What?"

"I'm talking with people who knew Larry and I'm not sure if
I should try Kelly again. I've left one message and want to be respectful. They were married so she could provide a unique per-
spective, but I don't know the best way to approach her. What
do you think?"

"The best way to approach Kelly is to be a man with money."

"Excuse me?"

"And she likes them semi-famous. You know, local celebs."

Unsure how to respond, I go with a soft "Mm-hmm."

"I'm not one to gossip but I heard Kelly's last husband died
under suspicious circumstances."

"I thought he accidentally drowned."

"That was the story."

"You don't think it was an accident?"

"Let's put it this way: how many forty-year-old guys with
twenty-five-year-old wives drown in their own bathtubs?"

"Did he have a heart attack?"

"Don't know. Supposedly, he was home alone. I do know there
were plenty of whispers when Kelly moved here and instantly
took up with Larry. Some people called her Black Widow."

I don't like describing women that way. I get that it's a reference to the female black widow, the most venomous spider
in North America, but common characteristics people attach to

them are wrong. I know this because in fourth grade we had to present a report on a spider or an insect. I picked the black widow. Well, I ended up with the black widow because spiders terrified me and my foster mother insisted I step out of my comfort zone. Seemed to me a child snatched from her mother and dropped in a stranger's home was already living outside her comfort zone, but who was I to argue? Anyway, I learned the female black widow's venom is fifteen times stronger than a rattlesnake. But bites are rarely fatal. And contrary to public opinion, female spiders are not constantly killing and eating their mates after sex. While it's been known to happen, scientists say it's not the norm.

"What's your take on Kelly?"

"She loves dogs and shopping. Both can be expensive."

"She was in sales," I say. "Didn't she make money?"

"Oh, sure. Kelly could get anyone to open their wallet. Doesn't mean she wanted to spend her own money though. Like I said, I'm no gossip. But you might want to check her husband record. She's two for two in the death department."

An online obituary for Kelly's first husband portrays an active community member. Jack McIntyre, known as "Jack Mac" to friends and business colleagues, served on the local chamber of commerce board and sponsored children's baseball, softball, and soccer teams. And he was a hit at Halloween. McIntyre didn't hand out those slivers they have the nerve to brand as fun-sized. He gave out full-size candy bars, which, based on comments from his obituary page, catapulted him to coolest adult in the cul-de-sac.

The *Buffalo Times* ran a front-page story with the headline "End of the Road for Snowplow King." The article had photos of McIntyre behind a desk and behind the wheel. He was the hometown boy who made the community proud. Turned a single plow operation into a regional powerhouse. McIntyre had contracts with Erie County and small towns scattered across western New York. The article didn't quote Kelly, but one of McIntyre's managers said the team hoped she would continue running the company "as Jack Mac did, with integrity and professionalism." I can't find any other stories about his death so I call the Buffalo newsroom and ask for the reporter.

"This is Dimitri Edmunds."

I tell him I'm working on a story with a connection to one he wrote six years ago. "Do you have a minute to talk?"

"You can have two."

"Thanks. It's about Jack McIntyre. He ran a snowplow business."

"Jack Mac. One of my first stories. What's your interest?"

"Looking for information about how he died."

"Is this on the record?"

"I'd like it to be."

"It can't be because I couldn't get anyone to go on the record. Show me your cards first. What are you working on?"

I tell him Larry Lemmon collapsed at work and it's been reported he was poisoned even though the ME still hasn't officially released anything. I leave out the part about Network scooping me on the cyanide.

"Now I get it," he says. "You're questioning whether Kelly kills her husbands."

"Since you put it that way."

"Can we agree that what I share is for your background only? That you need to come up with your own sources to go on the record with any of this?"

"Agreed. What do you have?"

"A lot of whispers after Jack Mac died about whether it was really an accident. No one came right out and blamed Kelly, but there was innuendo."

"What happened?"

"He'd been taking pain pills after back surgery. Supposedly, took too many, passed out in the bathtub, and drowned. Kelly said she found him and called 911, but it was too late."

"Any kids? Insurance?"

"No kids. Don't know about life insurance. Can't imagine a man like Jack Mac wouldn't have a policy but I couldn't confirm. Kelly got the whole business. Sold the buildings for seven hundred thousand dollars. Got another four hundred and fifty thousand for the trucks, plows, and other equipment."

"So, she collected more than a million, fled the cold, and moved to the desert?"

"Sounds that way."

I thank him and promise to follow up if Jack Mac's death makes it into any Phoenix stories. While contemplating Kelly's marriages, another spouse interrupts my thoughts—the husband who threatened Larry.

"Thanks for returning my call. I'm reaching out to people who knew Larry and—"

"That wife-stealing son of a bitch got what he deserved."

And I may have a solid suspect.

"Did you ever confront Larry?"

"Tried to," he says. "Coward ran away from me. I was just gonna scare him, but when I saw what a wuss he was it made me madder. I've worked hard to take care of my wife and kids. And she's going to leave me for a wimp like him?"

"Did you get to talk to Larry?"

"Nah, he jumped in his car. Can you believe it? Anyway, I got a good kick in." His laugh is sharp as a shank. "Too bad it was to the door as he sped away. Wish it'd been his ass."

"Did he call the police?"

"Of course. Whad'ya expect from a weakling? They came to my house, interviewed me. I told 'em what happened. I'm not ashamed of protecting what's mine."

"Did the police recommend charges against you?"

"They sent the paperwork to the county attorney to decide. That was, I dunno, about two, three months ago. Doesn't matter now. Since he's dead, I won't have to worry about it."

"I understand this happened while you and your wife were separated?"

A heavy breath enters my ear. "Five more days. Then, it's final."

"I'm sorry you're going through a difficult time."

"Not as sorry as me. You wanna know the saddest part? I'd take her back today if she'd have me. But I guess a guy who works overnights filling Amazon orders isn't fancy enough. Maybe she'll find what she's looking for with whoever takes Lemmon's place."

After hanging up, I study the list of names. Admitting to violence and showing no remorse might be an automatic red flag on paper, but my gut says this guy is heartbroken, not homicidal.

"Earth to Jolene."

Startled, the pen flops from my hand.

"Girl, you were in the zone," Elena says.

"Yeah, I'm overwhelmed with the Lemmon story."

Gina slides a chair next to me. "Let us help. What's going on?"

Elena leans over my shoulder. "What are you working on?"

I flip the notepad over to hide the list and explain I have names but no strategy.

Gina suggests talking to Larry's producer, Ralph. "He's got to have info that'll save you time."

"I can't reveal any names, but, as you know, Ralph was in the room when Larry collapsed. And, of course, you're a bright reporter so you could assume certain things."

"Yeah, yeah, we get it," Gina says. "Ralph's on the list."

"Yeah, what's the big deal?" Elena says. "You need to talk to him. Haven't they known each other like forever? Between the show and the animal shelter Ralph's going to know tons."

"You're right." I cast a look at the digital clock on the wall. "If the news gods are on my side, I might be able to catch him after his shift."

CHAPTER
17

Showing up unannounced at KFRK requires a photographer with patience and speed, someone who can wait calmly for an unknown length of time, then shoot and edit furiously under an unreasonable deadline. Someone like Nate.

"Sophie has chicken pox," he says as we climb into Live Seven. "She's scratching more than a dog with fleas."

"That's too bad. I know how much she loves kindergarten. Will she miss much school?"

"Yeah, we have to let it run its course. Doctor says about ten days. Brandy's going to take time off, but since she's only working part-time she can't afford to lose many hours. We're blessed her parents can help watch Sophie."

Brandy's parents weren't always so helpful. Especially when their seventeen-year-old daughter told them she was pregnant and marrying the eighteen-year-old father. It wasn't the path Brandy—or her psychologist father and medical doctor mother—had planned, but it's the path she chose and they came around. Nothing like a first grandchild to break down barriers. That was fourteen years ago. After their son, Brayden, was born, they went through challenging times, as Nate refers to it. He's never gotten specific, only saying he wasn't the best husband or father during the early years.

"I'll spend the rest of my life making it up to Brandy and Brayden," he once told me.

As for Sophie, she's only known a doting father during her five years.

"If Larry's producer agrees to an interview, we're going to be slammed the rest of the day," Nate says. "Every newscast producer will want something, so let's be proactive and fuel up."

We pull into a QuikTrip, and while he appraises the hot dogs, taquitos, and pizzas, I debate going half-diet, half-regular Pepsi. As the ice crunches into my thirty-two-ounce cup, a man barges to the diet nozzle and slams a sixty-four-ounce cup beneath it. Decision made. All sugar. Or more precisely, high-fructose corn syrup. Either way it's not healthy, but we all have our vices. Nate and I reunite at the register where he's balancing a sandwich, a soft pretzel with a side of melted cheese, and a bottle of iced tea.

"Already paid for your drink," he says. "Let's go."

"Thanks. I'll get you next time."

Nate tosses his sandwich in the cup holder and peels back the cover on the cheese sauce. "How do you want to play this?"

"Ralph's not expecting us and he hasn't responded to my calls or emails so I assume he won't be overjoyed to see us. Hoping to keep it low-key."

"In a truck with Channel 4 Eyewitness News all over it?"

"We can park in a corner, watch the door, and wait for him to come out."

"Whatever you want." He pops the last pretzel twist in his mouth and mumbles, "I got your back."

"And you have cheese on your chin."

Nate swipes a napkin across his mouth, unwraps a ham sandwich, sets it on his lap, and begins backing out. It makes me nervous when photographers eat and drive because it can be distracting. But since I'm not offering to drive, I keep my opinion to myself. The first and last time I drove a live truck was during an emergency—a TV news emergency. A truck died forty minutes before the reporter and photographer were supposed to go live. They were only five miles away and everyone else was under deadline so I offered to deliver a truck. Although we call them trucks, they're vans. Jumbo vans carrying extra fuel and loaded with equipment inside and out. I had to drive the oldest model with no rearview camera. Side mirrors were my lifeline.

"Only five miles, only five miles" was my mantra. After I arrived, it became "Never again, never again."

Nate finishes the sandwich as we reach our destination. We drink in unison while passing the memorial that's doubled in size. Candle wax drizzles on the sidewalk, handwritten posters are angled against the building, and, thanks to occasional gusts of wind, balloons crash into each other like bumper cars. Four people breeze out the door without acknowledging the cards and flowers. Presumably employees. Probably wonder when it will go away. Based on experience, I'd say a week. Taking it down sooner can come across as insensitive and cause someone to complain to the media, which could drive more coverage and people dropping off more items. On the flip side, leaving it up too long can get messy and come across as sacrilegious. It's a safe bet the scene will last through the memorial service.

Nate parks in a corner farthest from the back door. As he texts his wife to check on their daughter, Sexy calls me to check our status.

"Where are you?" David asks.

"Outside KFRK. Waiting for Larry's producer."

"You got an interview?"

"Not yet but I'm confident he'll talk."

"If not, we can just show the note and run the audio clips you got in the mail."

"No, we can't, David. I promised my source we'd hold off in exchange for new information."

"And what do you have that's new?"

"I can't say yet, but—"

"Again with the off-the-record stuff? None of this is helpful."

"It could put us in a better position when the cause of death is announced."

"The network already reported cyanide poisoning."

"I mean officially."

"Jolene, I'm not interested in days or weeks from now. We have newscasts to fill today."

"Just let me talk to Larry's producer and I'll get right back to you."

Clicking his fingers, Nate points to the door.

"Ooh, there he is. Gotta go."

I bail out and follow Ralph across the street. As he nears the coffee shop's entrance, a woman steps in front of him. She's on the thin side, average height, shoulder-length brown hair. Can't make out facial features—or words. Ralph broadens his shoulders and spreads his feet. Whatever he says makes the woman shrink, shake her head, and scuttle off. Probably asked for money. Panhandlers were among Larry's pet peeves. Ralph would find them annoying, too. Rather than add to his anger I hold back, watch through the window, and give him time to order. When he moves aside to wait, my sales pitch begins.

"I'm sorry for your loss and for intruding. I'd like to talk with you for a couple minutes."

"Not interested."

"I understand it's an awkward request and I hope you can understand my position."

"I couldn't care less about your position. I'm here to get coffee, not be interrogated."

OFF THE AIR   151

"If it came across that way, I'm sorry. I just want to talk with someone who was close to Larry."

"There are plenty of people who would be happy to talk to a biased reporter. I'm not one of them."

Ralph stomps to the counter. I stay on his heels.

"Would you be willing to share your thoughts about other people? I have some names I'd like to run by you." I lower my voice. "It's confidential."

He looks away but not before I catch the glint in his eyes.

"Can we speak privately?"

"I can give you five minutes."

He grabs a cup and I tag along. The table in the back corner is too small for his liking and too close to the restroom for mine. Flushing toilets and running water dilute the background music, but it's away from other tables, which is more important than ambiance. Ralph pulls at his shirt and offers an apology. Nothing personal, he says, not a fan of reporters.

"I talked to that bimbo JJ because Andy was excited about meeting her. Not much going on under all that makeup. Of course, that applies to the less attractive ones, too. You all want dirt on people. You aren't really interested in covering things that matter. That's why Larry was popular. He spent time on the issues, helping educate the masses. Giving them the real deal, not sugarcoating stuff, not spoon-feeding them government propaganda."

I've listened to more variations of media bashing than I can count and have a response ready.

"I agree with you—some reporters are uninformed and lazy. Frankly, it can be embarrassing—even shameful. I've learned the best thing I can do is ask good questions and gather as much information as possible, which is why I appreciate your help." I lean in. "What did you think when you heard about the cyanide?"

"There but for the grace of God go I."

"As you know, police want to talk to the woman who delivered the cookies. Do you have any idea where they came from?"

"Not a clue."

"Didn't you eat them? Did you ever get sick?"

"I didn't get sick, but I only ate the chocolate chip cookies. I don't like nuts. Larry ate both. Smart tactic on whoever's part to put cyanide in the almond ones to disguise the odor."

"Based on my research, cyanide sounds brutal. Any thoughts on who might want to hurt him?"

Ralph fixates on his drink. "Sometimes, Larry pushed the envelope. Some people didn't like it."

"Did he have trouble with anybody in particular? Or was he concerned about anyone?"

"Listen, I'm not going to get sued for talking bad about somebody. If you're nosing around for someone to point fingers, you got the wrong guy."

"I don't need you to point fingers. Somebody has already done that. I need your input as to whether I should keep my finger on them. Can you help?"

Ralph blows on the coffee before taking a sip. A toilet flushes. He checks his watch, smooths his mustache, and nods. "Under one condition. This is for your information only. You keep my name out of it."

We go over the list, starting with Darrell Arthur, the host covering Larry's shift. From what I've gathered, Darrell's political style is more George W. Bush. But that's his on-air persona. I need to know what he's like off the air.

"How did Darrell and Larry get along? Any problems between them?"

Ralph's mouth wilts in disbelief. "You think he poisoned Larry to take over his show?"

"I didn't say that. I'm just trying to understand the relation-ship."

"Never heard them argue."

"What can you tell me about Darrell outside the station?"

His lips coil into a sly smile. "You mean Dr. Arthur. He's an oral surgeon. We always thought that was pretty funny. A talk show host who operates on mouths. Larry sometimes called him Ben's brother."

"Ben?"

"After Ben Carson. You know, the neurosurgeon who ran for president? Trump made him Secretary of HUD."

"Yes, I know who you mean."

"They're both Black—excuse me, African American." He tacks on air quotes. "Both raised by single mothers, both conser-vative Christians and doctors."

He says Larry would use Dr. Arthur on the air although Dar-rell preferred his first name. He wanted listeners to consider him an ordinary guy, but Larry always made it clear that Darrell was nowhere close to average. He attended Johns Hopkins Univer-sity while Larry earned his GED in the army.

"Did that bother Darrell?"

"He asked Larry not to call him doctor on the air, but Larry told him no, that's who you are. You should be proud, he said. Darrell didn't much like Larry's style but he liked filling in on holidays and Larry's vacations. I know he wants his own week-day show." He leans back, arms across his abdomen. "Come to think of it, maybe he was too hungry, you know? It's a cutthroat business. I know people who would trample their mother to get ahead."

"How's he doing filling in? Any changes?"

His stomach bumps the table as his fingers find the cup. "Gotta give him credit. He's handling it okay. Can be a tricky balance between paying respect and being your own person. Darrell's problem is he can't attract hard-core loyalists."

Ralph lifts the cup. "See, Darrell is like this plain black coffee. It used to be the go-to, everyone accepted it. But not anymore. You gotta have oat milk and caramel. Hell, I even saw a kid order whipped cream and sprinkles. That ain't coffee." His face dares me to challenge. "But that's what it's come to. If Darrell wants to stay in Larry's slot, he's gotta add flavor. Spice things up." He takes a determined drink, a sip-swig combination. "That would contradict his style and personality. Then again, people aren't always what they seem, are they?"

"What about the angry husband who went after Larry?"

"Went after him? You're kidding, right? He got mad, kicked Larry's car, end of story. Larry only dated his wife for two, maybe three weeks—and that was months ago. Why would he target Larry now? Doesn't make sense."

When I mention Phillip Ellys, he sneers. "Mr. San Francisco. One of those West Coast elites."

"What do you mean?"

"You know, one of them tree huggers. Always crying the world's going to burn up, judging people who don't recycle every single thing."

"I understand some of his conversations with Larry were intense."

He spins his cup. "Oh yeah, Phillip hated Larry. Their feud started when Larry drove a Hummer—the gas, not electric model. He got it free—all he had to do was promote the dealership. Larry loved to pull up next to a Prius or electric car and rev his engine. You know, stick it to the driver?" His cup goes still. "One time it was Phillip behind the wheel. Of course, now he doesn't have a Prius or any car. He's always riding his bike or blight-rail."

He hesitates to make sure I caught the "B-word." To hear

certain leaders and business groups talk, you'd think Phoenix's light-rail system created utopian communities for all. But the reality is that the city prioritized putting money, services, and attention into specific areas and neglected others. Years of increased crime and drug use along portions of the line combined with too little, too late city action caused some residents to give up on elected officials and their neighborhoods.

"How did Phillip know it was Larry who pulled up next to him?"

"Didn't you see Larry's Hummer? Thought you interviewed him."

"We talked in the studio."

"Not much of a reporter, are you?"

"I was interested in what he had to say about issues, not cars."

"You really missed out. The Hummer had magnets on the doors. Both sides had station logos with Larry's face and Freaks Love Larry signs."

"Are you saying their on-air relationship started after Larry pulled up next to Phillip?"

He nods. "Phillip called the show the next day and we put him on the air. Stellar live radio. Larry joked he was going to drive the Hummer right over here for coffee instead of walking across the street. Just to burn gas. And when he was done, he'd throw the cup in the trash, not the recycle bin. Then, Larry said he'd drive to McDonald's—you know how those screwballs hate big chains—and order a bunch of Big Macs. Of course, Phillip is one of those militant vegetarians, thinks animals are equal to people. Larry would say, 'I've never eaten a person, but I can tell you cows and pigs taste great.'" He laughs and takes a sip.

"Phillip's posted some fiery stuff about Larry on Facebook."

"Yeah, I never figured out why someone who hated Larry so much would listen to his show. But Larry always said enemies

and anger help everyone—either through higher ratings or donations for a cause or campaign."

"Do you think Phillip would do anything worse than post
critical comments or argue on the air?"

Ralph tilts his cup toward me. "Personally, I don't think he
has the balls. Those liberals try to talk tough, but they never
walk the walk." He sets his cup down. "Larry carried proof he
was the real deal." He makes a gun shape with his thumb and
forefinger and pats a hip. "If you get my drift."

"I know he supported Arizona's open carry law. During our
interview he said he liked carrying his gun at grocery stores and
gas stations."

"He believed an armed society was a civil society."

"What about Ignacio Cortez?"

"Nacho? Now there's an hombre with issues."

Ralph says Larry and Nacho had a gentleman's agreement:
when Nacho called in to complain about something, they both
played their parts.

"It was a win-win. Nacho got to show people he was taking
on the man and Larry could always count on high-energy segments. We played loads of sound effects and mariachi music."

I say nothing about the anonymous package with the audio
clips but tell him I'm familiar with the Taco Bell Chihuahua
commercials.

Ralph slaps his thigh. "Those were hilarious!"

"Is it safe to say Nacho didn't find them as funny as you and
Larry did?"

"Oh, Nacho knew his place. We all have our roles. It's showbiz. And it was all fine and dandy until the station's anniversary
party."

Turns out the day KFRK designated to highlight its thirty
years representing "Arizona's true conservative voice" was also
the day Nacho chose to highlight his version of making Amer-

ica great again. The station had reserved a ballroom at the Willow Resort. While Larry was onstage, Nacho stormed in with a group carrying signs that read TAKE BACK OUR COUNTRY and chanting, "¡Sí se puede! Yes, we can!"

"How did Larry handle it?"

"Oh, he was caught off guard. But no one noticed but me. He tried to play along. But Nacho wasn't playing. Larry couldn't even be heard over all the heckling. Then our people started chanting, 'Build the wall' and 'Deport them!'"

Disapproval oozes from a customer's face as she passes our table. Ralph is unaffected.

"I thought fights were gonna break out, but Larry called security, yelled in the microphone for them to remove the party crashers, said they were here illegally." His smile reveals teeth fighting for space. "Man, that got some laughs. As security led Nacho away, he was bawling, 'This was our land first!' Larry called him a sore loser. Told him to read American history. Our fans went wild over that one, too. After Nacho's group left, the party got rowdier. If I didn't know better, I would've thought Larry planned it."

"Did Nacho ever call the show after that?"

"Oh yeah, lots of times. But Larry wouldn't talk to him. Never did another segment with him. Nacho even tried to get me to convince Larry to change his mind. Went on and on about how he'd helped Larry's ratings. When that didn't work, he said Larry should stop hiding behind the microphone, man up, and meet him face-to-face."

Sounds like someone with an ax to grind. Or poison to serve. I ask Ralph about Rosie Rangel. He grins and calls her Nacho's nemesis. "That's a good woman. Born and raised here in Arizona. Believes in God, guns, and country."

"Why ban her from the show?"

"Rosie got a little carried away. Called for armed residents to form their own border patrol. Can't blame her though. She's sick and tired of illegals sending their kids to our schools, filling our emergency rooms, not paying taxes, collecting welfare, you name it. And don't get her started about the drug cartels flooding our communities."

"She told me Larry gave her the nickname 'Run 'Em Out Rosie.'"

"Maybe that's what sent her overboard. She didn't always understand the showbiz side. Sometimes she could come across—I don't know if 'ornery' is the right word—more like she didn't know how to keep it entertaining, you know? Took it way too serious. But poisoning Larry? No way." He lifts his cup. "Your best bet is to look at Nacho."

That could happen sooner than I expected. I slide my vibrating phone off the table to read a text. Nacho is ready for the interview.

"Please excuse me, Ralph. I need to respond to this. I appreciate your time and promise to keep your name to myself."

He nods like he's seeing me for the first time.

"You know, you're not so bad for a reporter."

Alert the media! There's hope yet.

"Thanks, Ralph. I'll be in touch. And I'll see you at the memorial service."

Before I'm out the door, I text Nacho asking when and where.

Now. My house.

CHAPTER

18

I plow through the door and sprint across the street where Nate is heading my way.

"Hey, I was coming to check on you. Everything okay?"

"Yeah, got excellent background. Plus, Nacho's ready to talk."

I bring Nate up to speed during the twenty-minute drive to Nacho's home on the city's west side, known as Maryvale. Named after Mary, the wife of developer John F. Long, it was Phoenix's first suburb and master-planned community with its own shopping center, hospital, schools, and parks. Advertisements from the 1950s and '60s showcased single-story homes with customized interiors and backyard pools.

Today, Maryvale's reputation is less glamorous. Some call it "Scaryvale." Many shopping centers that catered to families with healthy disposable incomes are now filled with payday loan shops, smoke shops, and dollar stores. Parks that once drew children out of new houses to pristine playgrounds now attract people without shelter. Homes that could be marketed as retro are often viewed as run-down. Many people understand the possibilities for an area that's centrally located, but those people aren't developers with deep pockets, community connections, and long-term vision.

"Good vibes, please. I'm calling the producer line to let them know we have Nacho."

"Don't leave me out of the fun," Nate says. "Use the speaker."

The reaction is classic David.

"Ooh, sexy! Plan on being the lead in the early shows. We'll want different sound for each newscast. Remember to tweet and post to Facebook. The station will do the same. Don't worry about your web version until after your live shots. And we'll need to talk about what you can do for the late show once you finish the early news."

What I want to say: Can we pick up your dry cleaning, too? Maybe wash your car? Bring you dinner?

What I actually say: "Okay, talk to you later." I'd like to think I'm making progress in the "Don't let 'em get to you" arena but it's really because there's no time to argue.

As promised in Nacho's text, his house is easy to spot, courtesy of the striped green-white-red Mexican flag plastered above the front door. In the driveway we catch the first sign of trouble—a white SUV, its twin parked along the curb. Confirmation comes when we spot a guy dragging a metal roller case toward the house while another guy jogs to the driver's side.

"You recognize them?" I ask as Nate parks on the street.

"Nope. The SUVs are rentals."

My body twists to watch the jogger remove a black bag and return to the house.

"Nacho didn't say anything about sharing the interview with another crew. This blows. We're overdue for an exclusive."

"Still better than nothing, right?"

We scoot out of the truck. Nate hands me the tripod and collects his camera, and we hurry to the front door. After knocking, I press the doorbell. A full minute passes before a man speaks through a dark screen door that obscures most of his face.

"Yes?"

"Mr. Cortez? Hi, it's Jolene with Channel 4. This is my photographer, Nate. Thanks for inviting us over."

Nacho presses his nose against the screen and speaks so softly I strain to hear. "Listen, I'm sorry, but after I texted you CNN showed up. And they asked for an exclusive for twenty-four hours. I couldn't say no, you know how it is. The exposure could be a godsend to the cause. Can we talk tomorrow?"

I bite back a curse. "I'm sorry to hear that and hope you'll reconsider. We did have an agreement."

"I know, but this is our chance to be in the national spotlight. I promise we can talk tomorrow. Text me and we can set up a time. I'm sorry."

As the door closes, my stomach churns. We trudge back to the truck where I stare at my phone. Nate lets me munch on a thumbnail for a couple minutes before tapping my shoulder.

"C'mon, the sooner you deal with it, the sooner it's over."

Sexy's whine fills the truck. "You have nothing?"

"I have a lot of new information, just not anything I can turn for the newscasts—yet."

"But we're already promoting your exclusive interview."

I'd like to point out Sexy's failure to follow yet another journalism rule: never promise something until you have it. But I'm as miserable as he is so I keep my mouth shut while frustration pours out of his.

"If you can't come through, we'll have to scramble to fill the shows. If you get something—I mean legitimately get something—let me know."

"Ignore him," Nate says after we disconnect.

"He has a point though. I've left them in a bad situation. Got any ideas?"

"You said Rosie was more than willing to talk."

"Yeah, but I'd rather use her as a last resort."

"What about the host who's filling in?"

"His dental office is in North Scottsdale. Minimum forty-five-minute drive."

Nate checks his phone. "Even if he's there and willing to talk, we won't have enough time to turn a story for the early newscast. Anyone closer?"

I mentally run through the list. "Let's try Phillip Ellys."

"Who's he?"

"Environmental activist with a history of angry comments directed at Larry. His nonprofit is on Nineteenth Avenue."

Nate turns left onto Indian School Road, a major thoroughfare named after the former Phoenix Indian School. When it opened in 1891, the government-run boarding school focused on culturally assimilating Native children into white society. More than four hundred schools were part of a federal system that forcibly removed American Indian, Alaska Native, and Native Hawaiian children from their families. One of the earliest off-reservation schools, Carlisle Indian Industrial School in Pennsylvania became a model for others. Its mission, according to school superintendent and army officer Richard Henry Pratt, was to "kill the Indian in him, and save the man." Students were stripped of Native languages and tribal traditions, called by new names, and forced to cut their hair.

After the Tk'emlúps te Secwépemc First Nation discovered 215 unmarked graves at the former Kamloops Indian Residential School in Canada, the U.S. Department of the Interior introduced an initiative to record the painful legacy of similar schools. The agency has documented burial sites, but to prevent vandalism and theft of artifacts it will not publicly release locations. Only Oklahoma had more boarding schools in the federal system than Arizona. In the 1930s, enrollment at Phoenix declined when younger students left to attend schools on reservations. Over the decades, as more tribes built their own schools, the Phoenix curriculum and campus evolved and, in 1990, Phoenix Indian School officially closed. Today, original reclaimed floorboards from the grammar school make up a wall inside the Phoenix Indian School Visitor Center. Only two other historic buildings remain on the 160-acre site that's home to Steele Indian School Park: the dining hall and Memorial Hall, built to honor sixty-two students who enlisted in the army and navy during World War I.

"Do you want to call or just swing by?" Nate asks.

"Let's just show up. It worked for CNN with Nacho. Maybe it'll work for us."

The office for Save All Living Things (SALT) is in a two-story building that was saved but not nurtured. If someone had cared for the former motel, it might've earned mid-century jewel status. In its current state, it's more tired than trendy. The grimy directory behind cracked glass reveals that SALT is between an accountant offering $59 tax filings and a lawyer specializing in $299 divorces. We scale thirteen cement steps before reaching the landing.

"Left or right?" Nate asks.

"How about left for liberal?"

"What about right for righteous?"

"Let the record reflect that I, an independent, intelligent woman, have no qualms following directions suggested by a man."

"Hey, don't lump me in with guys who won't take direction. I'm secure in my masculinity."

"Okay, Mr. Masculinity, I'm going left and you need to stay back and listen." I flip on the mic. "Ready?"

"Good to go."

After passing two doors, I hesitate. No name, but the number matches the directory. It's locked. Dust peppers a black shade that covers the only window. I hold the microphone halfway down so it's out of Phillip's line of sight but close enough for Nate to hear what's happening. With my free hand, I knock three times.

Phillip Ellys looks nothing like his Facebook photos. For one, he's not wearing a bike helmet. Without gawking, it's hard to tell if he has a high forehead or receding hairline. Maybe both. Speculating he's thirty-five to forty years old.

"Hi, Mr. Ellys, I'm Jolene Garcia with Channel 4 News. I've left messages and haven't heard back so—"

"You haven't heard back because I have nothing to say. I'm not interested in joining your media spectacle. I have more dignified pursuits."

And I have a newsroom counting on this interview.

"I understand you're busy, and this won't take long at all. I'd really like to hear your thoughts about Larry Lemmon."

"The world is better off now that he can't spew his ignorance and hate. How's that?"

"That's direct. And something we haven't heard yet. My photographer is just down the hall. Can we do a quick interview? Two minutes and we're out of here."

"How about you leave now? All you reporters do is pervert and distort. It's all sound bites over substance. Like I said, I'm not interested."

"I can't speak for the whole industry, only myself. And I can promise you, I'm interested in telling the full story."

"Oh, I bet. What brought you here? The pictures? You think you can wave them in my face and get me to act like a fool on camera?" He pinches the doorknob. "That's not going to happen!"

The microphone slips in my damp palm. "Please, I don't know anything about pictures. I just want your input."

"I'm not stupid. All you want are ratings and clicks and I'm not going to be part of it." Spittle catches in the corners of his mouth as the door inches closer to my face. "You're on private property and I demand you leave immediately."

My stomach clenches and my throat closes. First, JJ got the exclusive with Ralph. Then, Network reported the cyanide. Right now, CNN is talking to Nacho. And I've got zilch. Damn it, I'm a better reporter than JJ and this is my turf. No more losing. My hand strikes the door.

"Mr. Ellys, did you know you're on a police list in connection with Larry's death?"

"What?" He points at Nate. "Hey, you stop right there!"

Phillip's eyes have changed from brown sugar to burnt toast. "I've told you more than once to leave me alone! You are officially trespassing and, if you don't leave, I will call the police. In fact, I'm going to file a formal harassment complaint. You'll be hearing from my attorney."

He slams the door, but I stay put. Need to make sure Nate has enough video. After silently counting to five, I turn around.

"Please tell me you were rolling."

"Only got the last part with him telling us to leave and threatening to call the cops. Nothing we can use."

"Says who? Now we have something new."

"Are you kidding? We'll come off like complete scum."

"Why would we look bad? We're not suspects or persons of interest."

Nate observes me for a moment. Doesn't speak.

"What?"

"Jolene, the guy's threatening legal action."

"For doing my job? That's not illegal."

"I don't know what's gotten into you, but you need to chill."

But chilling is not in the cards. A fire is. Alex texts the address of Cozy Ranch, an assisted-living center where someone called 911 to report heavy smoke. Nate heads north on Seventh Avenue through the Melrose District. A former haven for pawnshops, adult bookstores, and absent landlords, the one-mile corridor is known for quirky boutiques, locally owned independent restaurants, and the city's first rainbow crosswalk to support the LGBTQ+ community.

I read the station's text aloud. "They want a live shot."

Nate's nod is barely perceptible.

"I know you're upset with me, but if you were facing the same pressure you'd understand."

This time, he doesn't nod.

For the next few minutes, the only conversation takes place in my mind. The good me and the not-so-good me battle over whether to apologize to Nate or let it go. As we approach the scene, a third me pipes up and I declare her the winner.

"Are you at least going to talk so we can cover this fire as professionals?"

He releases a hard breath. "Yes, Jolene. I know how to do my job."

Despite four fire trucks packed into a circular driveway at the building's entrance, the scene is calm. No flames, no smoke, no one rushing to get in or out. Near the front, there's a cluster of firefighters. One motions to the roof but I notice nothing strange. Nate holds his camera, hands me the mic, and says he'll be listening. All without meeting my eyes.

I take a picture of three firefighters next to their truck and post the photo with a promise to report details during the newscast. My eyes glide across the parking lot, and settle on a huddle beneath a row of ficus trees. Roughly sixty people of various ages, about half using wheelchairs or walkers. Employees in medical scrubs dot the line. I ask a woman wearing a lemon-lime safety vest what she knows.

"Not much. They only evacuated the west side. That's where the kitchen is. And the dining room and TV room."

A grating voice interrupts. "Hey, do you know JJ?" The sound is like teeth scraping a fork. "She's my favorite reporter."

I reconstruct my face into something neutral before turning to the voice.

"Do me a favor, will ya, and tell her Jamie Cross says hi. Sure would appreciate a picture with her but they didn't give me a chance to get my phone when they herded us out. I see ya got your phone. Maybe you could take it?"

"You'll have to excuse us." Nate gets hold of my elbow and gives JJ's fan an earnest smile. "The fire department is ready to update us." He silently guides me to the media scrum where another aggravating voice takes over.

"Hey, Jolene, I didn't expect you to be here," JJ says. "Shouldn't you be working on a Larry Lemmon story? Or have you finally caught up with everyone else?"

"Excuse me." Nate steps between us and opens his tripod. I squeeze his arm in gratitude as the PIO begins.

"The call came in as smoke showing. First units on scene saw no visible smoke or flames, and evacuations were already under way. Our crews cleared the building with no reports of injuries. The smoke alarm went off in or near the kitchen. Based on the preliminary information, it appears there was something cooking on the stove that may have burned. The investigators are still inside. Once they give the all clear—that should be in the next thirty minutes or so—then residents and employees will be allowed back inside."

This story isn't going to make anyone forget I lost Nacho's interview. I can hear David pushing for a sexy angle, which reminds me of the last "fire" I covered. A pickup truck engine had ignited and burned the carport next to a house. No people hurt, but a cat was trapped, too frightened to move. A firefighter freed the feline and placed an oxygen mask on its furry face. Made for captivating video and the story, as our consultant would say, went viral. That's why I ask the PIO if there were any animals inside.

"You mean like pets?"

"Yeah."

"Highly doubt it. Some residents have compromised immune systems and other serious health issues. I can ask though, if you really need to know."

"That's okay. My producer is fishing for an unusual hook."

"Sorry I can't help you. This is one of our less exciting calls."

"Ooh, I think every fire call is exciting." JJ executes a Beyoncé hair flip. "You guys are willing to risk your lives to rush into burning buildings and save total strangers. It's truly heroic."

It's truly nauseating. And gets worse as we set up live shots next to each other. Yes, I have to report live from the scene where a pot of burned grits set off a smoke alarm. JJ imagines she's reporting on a raging wildfire threatening an entire Southern California town. She practices how she'll walk and talk, reminding her photographer to get a full-body shot so she can show off red-soled shoes that no Phoenix reporter could buy without a wealthy partner or parent.

"These are brand-new." She kicks up black pumps. "Only my second pair of Louboutins."

The other pair is red. I know this—along with her birthday—because she paraded around after "Daddy" sent them. JJ was disappointed when the photographer pointed out that the trademark soles wouldn't stand out in a live shot.

Minutes before we're supposed to go live, my phone chimes. I pray it's not the station asking why I'm not tweeting. I waver at the unfamiliar number but answer before it goes to voice mail. It's Kelly Lemmon, Larry's second wife. And she wants to talk. Securing an exclusive interview is cause for celebration. But when she invites me over tomorrow, the buzz fizzles out. Saturday is consistently the least watched day of the week for news. Barring a momentous event, few people tune in to early or late newscasts. Still, David manages a sexy hook.

"We'll run a short story after you get the interview Saturday, basically promoting a longer piece that'll run Sunday when our late show will have a killer audience thanks to the network's lead-in. It'll be perfect!"

Lead-in perfection, in David's view, is the network's highest-rated program, a pseudo-reality show with women fighting for the attention of some guy. I may not like the show but I'll take the extra eyeballs.

CHAPTER
19

The station won't pay overtime for Nate to come in the next day, so I'm working with weekend photographer Roger Hale, nicknamed Snail. When I find him loading gear, he says he'll be ready in five minutes. In Snail time, that's at least ten.

Roger is the best person to drive to Kelly Lemmon's house in Paradise Valley. It's home to the country's first police department to catch speeders by using cameras and radar devices streaming across roads. Besides hating speeders, Paradise Valley loves money. It's Phoenix's wealthiest suburb. But you won't find a Neiman Marcus, Whole Foods, or even a Starbucks. For those, you have to travel to the neighboring cities of Phoenix or Scottsdale. Paradise Valley is zoned for hillside mansions and resorts cradled between Camelback, Mummy, and the Phoenix Mountains. To be fair, there are a few homes valued under a million—mostly older, smaller condos.

"It's been ages since I covered a story in PV," Roger says.

"What was the last?"

"The Rock Burglar."

"Someone was stealing rocks?"

Even Roger's laugh is slow. "No, no. He used rocks to smash windows when people weren't home."

"Didn't alarms go off? These houses must have extensive security systems."

"He was smart. He targeted bathrooms."

"I don't get it."

"Think about it."

Roger waits as if I want to contemplate the possibilities. When he realizes I don't, the story continues, "He smashed windows in bathrooms. Easy access in and out. Who puts alarms in their bathrooms?"

"Bet they do now."

"Over the years, he broke into hundreds of homes and stole millions—I forget how many millions—in cash and jewelry. When cops caught him, it made national news."

Will national outlets want to run my interview with Kelly? Maybe I'll suggest we share it. Bob might question whether an alien has invaded my body, but how many reporters can claim two exclusives on such a remarkable story? That's worth promoting beyond our station. I wonder if anyone from college would see me. What would my high school classmates think about the dorky girl who lived with her grandma making national news? Would anyone connect the dots?

Kelly must have cashed in during her sales career, collected abundant alimony, or both. Though her house isn't built on a mountainside like the homes of corporate executives, professional athletes, and entertainers, it's still striking. Desert-friendly trees and plants adorn an impeccably maintained yard. The front door is four times the size of mine and, when she opens it, I can't help but notice so are her breasts. Kelly's so skinny it's surprising they don't cause her to topple over.

"Hello, you must be Jolene."

"I am. Thank you for talking with us, Kelly. This is Roger. He'll be shooting our interview."

A teeny dog nestled in Kelly's left arm is on the verge of falling into cleavage. To go along with the implants, she has plump lips and a forehead as smooth as her nail polish. A spray tan diminishes but doesn't erase freckles.

Clop, clop.

The physical appraisal stops and staying alive takes priority.

Clop, clop, clop, clop.

A wolflike creature skulks toward us, ears and tail at attention, ready to attack. I hide behind Roger.

"Oh, there's Trouble. Mommy's sweet protector. Don't worry, she's harmless."

Trouble's growl says otherwise.

"We don't want your sweet protector to get the wrong idea," Roger says. "Would you mind keeping her in a separate room while we're here?"

She coos at the creature, "Does baby girl want to go to her playroom?"

As Kelly leads Trouble away, she directs us to something called a drawing room. I wave Roger ahead, using the minute to catch my breath. Then, the sunken room takes it away. It could've held my grandma's entire house. Floor-to-ceiling windows open onto a putting green and swimming pool that goes for miles. I've only caught glimpses of places like this in movies and on TV. Without that buffer, awe shifts to envy. What stands out most is what I don't see and what I don't hear. No other houses or apartments. No planes or helicopters. No buses or motorcycles. No barking dogs or shrieking children. In my neighborhood, wisps of quiet come only after most people are asleep—even then, there's a persistent soundtrack of stray cats yowling, skateboards slapping concrete, and sirens slicing the stillness. Rich quiet is different.

Above the marble fireplace hangs an oil portrait of Kelly and

Trouble. The dog's gold coat gleams against Kelly's emerald gown.

"What a beauty, huh?" Roger says.

"Trouble or Kelly?"

"I got nothing against dogs, but I'm a sucker for redheads."

"It's almost natural," Kelly says.

Roger's face turns two shades darker than her hair.

"I'm sorry. I meant no disrespect."

"None taken. I've invested a tidy sum in this." Her hands dance around her face and torso. "Years ago, a psychologist suggested I was overcompensating for growing up without money and being, shall we say, less than attractive."

She glances at a mirror on the wall, her professionally tweaked profile outlined by glossy hair.

"Short, flat-chested, with a face full of freckles and a mouth full of crooked teeth." Her eyes travel far away from her multi-million-dollar home. "That was me."

Her somber expression falls, replaced by a smile that's sealed a thousand deals.

"The shrink was right, but there's nothing wrong with wanting to like what you see. And I do. Can I get you two anything to drink? I have sparkling water, lemonade, an assortment of sodas and juices."

Roger asks for water and she invites us to set up anywhere. Creamy chairs surround a U-shaped bar with enough bottles to satisfy the newsroom for a year. Roger opens his tripod near a charcoal-gray couch and positions the camera to face a matching chair. The sofa table holds framed photos of Kelly with dogs who look nothing alike and Kelly with friends who look eerily similar. Like the cast of *Real Housewives*, pick any city. On impulse, I brush the seat of my pants to avoid cross-contamination between the stained cloth in our truck and custom-made furniture. Settling into real leather is like experiencing a gentle hug. A refreshing scent hovers, but there's no sign of candles or a diffuser. My grandma used to stick scented dryer sheets under cushions. Does Kelly? I take three short sniffs. It's not generic Bounce. Maybe rich people hide freshly printed cash under their cushions. My fingers worm between leather, digging for the answer.

"I hope Perrier is okay."

My body snaps back as Roger accepts a green bottle and frosted glass.

"I have San Pellegrino if you prefer," Kelly says.

"This is great, thank you."

The ice in Kelly's lemonade clinks as she sets it on a low table made of stainless-steel slates. Reminds me of a sewer grate without the gunk. Since I don't know how she'll react to questions about her first husband, I'll ask them last. Best to begin by talking about Larry. That's what she expects.

"Ready when you are," Roger says.

"Thanks again for meeting with us. Let's start with how you and Larry met. It was at KFRK?"

"Yes. He was quite charming."

"In what way?"

She giggles. "I know it may surprise you to hear Larry described that way, but he was such a gentleman. Always complimenting me, holding doors, buying flowers. He knew how to treat a lady. Too many men don't. Or maybe they just don't want to."

"What else attracted you to him?"

Kelly takes a sip, licks her lips, and returns the drink to a coaster. "You know the adage 'You can tell a lot about a man by the way he treats animals'? I've always adored dogs and I'm an avid supporter of the Arizona Humane Society. When Larry found out I organize the group's annual charity ball, he wrote a check for ten thousand dollars and told me to use it however

I saw fit. And I was incredibly touched when Larry supported Ralph. Did you know he financed Ralph's shelter?"

I smile and nod.

"Not many people do. Larry was a generous friend. They went to high school together. When Larry got his job in Phoenix, he brought Ralph with him. He could've easily left him in that small town."

Like he did his first wife and son.

"When did you marry?"

"Eight months after we met. Sadly, our courtship lasted longer than our marriage."

She places her left hand over her heart and turns away. Whether the reaction is genuine or done for the camera, I can't tell. Kelly removes her hand and admires it. The finger where a wedding band would go is ringless, but next to it, sapphires circle a colossal diamond.

"We both realized we rushed into marriage," she says. "Our interests, our personalities were just too different. I favor cocktail parties, shopping, and society events. Larry's into what he called the three G's: God, guns, and government." She smiled. "Or, more precisely, praising God and guns and slamming the government."

"Sometimes people crank things up or say things they don't fully support to gain attention or get reactions from guests. Did Larry?"

"Oh, no. He believed what he said. Another admirable trait. When we first started dating, I'd listen to his show and sometimes think, 'Oh, this is an act.' But that really was Larry."

"Did you ever think he went too far criticizing people? Or crossed the line with his comments on immigration?"

She tucks auburn strands behind an ear. "You have to understand where Larry came from. What do you know about Douglas?"

"I thought he was from Sierra Vista."

"He moved there for high school. But the damage was done in Douglas, just a mile from the border."

"What damage?"

"Growing up poor wasn't Larry's problem. It was being one of the few white students witnessing kids in the country illegally getting more attention from teachers. Outside of school, too. Churches and various groups were always organizing toy drives and clothing donations for immigrants—as if children born in the U.S. need no help. Too many American children don't get the support they deserve. And others get more than they need."

Like Kylee Kim from my high school. Her voice still sounds like sunshine in my head. Every day I watched her shiny black ponytail caress her back as she floated through the halls. By sophomore year, Kylee had racked up as many awards and accolades as the senior class president. And then, Kylee's life changed. She went from the girl everyone wanted to be to the girl whose dad died in a car crash. The glut of love and support gutted me. How does a girl who had everything—everything—for sixteen years get even more? At times, I had to fight the urge to trip her ballerina legs or chop off her ponytail.

Then I got smart and borrowed Kylee's misfortune for myself. Why do I live with my grandma, you ask? Because my parents were killed in a car crash. Cue the condolences. And no more intrusive questions. The cover story worked then and works now.

"To us, it may sound horrible," Kelly says. "But for Larry, the reality was being a poor white kid with no ties to Mexico worked against him."

"Did he share that with you?"

She scoffs. "Larry share his feelings? No. That's what I diagnosed from years of exploring my own childhood. I suggested Larry try therapy but he wouldn't have it."

Can't blame him. What's the point in rehashing your

childhood? Can't change it. I scan my notepad even though I know where the interview is heading.

"And you divorced about six months ago?"

"Yes, we went our separate ways—amicably. We like—I mean we liked and respected each other. As civil a divorce as you can get."

"Did you quit your sales job while you were married or after the divorce?"

She bristles. "In other words, did I marry Larry for his money?" She brandishes a fingernail decorated with rhinestones. "To be clear, I earned my own money and didn't need Larry's." She folds her hands and relaxes her face. "However, when we divorced, he offered to provide a modest alimony so that I could continue to live in the manner to which I've grown accustomed. Larry never fully felt at home living here. He needed more space, more land. That's why he kept the range in southern Arizona after opening one in Phoenix. The only surprising thing was, he wanted me to have the dogs. Larry's much more of a homebody and I thought they'd be good for him, keep him from getting lonely, you know. But he insisted I take them." She sits back and her eyes float toward the hallway. "I'm thankful he did. It's reassuring to have them watching over me."

I ask if she can think of anyone who would want to hurt Larry.

"I'm sure plenty of people wished him harm, but to carry it out? I don't know. I saw that Mexican guy on CNN. He was pretty volatile. I remember he showed up at a station event and they had to kick him out. But not before they stormed the stage where Larry was speaking."

"What happened?"

"They unfurled a banner. Of course, it was written in Spanish so nobody understood it. But Rosie told us what it said: 'Gringos, get out of Mexico.'" She shakes her head. "Like it or not, this is the United States, not Mexico. It was all very tacky."

"Did you know Nacho? Or I guess I should say Ignacio."

"Larry called him Nacho. We never met personally. He and Larry had a tremendous thing going. I don't know what made him throw it away. After the way he behaved at the station party I don't care to ever see him again. It wasn't just rude, it was scary."

"What scared you?"

"The anger on his face. And his voice. I thought he was going to incite that mob to turn violent."

"What do you know about a guy named Phillip Ellys?"

Kelly twirls a finger around her temple. "Kind of cuckoo, if you know what I mean."

"No, I don't."

"Very extreme in his views."

She waits for a response. I say nothing.

"I know what you're thinking. Larry was extreme, too. But Larry understood reality. While his show attracted a certain audience and generated controversy, he also knew when to scale back. He told me the trick was making it look like you weren't backing off. That's what made him so successful."

"This Phillip guy doesn't know when to stop?"

"Exactly. If you don't recycle everything you touch, or don't take public transit everywhere you go, then you're destroying the planet. Honestly, that guy needs to lighten up."

"Did Larry get a lot of hate mail or calls?"

"A lot? I don't know how to quantify that, but there are nasty people out there and he certainly heard from some of them."

"Did anyone ever threaten him?"

"You mean did anyone ever say, 'If you don't stop, I'm going to poison your cookies'? Not that I know of."

"Any idea who might have delivered the cookies?"

"No. And neither does Ralph or Andy. We're all confused. Poor Andy's just a kid trying to figure out a career and now he's involved in this. And Ralph is devastated. He lost his best friend."

"No problems ever between Ralph and Larry?"

"Like any relationship, they had their ups and downs. I imagine Ralph got tired of Larry getting all the attention. He was much more than Larry's sidekick. He did a massive amount of show preparation and behind-the-scenes work. Things like research and booking guests. People think a show like that is easy to do—waltz in, turn on the microphones, and start talking. But there's so much that goes into it. Occasionally, they disagreed over topics or guests, but it was never anything earth-shattering."

"What about Darrell? An oral surgeon and a talk show host. Sounds very ambitious."

A flicker appears in her eyes. "I don't think ambition is a crime. And Darrell is too much of a gentleman to do anything so crass."

I switch the cross of my legs, a signal Snail and I discussed on the way here, a cue for him to get a close-up shot.

"Kelly, I'm sorry to bring up another painful topic, but I need to ask about your first husband."

"You *need* to?"

"I wouldn't be doing my job if I didn't ask. As you may know, some people have raised questions about how he died."

"First, he had a name. It was Jack. Second, I'm aware of other people's jealousy and cynicism. That is their problem, not mine. I loved Jack with all my heart."

"I'm sorry. It's just the accident—"

"That's exactly what it was—an accident. How dare you come to my home and insinuate I had something to do with Jack's death?"

"No, that's not what I meant. I just needed to—"

"To what? Paint me in an unflattering light? You know, Larry was right about you so-called journalists. You look for the worst in people. And if you can't find it, you make it up." She unclips the mic from her shirt and it clunks on the table. "Now, you'll have to excuse me. I need to get ready for an appointment. Please show yourselves out."

Fearing Kelly might return with Trouble, I snap up Roger's tripod—he can handle the camera and light case on his own—and jet to the door, nearly knocking over a lamp.

"Hey, watch it," Roger says.

After escaping the house, I crouch behind the SUV. If Trouble gets loose, I can climb on the bumper and up to the roof.

"Geez, Jolene. What's your problem?" Roger sets his gear down and opens the back. "I know you're not a fan of dogs, but it's not like she's going to sic 'em on us."

"You never know. I didn't expect her to react the way she did to some of the questions."

"I don't blame her. You practically accused her of killing her first husband."

"I did not!"

"That's how she heard it."

"She was already shutting down when I mentioned Darrell Arthur."

"Maybe they have a thing going on."

My mind flashes to the day Larry died. Kelly crying on Darrell's shoulder. "That could be a problem since he's married. Separated, but still married."

"If he's separated or getting a divorce, who cares?"

"Some listeners might. And that could hurt his chances of getting a show in a better time slot."

"So you think Darrell poisoned Larry to take over his show?"

"Just making observations. Several people seem to have agendas."

"My agenda calls for pizza and beer so let's put this story together as fast as we can."

And with that, Roger channels his version of Formula One driver Lewis Hamilton. The speedometer zooms past the posted limit to forty-one miles per hour. Then forty-two. Forty-three. He coasts at forty-four. I reach for my phone and push the seat back, angling the camera to catch the speedometer. Roger's eyes never leave the road.

I text the photo to Gina and Elena.

Breaking News: Snail's going 4 mph over limit! C u soon.

Since tonight's story is nothing more than a glorified promotion for Sunday night's report, it doesn't take long to produce. Roger's able to order his meat lover's pizza before the early newscast while I slide into a corner booth at Welcome Diner. An overhead mural features Franklin Pierce, the fourteenth U.S. president and namesake of the street that hosts the restaurant. The twentieth president, James A. Garfield, makes the mural for having a nearby street named after him, along with the neighborhood moniker, Garfield Historic District.

"Happy hour's almost over," Gina says. "I ordered hurricanes for you and Elena."

Gina introduced Elena and me to Welcome Diner's signature drink, a delicious blend of fruit punch and rum served in mason jars.

"What about you?"

Her smile drops. "Lemonade."

"She doesn't want to show up with liquor on her breath," Elena says.

Gina is meeting us before she heads to the Westin downtown to emcee a charity gala that awards college scholarships to deserving students. After our main anchors, she gets the most requests to host events. Gina is intelligent, gracious, and, as every person in the restaurant has noticed, a knockout. Her orange dress makes you think of luscious peaches on a warm summer day. On me, you would think overstuffed Halloween bag. Next to Gina, Elena models the girl next door with a white cotton shirt, blue jeans, and a face that says she's genuinely interested in hearing your story about being stuck in traffic.

"What are we eating?"

"Little Birdy sandwiches, chili fries, and the fried green tomato platter."

"Protein, carbs, and greens," I say. "Thanks for taking care of us."

"Don't give her too much credit," Elena teases. "She's also tending to herself."

"True," Gina says. "I never eat at events. It's impractical. The second you take a bite, someone asks a question. Or they want to shake your hand as you're buttering a roll."

"You are free to pay us no attention and eat to your heart's content." I turn to Elena. "What's new with you?"

"We were just talking about Gina's wedding."

My head boomerangs. "What?"

"Relax, not mine," Gina says. "My best friend's wedding. I'm the maid of honor. My first time in that role—a virgin, if you will. Elena's giving me advice from both sides—maid of honor and bride."

"My best friend was a wreck on her wedding day." Elena picks up a fork and mimics a teacher holding a pointer stick. "Being the person to lean on is a major responsibility. I think it prepared me to be extra kind to my maid of honor. Anyhow, I tried." She smiles at the memory. "We're still besties so it all worked out."

It feels like a dry chunk of cake is lodged in my throat. Gina and Elena are the closest friends I've ever had. But does it count if it's not mutual? Based on their friendship scale, I'm on par with a wedding caterer.

Gina's bracelets jingle as she places a napkin on her lap. "I can't believe it's been, what—two months—since we got together like this."

"You're the one with the packed social calendar," Elena says. "I'm the boring, married one."

"And I'm just the boring one."

Elena elbows me. "You know what I mean. Gina leads the glamorous life compared to us. Manny thinks taking me to a station-sponsored event counts as a date."

"C'mon, he's the promotions manager at Univision," Gina says. "There must be upscale events."

"I guess. The private parties for top-tier clients usually have tasty food. I'm just saying it would be nice to do something not work-related, you know?"

"Tell him," Gina says. "You better do all you can now before the kids come along."

"Please. You sound like my mother. Ever since I turned thirty, she's been on me like white on rice. 'Mija, when are you going to bless me with a grandchild? Your sister has blessed us twice. And she's two years younger than you.'" Elena sinks back into the booth. "I love my family, I really do. But I'm also relieved they're in El Paso. Too much pressure! We'll start a family when the time is right for us."

"That's right," Gina says. "You just tell them you're having too much fun going on all those hot dates."

"Ha, ha. We can't all be Gina Robinson, the reporter every successful man in Phoenix wants to wine and dine."

"Who's the latest contender for your heart?" I ask.

"Nobody." Gina wags a finger. "I told you I'm swearing off men for a while."

"But it's been three weeks since you broke up with the hockey player," Elena says. "Think about all the guys sitting home alone, waiting for you."

Gina rolls gold-flecked eyes as our drinks arrive.

"Here's to Jolene." Elena raises her cocktail. "The most dedicated reporter I know."

Gina taps my glass. "Cheers."

"Not sure about dedicated. Maybe not smart enough to know when to quit."

"Hey, your friends just toasted you," Gina says. "Show some manners."

I apologize and take a long sip.

"You need to end that kind of talk," Gina says. "You just finished an exclusive interview today and you're the last reporter who interviewed Larry Lemmon. No one can take that away from you."

"Thanks, guys. I don't mean to throw a solo pity party."

"We're all going to be feeling sorry for ourselves when SMH time takes effect." Elena prods an orange slice with a straw. "I wonder how much the station pays her."

"No raises for us but they always find money for consultants," I say.

"So glad journalism school is paying off," Elena says. "Oh, wait, it's not. I still owe nineteen thousand dollars in loans."

"Maybe Rick can address student debt in his first commentary."

Poking at ice, Elena says, "We can't get an extra ten seconds for our stories but somehow there's time for his opinion?"

"Don't forget the comments from our Facebook friends," I say.

"At least it's not as bad as the station in Dallas," Gina says. "That would be the worst."

She knows I don't keep up with a lot of industry chatter and continues without me asking.

"FTVLive reported it. Every day the station posts a list showing who had the most social media engagement the day before. It's crazy competitive. Reporters call it 'Squid Game.'"

"Prepare for management's fake shock when that doesn't end well," Elena says.

"I hear you," Gina says. "But you guys have to consider Bob's view. Hardly anyone under forty watches local news with any consistency, and no one's been able to figure out how to make money off websites."

"That's not our fault," I say. "Blame the geniuses who started giving everything away for free a zillion years ago. Generations have grown up getting news however they want, whenever they want, at no cost."

"No one could have predicted how the internet was going to change everything," Gina says.

"If that's true—and I'm not sold—it was a failure of imagination."

"All right, you guys, who's in a betting mood?" Elena asks.

"An internet bet?"

"No. I bet both of you will end this negative talk in the next thirty seconds."

"What makes you say that?" Gina asks.

"That."

Elena was close. Twenty seconds later, our mouths are full of fries.

CHAPTER
20

The next day, as I'm leaving for work, I nearly run over Tuffy.

"Stop! Stop!"

A man blocks my exit, then disappears from the rearview mirror before lunging through my window. I jerk away, and if not for the seat belt, the gear shift would've impaled my waist. Tuffy seems amused.

"I am very sorry. Tuffy got loose."

Why does this stranger have Norma's baby? Keeping eyes on his pale face, my fingers claw for the phone.

"Allow me to introduce myself." He juts out a hand that I reject. "I am Oliver Greer. It is a pleasure to meet you, Jolene." His smile exposes giant gums and tiny teeth.

I squint at Tuffy for guidance but can't read doggie minds.

"Norma has told me splendid things about you."

"Where is Norma?"

"She's getting a manicure and asked if I wouldn't mind taking Tuffy for a walk. She suggested we might have a chance encounter, and here we are."

Unlike Norma, his wink is obvious. Tuffy is absolutely amused.

"Please excuse me, I'm on way my out."

"Will you be appearing on a television program tonight?"

What kind of twenty-something says "television program"? A serial killer, maybe?

"I really need to go."

My foot releases the brake pedal but Oliver isn't done.

"Excuse me, please, if you'll allow a request."

To avoid running over his feet, I have to stop.

"Might I interest you in murder and a meal?"

Is that blood on his gums?

"It would be very gratifying if you would accompany me to a dinner theater show featuring a murder mystery."

I aim for polite but not encouraging. "No, thank you. I'm late and have to go."

Between Oliver and Norma and Larry and Kelly, my mind swirls all the way to work. I'm on autopilot and don't remember seeing one light or making a single turn until I swing into the station's garage. Although it's Sunday, our weeknight anchors are working. Management's latest ploy, which they think is incredibly innovative, is to have Rachel and Rick anchor Sunday through Thursday. Belatedly, the powers that be grasped what everyone else has known for years: few people watch Friday night news compared to Sunday nights, when people are catching up and preparing for another week.

After some quick hellos in the newsroom, I text Jim.

Running more interview tonight. Got anything new?

He never responded yesterday, but I'm confident a new week will bring fresh details. Twenty minutes before the newscast, I enter the makeup room, where Rachel and Rick are discussing the latest events in the Middle East. Just kidding. Rick is contemplating whether he should add "a touch" of gray to his temples.

"Go for it," Rachel tells him. "You'll look more distinguished."

And make her look younger. Rachel has always been an anchor, never a reporter, and her priorities have always been her appearance and delivery. I don't mean to sound jealous. I get it. Some people are born with anchor faces. Mine has been described as approachable. And that's okay. Average can be as valuable to a reporter as beauty is to an anchor. Rachel got her first job in Tucson, about 115 miles south of Phoenix, and two years later moved to Phoenix, where she's worked for thirteen years. She's aging in an industry that not only values youthful appearances but the smaller paychecks less-experienced job seekers gladly accept. Thousands of twenty-five-year-olds are gunning for a limited number of anchor seats. Rachel knows this because she was one of them.

"I had a co-anchor who wore glasses even though he didn't need them," she tells Rick. "The consultant said he came across as more trustworthy and viewers loved it."

Rachel's been through three male co-anchors in Phoenix. Two moved to bigger markets. One was fired for having sex with an intern. Not specifically for the sex, because the intern was twenty-one years old and the company has no policy banning relationships between consenting adults. It was the location that did him in. A security guard found them on the roof of the parking garage. Mr. Romance brought an air mattress for their rendezvous under the stars. Someone said he's anchoring morning newscasts in Davenport, Iowa. Not sure where the intern landed.

Rick's fingers circle his eyes. "Glasses, huh?"

"Paul Coleman was the last main anchor to wear them in this market and he got hired at the ABC affiliate in Chicago. They adore him there."

Rachel's longevity in Phoenix is her armor and she dons it when a new co-anchor arrives. When Rick and his family were house hunting—before he appeared in a newscast—the station ran promos inviting viewers to "Stay informed with Rachel and

Rick." Rumors circulated that he asked the station to use "Rick and Rachel," claiming it sounded better. Not the best way to kick things off with the person you sit next to five days a week. And it hasn't improved. They're civil to each other in the newsroom, but nothing close to the "We're best friends" persona they present when the cameras' red lights come on.

Rick dangles a striped blue tie and solid red tie in front of me. "Which one do you like?"

Clearly, he's confused me with Gina, queen of accessories. Rachel suggests the blue since she's wearing a maroon dress. Rick's fingers dance around his neck, and when they rest, a knotted tie takes their place. He pulls a jacket out of the closet and says he's going to run through scripts at the social media center before the newscast.

I turn to Rachel. "Wait, that's tonight?"

"We're doing a soft rollout so David can make adjustments before the promotional campaign starts tomorrow."

With Rick positioned at the social media center, I take his seat on the set. The station's previous consultant was all about anchors engaging with reporters. The problem is our anchors don't always care about our stories—or have time to review them. At first, management encouraged anchors to come up with their own questions to ask reporters, but frankly, some were pretty dumb. Or the anchors would ask something that had already been addressed in the story and instead of appearing involved, it smacked of not paying attention. Now, we write the questions for anchors to ask. Mostly they stay on script.

Rachel watches a monitor that's positioned over my shoulder and out of viewers' sight. When the edited story ends and our faces fill the screen, she says, "Jolene, when will we learn the test results for cyanide?"

"It could be as soon as the next couple days or it could take a few weeks. However, it's unlikely we'll learn anything new before Larry Lemmon's memorial service tomorrow."

Rachel thanks me and introduces Rick in the social media center, where it appears he's downed a Red Bull since leaving the makeup room.

"We're so excited to give you the first look at our brand-new social media center." He springs across the newsroom like Tigger. "It's all about hearing from you. Check this out!"

The camera spins to reveal the station's Facebook page displayed on a sixty-five-inch screen.

"Here's how it works—as you watch Channel 4 Eyewitness News, we'll invite you to post your thoughts about our stories. Tell us what you like, what you don't like, what you'd like to see more of. We'll read your comments live during our newscasts. Sound like fun? We think so! Let's get started with a post from our friend Winnie."

She says Larry's ex is on a quest for a sugar daddy. Vivek asks people to pray for Larry's friends and family. Lawan suggests people pray for the immigrants and refugees Larry belittled. As Rick reads a comment from E.D., he hesitates mid-sentence and realizes it's an ad for erectile dysfunction. Next to me, Rachel stifles a laugh. After a beat of silence, he proceeds to Vanessa, who says she's worried about how fractured our country is and wonders what it means for future generations.

"This has been a thrill." The camera shot widens to include Rick standing next to the monitor. "Thanks to all our friends who posted. Please keep your comments coming. We'll be sharing your thoughts in every newscast, every day. Be sure to tell your friends and family to tune in and join the conversation live on Eyewitness News."

Back at my desk, I find two texts. Neither from Jim. The first is from Elena.

Congrats! Fab interview.

The second is from Gina, who despises getting news releases in all caps and exclamation points as much as I do.

THAT LOOKED SUPER FUN!!!

I spend too much time debating which emoji to use and opt for a poop image. She'll understand. When I reach into the top drawer for my keys, my fingers graze the padded envelope still holding the thumb drive and copy of the anonymous note. Jim sent an officer to pick up the whole package, but no way am I giving up the original envelope and thumb drive, not if there's the slightest chance to use them as visuals in a future story. A copy of a typed message, I can deal with. I leave the drive in the drawer and stuff the envelope into my bag.

Hitting the gym would be the smartest way to handle stress, but I choose second best. I pull out of the garage and head toward Twenty-fourth Street, my destination less than two miles from the swanky Biltmore District. Gentrification is more subtle here. Developers haven't yet taken over entire intersections and raised rents to bring in tenants they consider more respectable, like Planet Fitness, Pita Jungle, and Banner Urgent Care. At ten thirty on a Sunday night, a stoplight offers the most illumination at Osborn Road. A corner store with metal bars on doors and neon decals on windows is next to a biscuit-colored single-story building that could be mistaken for the best house on the street. Helvetica font on a lamppost sign invites me to try craft cheese, wine, and fresh pasta, but a yellow arrow beckons me to the twenty-four-hour drive-through at Dos Vaqueros.

It's another reason I appreciate Nate. My first week in Phoenix, he introduced me to carne asada fries, and it's no exaggeration to call it a life-changing experience. Lolita's Mexican Food in San Diego is usually credited with creating the dish. Some describe it as nachos with fries instead of chips. Fries make up the first layer, followed by melted cheese and grilled steak. With scoops of guacamole and sour cream strategically positioned in opposite corners, you can control the amount in each bite. It's not a snack, it's a meal that easily contains an entire day's worth of calories—maybe two. The ultimate reward for hard work. But feasting on my favorite food will have to wait because my neighbor has other plans.

"Are you ready for my report?" Norma asks before I'm out of my car.

"On what?"

"Your mystery note, of course. Remember? I texted you I would investigate."

I vaguely remember asking if she'd seen anyone around. No way would I ask her to play detective and dig into my life.

"First, I was surprised to learn most of the residents here didn't know you were on TV. They couldn't believe we have a local celebrity living among us. And such a young one."

Please let there be only one nosy Norma in the club.

"But some people know who you are. Miss Kathy—she lives at the end of the road—she watches your station quite a bit. And Mr. Lee told me he's impressed with your reporting. Isn't that fantastic?"

"Yes." I smile and wait the obligatory two seconds. "Did anyone see who left the card at my door?"

"No, unfortunately. But if you let me take a look, that could help with my next step."

The next step should be me walking through the door. Maybe Mr. Lee or Miss Kathy left the card. Maybe an anonymous note of admiration is acceptable for a generation that grew up in less stalky times. Possibly, I'm overreacting. Definitely, I plan on overeating.

"What do you say? Ready to play Cagney and Lacey?"

"Who?"

"*Cagney and Lacey*. It was a popular TV show in the eighties. They were police detectives in New York City. My Thomas, rest his soul, and I never missed an episode. You would make a terrific Cagney because she was very career-minded."

"Thanks for the TV show trivia." I lift the container of fries. "Gotta get inside before dinner gets cold."

"I'll be here if you change your mind."

Before setting my keys in the fruit bowl, I remove the anonymous card left at my door and compare it to the envelope sent to the newsroom. The card's message is written in all capital letters while the envelope's address is not. And the writing on the card is significantly bigger. But the black marker matches and both writing samples are upright, no slanting. Could be the same person. Upon closer inspection, I notice the "G" on the card is sloppier and the "J" on the envelope is missing its top line. So, not the same writer? My stomach unleashes a savage growl. I toss the card back in the bowl and the envelope in my bag.

Oscar spurns my apology for being late and gulps his food. I settle on the couch, drape a paper towel over my chest and ingest a forkful of happiness. In between bites, I call out letters to *Wheel of Fortune*. It's not my strongest night. Would never have made it to the bonus round, where the puzzle is "What are you doing?"

_ L _ RT_NG _ _TH _ _ S _ STER

With four seconds left on the clock, the contestant calls it.
Flirting with disaster.
If I were paranoid, I might take it personally.

CHAPTER

21

After hitting the snooze button three times the next morning, I slide my phone off the nightstand and command my eyes open. Crap. No power. I force myself out of bed and rummage through a drawer for a charger. As soon as it's plugged in, a string of messages lights up. It only takes one to jolt me awake. It's from JJ's station.

> **BREAKING: Medical Examiner to announce talk show host Larry Lemmon was poisoned. Watch the news conference live at 9:30 a.m.**

Double crap. It's almost seven thirty. No way I can cover the ME's announcement and Larry's memorial service. Nate and I planned to meet at eight thirty. I call the newsroom.

"Did someone oversleep?"

"Oh, Alex, so glad it's you." I tug a navy dress off a hanger and toss it on the bed. "Listen, my phone was dead, just saw the texts. Who alerted us and when?"

"The ME's office emailed a press release at six thirty this morning. The constant cyanide coverage must have gotten to them."

I drop the dress over my head and drag it past my hips. "So no one beat us, right?"

"A couple stations did on text alerts and social media posts, but no indication anyone knew this was coming."

"Not me, since I guaranteed everyone last night we wouldn't hear anything about poison today."

"That's the way the cookie crumbles," Alex says.

"Or the way poison is delivered." My fingers catch the side zipper. "How are we covering it?"

"Sending a morning show crew to the newser, and a dayside reporter will turn stories for the early evening newscasts. Are you and Nate all set?"

Halfway up, the zipper's teeth bite into fabric. "Yes, and I need to go. Thanks." I toss my phone on the bed, roll the dress down, and pull on black pants. A brown sweater completes my funeral attire. Forty minutes later, I find Nate loading the last of his gear into Lucky Seven. Maybe it's a good omen.

"Are we okay?" I ask.

"I don't know." He faces me. "Are you going to behave?"

"Probably not forever, but I will today."

Nate doesn't respond immediately as he considers my response. "You better." He pings my shoulder. "Let's go."

Larry's memorial service is scheduled to start at ten o'clock, but most stations have been here doing live hits for morning shows. Our crew leaves when Nate and I show up. It's also when protestors start gathering. They're not allowed on church property, but public sidewalks are fair game.

"Give me five minutes to spray this," Nate says.

Near the parking lot's main entrance he shoots video of ten people with signs propped against their legs and secured under arms. One woman notices Nate and mounts a sign above her head. It reads, REAP WHAT YOU SOW.

A Baptist church in Phoenix is hosting the service. Not because Larry was a member—he didn't attend religious services—but because it's so large. Asphalt wraps around the building, covering as much space as a football field. There's enough parking for his fans, colleagues, politicians, and media outlets. In addition to local and national media, the BBC hired a freelance crew. And there's gossip Univision News anchor Jorge Ramos might make an appearance.

"All done," Nate says. "I'll feed this to the station later and they can use it however they want. Let's scope out the space."

Inside the sanctuary, along the back wall, there's a riser currently supporting five TV cameras. Safely, it can hold seven. Eight will test professional relationships and nine could lead to jabs, both verbal and physical. Nate sets up his tripod and rips off wide strips of masking tape. Using a red marker, he scrawls the station's call letters across the tape, and places the strips around his gear. Once the photographer's version of marking territory is complete, I proceed with the reporter's version. The last row is designated for media. In hopes of securing a quick exit, I scribble "Reserved" on a legal-size notepad and leave it on the aisle seat.

There's no casket, but there are three blown-up photos on easels: Larry smiling behind the microphone, Larry holding a shotgun by his side, and Larry standing with a boy, presumably his son, Travis, when he was about five years old. Based on Travis's spotless shoes, creased pants, and uncertain smile, could be his first day of school. I wonder if he'll show up. As guests arrive, the hum of voices swells, like a choir warming up. It wanes as everyone stops to read the same alert on their phones: the ME's office confirms cyanide poisoning as the cause and lists homicide as the manner of the death. This just became the must-attend service of the year.

An obnoxious squeal makes me cringe. The master of makeup, miniskirts, and men is fawning over a network reporter who thinks he's nailed the blazer and designer jeans. An East Coaster who packed under the assumption everyone in the Southwest dresses in boots and bola ties. It's a memorial service, not a rodeo.

"Excuse me. Jolene, isn't it?"

Turning around, I face the program director from Larry's station. "Yes. And you're Shana. Thanks for all your help during this trying time."

Her eyes cut to the cameras and she leads me away from the media section.

"I saw your interview with Kelly," she says. "Got defensive, didn't she?"

"Well, I was glad she agreed to talk."

"That's a diplomatic response, but I get it. You've got to act like you don't have an opinion." Her voice drops. "But we both know there's something shady going on there."

Did I miss something with Kelly? Or am I missing something now with Shana?

"I appreciate your information. Please let me know if you think of anything else that would be helpful."

"Another bland line. If you get tired of reporting you might have a career in politics. You have a knack for not saying anything." She pushes a program toward me. "This has a list of speakers and musical selections. We're going to adhere to this as closely as possible because we're carrying the service live on air and streaming video on our website."

Several recognizable names make the list, including a former Arizona governor, a current member of Congress, and the founding member of a prominent rock band from the 1980s. No ex-wives and no son. I ask Shana if any family members will speak.

"They're not scheduled, but if they want to speak, naturally I'll allow it. Larry's parents have passed and he had no siblings. I'm told his son is coming, but I haven't seen him yet. Now, if you'll excuse me, I need to make sure everything's in order."

Alex answers the phone when I check in with the station. Although he serves as Sexy's megaphone, the level is tolerable.

"We need you posting throughout the service," he says. "We'll use your photos and information for the station's social channels."

"You may want to give the digital team a heads-up to monitor comments. Protestors are gathering outside. As you know, emotions can be raw and someone could go off script."

"Understood. I worked the day of Pat Tillman's memorial service."

I was a kid when Tillman died and didn't learn about his sacrifice until I moved to Phoenix and covered Pat's Run, a fundraiser for the Tillman Scholars program. Tens of thousands of people take part in the 4.2-mile run/walk that ends at the forty-two yard line at Arizona State University's stadium, where Tillman wore number forty-two on his football jersey. After the terrorist attacks of September 11, 2001, Tillman left a lucrative NFL career with the Arizona Cardinals and joined his brother Kevin in the U.S. Army where they served as Rangers. When Pat was killed in Afghanistan in 2004, the army quickly blamed enemy fire. Later, it was revealed the army tried to hide what actually happened—the twenty-seven-year-old was killed by friendly fire, shot in the head.

Before Tillman's family learned the truth and publicly criticized military leaders for the cover-up, Pat's memorial took place. Politicians, celebrities, football players, and league officials offered condolences, and some implied Pat was in a better place. Then, his youngest brother, Richard, stepped to the microphone. After thanking the speakers, he pointed out Pat wasn't religious and, using curse words, described his brother as dead, not with God. The language was broadcast live by media outlets across the country.

"That's why we'll be on a six-second delay," Alex says. "There's one more thing we'd like from you."

"We? Or Sexy?"

"Yes, David. A short scene setter after the service wraps up for the web and social media that'll carry us through until the early newscasts."

"We'll try, but keep in mind we'll be running after people to interview, so it may not happen as fast as some would like. And by 'some,' you know I mean David."

"I trust you. Send us what you can when you can."

I spend five minutes taking pictures of flowers and Larry's photographs to accompany my tweets. As ten o'clock approaches, the trickle of guests turns into a stream. The sheriff who proudly boasts about spending more per meal on abused animals than people in his jails is shaking hands and slapping backs while making his way to the front. Even though his next election is two years away, the campaigning never ends. An usher guides Larry's first wife and a young man in a dark suit to the front row. Given Annabelle's comments, I'm surprised to see her. Apparently, her love for her son outweighs her hatred for her ex.

On the way to my seat, I spot Jim standing in a back corner. "Hey, I texted you over the weekend. Never heard back."

"That's because I have a life outside of work." He surveys the crowd. "And so does my son. It was his birthday. We were busy hosting a party with seven-year-olds eating pizza and cake and running around the house."

"Sorry. Didn't realize you had family stuff going on, but I can't keep missing things, you know? JJ got the interview with Larry's producer, CNN got the community activist. Now the ME is calling it homicide and you keep telling me to hold off."

I watch him watching Larry's second ex-wife arrive with Darrell, the fill-in host. Unlike the day of Larry's death, there's no patting shoulders or leaning into each other. There's more distance and professional demeanor.

"What's the deal with them?" I ask. "How long have they been dating?"

"They tell us about two months. Others suggest it's been longer."

"Like how much longer?"

"Like before Kelly and Larry's divorce was final."

"I know Darrell is separated from his wife. What else can you tell me about him?"

"Just to be careful."

"Has he changed from person of interest to suspect?"

"Darrell is as much a suspect as Phillip Ellys." Jim swivels to face me. "Remember him?"

It takes a minute to register his question. "Listen, Jim—"

"You told him we were looking at him in connection with Larry's death. Your word doesn't mean shit."

"I'm sorry. I—"

"I don't want to hear it. The guy claims you trespassed and wants us to investigate. You can expect an officer to come by the station and take your statement. If I were you, I'd cool it before you become the story—or worse."

"I'm just trying to do my job."

"So am I, Jolene. And I'm telling you to back off."

And I do—for now, because the show is about to begin. Shana is up first. She strides to the podium, removes note cards from a pocket, and shares how she met Larry Lemmon.

"I had been offered, but not yet accepted, the position of program director. As some of you know, the job requires close contact with talk show hosts. I wanted to get a feel for how Larry and I might work together so I invited him to lunch. Did I mention I don't eat red meat?"

A hoot of laughter from the audience makes her smile grow.

"I later learned red meat was Larry's favorite food. Anyway, I figured he's a well-known host, enjoys being seen at the hot spots, so I suggested a place that was all the rage at the time. But Larry . . . oh, that Larry, he had no interest in trendy restaurants. He wanted Rito's."

A grin devours her face.

"But not Rito's at Seventh Street and Bethany Home Road. When it came to lunch, Larry could not care less about admiring timber trusses or floral displays. He wanted good food with no architectural distractions. And so, we paid a visit to the original location at Fourteenth Street and Roosevelt. For those of you unfamiliar with Rito's, it is a Phoenix institution with the best burritos this side of the border. The original Rito's is about a food's soul, not a building's style. It puts the 'no' in no-frills. You order inside and eat outside—that's if you're lucky enough to claim a metal seat without pigeon droppings."

A man in a middle row throws out a spirited laugh.

"See, he knows what I'm talking about. As I held a plastic fork in one hand, and a Fendi bag in the other, Larry said, 'Listen, I'm a simple, straightforward guy. Just tell me what needs to be done to win.' That philosophy helped us succeed as a team for five years. As my ex-husband will attest, inviting me to tell it like it is may not be the most productive approach in a marriage." She pauses for polite chuckles. "But it served Larry and me well. And for that experience I will be eternally grateful."

Shana leaves the podium and the pastor lobs generic terms of comfort. It's obvious he didn't know Larry but does an acceptable job of showing empathy and demonstrating compassion for those in attendance.

"Our fellow Christian has been called home," he says. "Larry's constant fight for the rights of the faithful makes this next song especially fitting. It's called 'Another Soldier's Coming Home.' Please sing along if the spirit touches you. If you don't know the words, please refer to your program. Or simply soak in the powerful message."

As music fills the room, dozens of people, including Darrell Arthur, sing about making room for another soldier at heaven's table.

"Such touching lyrics," the pastor says. "As the good book tells us, and the song reminds us, death is not the end. Rather it is the beginning of an everlasting life filled with love. For believers, leaving the earthly world is a joyful time. While it can be distressing for those left behind, you can find peace knowing that Larry, like all faithful Christians, will be welcomed home."

Annabelle's posture doesn't bend but her son Travis bows his head. The pastor introduces Larry's producer as the next speaker. On his way to the podium, Ralph struggles with a three-button suit jacket, managing to fasten the top before giving up on the rest.

"People are not always what they seem."

Ralph's gaze settles on the back on the room. He says nothing more. The silence drags so long people start squirming. What's he mean? Larry wasn't a good Christian? Some people turn around, itching to see what's captured his attention. I start counting. At four Mississippi, Ralph breaks the silence.

"Larry was not just my boss. I also called him my best friend. Some people thought Larry was an angry, pigheaded man. And they would not be completely wrong."

This time the silence only lasts only two Mississippis before Ralph smiles. "Come on, you gotta admit he could be opinionated."

Relief ripples through the rows.

"But Larry could also display generosity. As some of you know, I run a shelter for abandoned dogs. Larry opened his wallet and provided the seed money to get the shelter off the ground. And he continued to provide financial support every single year."

Ralph goes on to describe Larry's commitment to supporting military families.

"Some of you may not know Arizona is home to more than

half a million veterans. As a veteran himself, Larry understood the unique challenges these families face and found his following with the pro-USA mindset. Before President Trump used 'Make America Great Again' as a campaign slogan, Larry was living it. He understood the hardworking, patriotic Americans who felt ignored by career politicians and ridiculed by the liberal media. That's why Larry was loved. He gave voice to those whose voices had been scorned and silenced. I'd like to close with one of Larry's favorite songs, an oldie but a goodie. 'The Fightin' Side of Me' by Merle Haggard."

An older white guy bolts up and waves an American flag. "Amen! Love it or leave it!"

As Haggard sings a warning to war protestors, Ralph leaves the podium, passes his seat, and exits the room. I skim the program. The former governor is up next. He's not expected to say anything of consequence, and if he does, Nate will let me know. I follow Ralph as he walks out the front door.

CHAPTER
22

Outside the church, next to the stairs, Ralph is pacing, staring at his shoes, and pulling on a cigarette.

"Excuse me. Ralph?"

He answers with a frown.

"I saw you leave and just wanted to check on you."

"You checked." He blows a stream of smoke my way. "I'm good."

"Glad to hear that." I step down. "I apologize for intruding, but wonder if you could to talk with us after the service. My photographer can meet us somewhere private."

Ralph stabs his cigarette at the church. "I already did my talking in there."

"And it was very moving. That's why I'd like to do an interview."

"Not interested."

He takes a drag and crushes the butt, along with my hope for reporter redemption.

"I promise it won't take long."

Smoke clogs the air as he brushes by me, climbing two steps at a time.

"I was surprised to learn how much Larry supported your

shelter. His first wife told me he wasn't much of an animal lover. Did you help change his mind?"

Ralph stops hard and I nearly slam into him. He whips around, forcing me to clutch the railing to keep from falling backward. The stink of an ashtray hits as Ralph sticks a finger in my face. "This is the last time I'm going to tell you. I'm not interested in doing an interview. Now leave me alone."

The front door swings open. I've never been happier to see Jim.

"Everything okay here?"

Ralph drops his hand and turns to Jim. "Just came out for a quick smoke. I need to get back inside."

Jim holds the door for Ralph but shuts it before I can slide through.

"What do you think you're doing?"

"Talking to him."

"In the middle of a memorial service? Jolene, try showing some decency. If you want to harass people for interviews, at least wait until the service is over."

"I'm not harassing anyone."

"Really? Phillip Ellys was lying?"

"Like you said, we're in the middle of a service." I catch the handle. "Maybe we should talk when it's over."

As I pass, he says, "You really need to think before you act or you're going to do something you'll regret."

I wish I could make him understand. While cops and reporters often rely on each other to do our jobs, our duties are distinct and each situation is unique. It's not like Jim has to compete against other officers to break a case first and post it on social media.

Back inside, the ex-governor who once featured Larry in his campaign commercials as a hunting buddy is leaving the stage. The pastor introduces a congressman whose fifteen minutes of fame came when he compared Obamacare to slavery. The seventy-five-year-old from rural Arizona wants to return to the "good ol' days" before the Affordable Care Act.

Standing in front of the riser, I tug Nate's pant leg. When he leans down I whisper, "Larry's producer is a no. Let's try others after the service."

A crowd of hundreds assures no shortage of interviews, but I'm not interested in just anyone. I want persons of interest. And that narrows the possibilities. Since I've already interviewed Annabelle and Kelly, they're off the list. I could try Andy, the board operator who was working with Larry the day he died, but doubt he would contribute much. That leaves Darrell. My eyes stay on him as the service concludes with Larry's own words from his fifteenth anniversary show.

"Before I say good-bye, I want to thank you from the bottom of my heart. If it weren't for you, there'd be no me. To all the freaks out there, I express deep appreciation. God bless you, God bless Arizona, and God bless the greatest country in the world, the United States of America."

Darrell cruises through the crowd, exchanging pleasantries. Nate and I should catch him before he leaves the sanctuary so other stations don't glom on to our interview. But with Jim's alarm playing in my head, I suggest we hold back a bit to give Darrell some space. The gesture of respect turns out to be a mistake because it gives JJ an opening to reach him first. A kick in the gut would be less agonizing than watching her performance. First, the head tilt, followed by the handshake–shoulder touch combination. Then, the most critical line—requesting, "Just a minute of your time." I can easily read her lips because I've said it countless times. Darrell checks his watch, says something that causes JJ to hold up five fingers. Don't believe her, Darrell. It'll take five minutes just to record video of her attempting to emulate a serious reporter.

"C'mon, Nate." Before he can finish breaking it down, I nab

the tripod and hold it against my body. "I'll lead." Shuffling past local politicians and loyal listeners, my mouth plays a continuous loop of "Excuse us, please, excuse us."

Nate supplies directions. "Take a right by the woman in the green dress, then go through the side door."

The tripod's metal plate digs into my elbow, but I'm committed to the prize—professional salvation and atonement for the missed interviews. I'm almost within reach when someone obstructs my path.

"Hey there, I'm Rosie Rangel. You called me to talk about Larry because I was a regular show guest and a fan favorite. I saw you before the service started but couldn't make it over in time to say hello. What'd ya think of it?"

"Hi, Rosie," I crane my neck toward the door. "We need to catch up with someone so please excuse us."

"Oh, if it's an interview you're after, here I am." She does a ta-da thing with her hands.

"Thanks, but we've got to reach him now. Maybe we can talk later. Excuse us."

As we resume wading through the crowd, Rosie says, "Give me a call. I'm ready whenever you are."

At the door, I give a brisk knock before opening. It's an office. An empty office.

"Where'd they go?"

"Oh, man," says Nate. "Once I saw them go in, I quit watching. Maybe they're outside."

My words are still "Excuse us, please," but my tone is more "Get out of the way." The hall is as full as a movie theater for a *Star Wars* premiere. An aggressive shoulder tap directs my attention to a middle-aged woman wearing a red skirt, white shirt, and blue blazer.

"What station are you with?"

Before I can answer, she embarks on a speech about the

corrupt media. Nate pulls me away and suggests we check the parking lot. And that's where any faith in redemption vanishes. JJ is waving good-bye as Darrell drives off in a silver Lexus.

She catches my eye and shouts, "You just missed it! The. Best. Interview." She positions her hands like she's holding a trophy and kisses the air. "Like Emmy Award–winning."

My hand jets up, exposing a solo finger.

"Hey," Nate says. "We're at church."

"She started it."

"My five-year-old wouldn't even say that." His head shakes in disgust. "When you're ready to be professional, meet me at the truck."

JJ smiles and twists her hair. With her middle finger. I settle the tripod on a shoulder and trudge to the truck, teeth grinding the whole way. I apologize, but Nate's not having it. Shouldn't he be more forgiving since, as he pointed out, we're at a church? We shoot the scene setter Alex requested and report live for the early newscasts, speaking only when necessary. By the time we get to the station, I'm in such a horrible mood I can hardly stand to be around myself. Gina and Elena coerce me to the greenroom.

Gina hands me a Pepsi. "To drown your sorrows."

Elena drops onto the couch and rests a hand on my arm. "We heard what happened."

"That's what I get for being polite. Missing another interview." As I crack open the can, a look passes between them. "What?"

Elena clasps her hands and steals a glance at Gina.

I set the Pepsi down. "Out with it."

"We're worried about you," Gina says. "We know how much you like working with Nate."

My insides tighten. "You're taking his side?"

"No one's taking sides," Elena says. "We're just able to see it from both sides."

"Then you understand the pressure I'm under."

"Of course we understand."

But I don't think they can. Elena's always been more interested in lighter stories, and sidesteps crime and investigative reporting. And Gina doesn't have to worry about breaking stories because she's on the anchor track. She's the primary fill-in when Rachel is off, much to the dismay of the weekend anchor who used to be the chosen one. All signs point to Gina becoming the next weekend anchor when the current anchor's contract expires.

"We know how much this story means to you," Gina says. "But we can also see how your behavior is pushing Nate away. Do you want to work with Woman Hater or Snail every day?"

"What I want is to no longer be second best. Or third best." My voice bounces off the walls. "You guys just don't get it."

Elena stands up. "You're right. We don't get why you're willing to alienate the best photographer at the station. But you do you, Jolene."

Gina's jaw drops in surprise—whether at Elena's comments or mine, I don't know. As they leave, I lean back on the couch. Flakes of mascara dust my cheeks as I rub my eyes. I guzzle the Pepsi. I need to get out of here. It's time to return to the gym. But before I can get on a treadmill, I have to clear a newsroom hurdle.

"Why did JJ have Darrell and you didn't?" David asks.

To avoid the judgment in his eyes, I gather my phone and bag. "She got to him before we could. I'll try again tomorrow."

"What about the anonymous note and audio clips from Larry's show? Why are we still sitting on those when no one else has them?"

"Can we discuss this tomorrow?"

His expression says I'm being unreasonable.

"David, I'm really wiped out."

And about to go off on you, so please let it go.

"Okay. But let's not put it off any longer. Your track record isn't the best."

"Hey." Alex steps between us. "I appreciate all your work today. I haven't seen Nate. Be sure to thank him for me."

Doubt he wants to hear from me ever again. I need to wipe anything and anyone related to Larry Lemmon from my mind and take a page from Elena's playbook. She's devoted to *The Johnjay and Rich Show*, often recapping things she heard or sending links to segments like "Whatcha Wanna Know Wednesday." I listen on the way to the gym.

"I want to know why my colleague stole my idea," a caller to the show says. "It was worth five hundred dollars."

"How do you figure that?"

"We had a contest to come up with a slogan for a new client. The winner got five hundred bucks. But I never got to pitch mine because Caitlin stole it."

"What makes you think she stole it?"

"Okay, so here's what happened: everybody was supposed to get sixty seconds to explain their slogan. But my manager had like, a family emergency, and had to leave before everyone got to pitch, so I was going to change my font color but then I decided to think it over, so I ran to Starbucks. When I got back, I realized I'd left my laptop open and copies of my notes on my desk. Nothing was missing and everything was like the same—until the next morning."

"Uh oh," Johnjay says. "I think I know where this is going."

"I feel like we need sinister background music," Rich says. "Does Caitlin have an evil laugh and twirl a mustache?"

"No way. Caitlin is like, perfect. That's why I don't understand why she stole my slogan. I mean, everything in her life is perfect. Her hair, her clothes, her car, her boyfriend. You know what I'm saying?"

Why, yes, I do.

"I mean, why couldn't she let me have my thing?"

"Before we call Caitlin, we gotta know, what was the slogan?"

"Always honest."

When the laughter subsides, she says it was for a plumbing company. "They ended up not using it, but Caitlin still got the money."

I'm surprised Caitlin gives permission for Johnjay and Rich to put her on the air without asking why. But if her life is as fabulous as described, she probably expects to hear she's won an all-expense-paid trip around the world.

"I did not steal your dumb slogan," Caitlin says. "Why are you so obsessed with me?"

The segment ends after Caitlin realizes there's no free trip coming, threatens to contact HR, and hangs up. I'm still questioning why Elena sent me that link as I scan the QR code on my gym app. I take the latest *People* magazine from the rack and program the treadmill for a moderate walk. Flipping pages transports my thoughts from Larry Lemmon's death to the Kardashians' latest drama. After a five-minute warm-up, I'm ready to push myself. I hop off and return the magazine to the rack. With my mind on Hollywood, not Phoenix, I step back on the treadmill.

And that's the wrong move. My body tumbles, takes flight, and thwacks the wall. Lying flat on my face, breathing in musty carpet, I'm dumbstruck for a moment. My eyes shoot daggers at the merrily running treadmill. Two spots over, a guy grips the handles on his machine before asking if I'm okay.

"Yeah." I sit up, trying not to grimace.

The high school student working the front desk bounds over. "Oh my gosh! Someone call 911!"

"No, no." Leaning on one foot, I push myself up. "I'm okay."

"Um. I don't think you should move."

I can practically see the employee orientation lecture on liability running through her head. She's struggling between overreacting and being written up for violating policy.

"Maybe we should wait for the paramedics."

I soften my voice hoping she'll do the same. "No need. Really, I'm fine."

To prove it, I hit the treadmill's emergency stop button, pick up my bag, and stagger to the exit. Soon enough, my ankle will be as bruised as my ego.

CHAPTER
23

Overnight my left ankle expands to the size of a softball. I hobble to the kitchen and watch Oscar nearly leap out of the water to ingest the flakes.

"Show-off. What are you in the mood for? Music? Or NPR?"

Until Oscar learns to bark, the stereo is my best burglar deterrent. Sliding on flip-flops, I catch NPR's recap of Larry's service. Their report includes no scoops or exclusive interview, so, yay, I'm still ahead of one news outlet.

Visiting Walgreens to pick up pain reliever gets me thinking about the murders I discovered while researching cyanide. In 1982, Chicago-area investigators concluded someone had taken Tylenol bottles from various retailers, injected cyanide into the capsules, resealed the packages, and returned them to store shelves where they were sold to unsuspecting consumers. Seven people died. They never caught the killer. The murders are why pill bottles are so hard to open—they led companies to make tamper-resistant packaging. I double-check the seal on the bottle and totter to the next aisle to browse braces and wraps. The idea of putting anything around my ankle makes me wince. A pair of crutches enters my peripheral vision. The pads smash my underarms and my hands can't reach the handles. I loosen a nut and adjust the handles. Better. I push a button to lower their height. Now, I'm ridiculously hunched over but the pressure is off my ankle as I make my way to the pharmacy counter.

"Need help?"

"Yes, please. Can you adjust these?"

After some twisting and sliding, the clerk says, "Give them a try."

The crutches come below my underarms. "Now they're too low."

"No," she says. "Crutches should fall three or four inches below the armpit. You don't want to damage nerves or blood vessels there. The weight should go on your hands."

I take several gawky steps. "Does my hurt ankle go in front or back?"

"Whatever works for you. People usually bend their knee. Then, it's crutches forward and swing your leg through. Crutches, then leg."

Halfway down the aisle, I turn around. "How's that?"

"If you want, you could try children's crutches. They work for people up to five feet two inches."

"Do they come with cartoon or Disney characters?"

"No, but they'll save you ten bucks."

"Sold."

As soon as I enter the newsroom, Alex demands details.

"I wish I had a delightful tale, but it's humiliating. How about we skip it and instead talk about how you can help me?"

"10–4."

"First, I may need you to run interference. A cop might show up asking for me."

"Uh-oh. What'd you do?"

"Long story short: Phillip Ellys, the environmental activist you ran background on, claims I harassed him, and the police want to interview me."

"It's too bad you'll be out in the field. Far, far away. On assignment. All day. Maybe even into the night. No worries though, I'll let the cops know if they show up."

"I'd say you're the best but you already know."

"Roger that."

"Can you work your database wizardry on Larry's producer and the host who's been filling in? I sent you an email with everything I know."

"You got it."

It's early and the crews that cover late-afternoon and early-evening newscasts haven't arrived, which includes David. I savor the respite from sexy-angle demands. Setting the crutches against my desk, I notice a manila envelope next to my computer. No return address. Capital letters in thick, black marker spell out my name and the station's address. Postmarked two days ago in Phoenix. Just like the envelope with audio clips on a thumb drive. I run my fingers over it. No lumps or bumps. Not only do I want to know who's behind the correspondence, but also whether I'm the only reporter getting it. What if I'm part of a mass mailing? If I had sensitive information and no personal relationship with a reporter, I would send to several newsrooms to improve my coverage chances.

I cut across the top, reach inside, and pull out eight-by-ten photographs. Phillip Ellys is the star. There's a picture of him driving a Cadillac Escalade, another shows him parking the SUV, followed by a shot of him exiting the driver's seat. Not the best transportation choice for someone who makes a living telling people to reduce their carbon footprints. The next batch shows Phillip hiking with bottled water. No crime there. That's being prepared. But when I flip to the next photo, the big picture develops. Phillip is tossing the plastic bottle on the trail. The last photo shows the bottle falling, halfway between a cactus and the desert floor. These must be the pictures he was so upset about when we hit his office. Embarrassing, sure, but a motive for murder? I side with Ralph on this one. Phillip doesn't have a killer instinct.

What about Ralph? Was he sick of all his behind-the-scenes work that made Larry the star? Over the years, feature stories described Ralph as the producer and "loyal sidekick" while Larry was the good guy who brought his high school friend along for the ride. Could Ralph have resented Larry enough to kill him? But then he could lose his job because the next host would bring in their own producer. Plus, Larry supported his dog shelter. Or did Ralph think he could replace Larry as host and collect a bigger paycheck?

In most TV newsrooms, people adhere to the hierarchy: reporters and photographers work in the field, producers assemble the newscasts, and anchors present everyone else's work. Think of a newsroom like a TV drama, which it often is. Behind the scenes are writers, camera operators, and directors all supporting the people on camera. Every role is essential. But not equal. At the end of the day, everyone knows who gets the most credit. Ralph's not a moron, he must understand his role.

However, Darrell is different. A two-year-old profile in the *Phoenix Business Journal* has a picture of Darrell seated in a studio with the microphone to the side of his face. The headline reads: "Meet the Mouth Doctor with a Mouthpiece." In the article, Darrell talked about filling in for Larry and how important it was to have more people of color on the air, especially discussing conservative values. Without naming Larry, or anyone else, Darrell said extremists across the political spectrum who make outlandish statements harm the country. Was Darrell's drive for a daily show strong enough to eliminate Larry?

"Knock, knock."

I toss the pen down. "Sorry, Alex. I'm kinda spacey. It's not easy pinpointing who could be a killer."

"Can't help with that, but I do have information about Ralph and Darrell. Who do you want first?"

"Let's go with Ralph."

Alex reads from his notes. "It doesn't look like he's ever been married. Going back five years, there's no civil or criminal court cases against him. Busted twice for 5–10 in three years."

"You lost me with the numbers."

"5–10 is speeding. Two tickets in the past three years. Credit score's average."

"What about the shelter? Any financial problems?"

"Nothing I could find. He's current on property taxes. House is under two thousand square feet. His property covers roughly two acres, so there's ample room for the shelter away from neighbors. Nearest house is a quarter mile from his property line."

"Okay. What about Darrell?"

"As you know, he's separated from his wife of eleven years. Based on Kelly's Instagram and Facebook posts, she and Darrell started dating before the formal separation."

"Their relationship could have led to the breakup. What about kids? Kelly doesn't have any. Does Darrell?"

"He has eight-year-old twins with his wife. A boy and a girl. And I found another boy who lives out-of-state. For fifteen years, Darrell's been paying child support to a woman in South Carolina. I don't know what kind of relationship he has with the boy beyond financial."

"Any other court cases?"

He shakes his head. "Not even a 5–10. No complaints to the state dental board. No malpractice suits. And no financial problems I could find. His practice appears solid."

"Thanks. You've given me a lot to think about."

"Think fast because David's hunting for an exclusive."

Having new information about Ralph and Darrell makes me feel like a benchwarmer gifted a chance to become the hero of the game. Maybe Darrell's details will be enough for Ralph to publicly point the finger at him. Escaping to the greenroom, I recline on the couch, prop a pillow under my ankle, and perch a laptop on my legs. Thanks to Alex running interference, I should manage to evade the police. No one's going to stop me from owning this story. Not JJ, not Network. No one. I leave messages for Ralph and Darrell.

"Come on, guys, call me back."

"Who are you talking to?"

An uninvited guest with an insatiable appetite for sexy stories shatters my refuge.

"What do you have today?"

I adjust the laptop to hide the photos of Phillip Ellys. Sexy would want to do a whole segment on what we've received in the mail.

"I'm hoping to talk to Ralph or Darrell."

"Hoping? My producers have newscasts to fill."

I point to my ankle. "Oh, this? Thanks for asking, David. It hurts, but I'm a fighter."

"What happened?"

I blow off the question and tell him I can turn a story about persons of interest.

"Can we call them suspects?"

"Not until police do. The PIO sent an email saying the department is not commenting on the ME's homicide conclusion. All they'll say is they're still investigating."

"What can we go with today?"

"I can report cops have a short list of people they're watching without identifying them."

"That might be jumping the gun a bit."

My mouth flops open but nothing comes out.

"Maybe your injury's turning me into a softie—just for today though. Considering your current position, it would be an ideal time to start working on the dry-cleaning investigation—you know, come up with a list of locations to hit."

A noncommittal sound comes out of my mouth.

"I need to make some tweaks to our social media plan," he says. "See you later."

Thank you, SMH.

I haven't heard from Jim since the memorial service and send a text.

Checking in. Please let me know if there's anything new.

And while I'm thinking of men I've alienated, I text Nate.

Sorry I've been an ass.

"Is this a trick to gain sympathy?"

"Or is it karma for being rude to your co-workers?"

Gina and Elena stand in the doorway, arms folded across chests.

"She could be faking," Elena says.

"I don't know. She's got crutches."

"Reporters should be skeptical," I say. "But I am not faking. Gina, you can decide if it's karma after I tell you what happened—as long as you promise not to repeat it."

Their opposite reactions are expected. Gina urges me to visit a doctor while Elena's giggle builds to a full belly laugh.

"Enjoy it while you can," I say. "Doubt we'll be laughing when the consultant's plan is fully executed."

"Oh, ye of little faith, I expect to laugh even more," Elena says. "Rick's encounter with E.D. at the social media center was just the beginning."

"Speaking of beginnings, I have a story that needs one," Gina says. "Along with a middle and end."

"Thanks for stopping by. And for putting up with me."

I turn up the volume on my phone and inspect the battery

level. There's no text from Nate accepting my apology, no response from Jim, and no email confession from Larry's killer. A soft knock at the door gets my attention.

"Excuse me. Jolene?"

"Hi, Hussein. Do I have another package?"

"No. There is a woman at the front desk. She does not want to leave. She says you will talk to her."

I set the photos and laptop on the table and reach for the crutches.

"I did not know you were hurt. Do you need help?"

"Thanks, Hussein, I got it." I raise myself up. "What's her name?"

"Rosie. Rosie Bangle, maybe?"

"Rangel?"

"Yes, that's it. Do you want me to tell her you are busy?"

"No, I can talk to her. Thanks for letting me know."

I don't recognize the woman standing on the other side of the glass doors. Maybe it's because I spent a total of three seconds facing her at Larry's service. Or because she resembles so many other women. Forty-ish, medium height, medium build, medium brown hair that falls between her jaw and shoulders. Her baggy shirt and roomy pants look comfy to me, so they're probably a fashion don't.

"Hi, Jolene," Rosie says. "What happened to you?"

"No big deal. Just clumsy."

"That's good." She laughs. "Not the clumsy part. I mean the no big deal part."

"Did you need something, Rosie?"

"Since we didn't get to talk at Larry's service, thought I'd swing by and do the interview."

"I'm pretty busy."

"No worries. I'm flexible. I can hang out for a while."

"I don't even have a photographer so today's not going to work."

"Okay," she says without missing a beat. "We can schedule a time tomorrow. I can come to you. Save you from having to deal with traffic. How's that sound?"

"Rosie, I don't know what I'm going to be doing tomorrow. I could be assigned a different story."

Her jaw tightens. "Why don't you tell me what works best for you? I guarantee you'll like what I have to say. Remember, I spent two years on Larry's show. I was the guest of honor at station events. People know me. They respect me. What do you say?"

"I appreciate you dropping by. I have your number."

She moves forward, so close I smell her spearmint gum.

"Why are you blowing me off?"

"I'm not, Rosie. It's a bad time. I need to get back to work, okay?"

She grabs my bicep. "No, it's not okay. You think you're special because you're on TV? Well, you're not."

I shake her off my arm. "You need to leave."

"You need to wake up. I could've helped you. Guaranteed high ratings." Her thumb strikes her chest. "People love me. When Larry kicked me off his show, my fans flooded the station with calls and emails. People want to hear from me. I'm Rosie 'Run 'Em Out' Rangel. Who the hell are you?"

"Excuse me, please. Is something wrong?"

"Oh, Hussein, thanks for asking." I step back. "We're okay. Rosie was just leaving."

The UPS guy can hear boots pounding the floor but can't see over a stack of boxes. Rosie barges past, knocking down packages. Halfway through the door, she wields a finger toward me.

"No one cares about you or your pathetic station."

Rosie's outburst may be evidence of a short temper and deep desire for attention, but if she killed Larry, she'd be in a similar position as Ralph with no guarantee the next host would put her on air. She'd have to know that. Wouldn't she? Unless I'm missing something. And I am. A text alert from JJ's station promoting another exclusive. I click the link triggering Mr. Movie Trailer's voice.

"It's the latest twist in the death of a controversial radio host. We'll bring you exclusive video of a mystery woman delivering what might be deadly treats."

JJ appears on camera. "Join me tonight for my exclusive story." She's doing her beauty pageant pose. Standing at a slight angle with one foot in front of the other. About four months ago, while waiting for a PIO at a crime scene, JJ demonstrated the stance, explained she learned it at modeling school, and used it while filming an infomercial for a self-tanning lotion: "It takes five pounds off you!"

I feel fifty pounds heavier. My body wants to collapse on the couch in the greenroom, but if I stay, I'll have to face my colleagues' questions. I text Alex I'll be 10–7 for the night. Once he reads the code for out of service, it'll make sense. He gets our competitors' texts.

As I approach the carport separating my apartment from Norma's, I turn off the headlights and creep forward. After pushing the seat back as far as it will go, I maneuver my leg out the door, carefully setting my feet on the ground. I heave myself out and knock the door with a hip. It takes three bumps before it connects with the latch.

"Yoo-hoo!"

Knots in my shoulders bulldoze up my neck as I open the back door to get the crutches.

"Jolene!"

A burst of air erupts from my nostrils.

"Hi there." Norma is no longer yelling because she's three feet behind me. "My goodness, what happened to you?"

Deep breath in before I turn around.

"Just sprained my ankle. I'm okay."

"Oh, I'm sorry to hear that. Glad you're going to be okay though. Hey, have you seen that woman who killed Larry Lemmon? Can you believe it? The killer caught on tape! Do you still say tape? Or is it caught on video?"

"Either. Have you watched it?"

"Sure have." She picks up Tuffy. "I'm Facebook friends with JJ. She posted it tonight. Not the whole video. They want me to tune in at ten o'clock to see that. What do you know about the woman who delivered the cookies?"

"Nothing. Police are still trying to locate her. You know, Norma, just because she delivered something doesn't mean she's a killer."

"Maybe not, but she delivered the cookies that were poisoned and that's what killed Larry." She and Tuffy share puzzled looks. "Don't you know this already?"

"What I know is police are still investigating."

"Do you think she was an angry listener?"

I don't know about an angry listener, but I'm becoming an angry neighbor.

"I have no idea who she is."

"On Facebook people are saying Larry's ex-wife may have killed him. There are rumors she wanted his life insurance money. I'm not sure why she would get it since they were divorced, but who knows, maybe it was part of the settlement. Other people say Larry faked his death to somehow collect the policy himself. Not sure how he'd do that. I even heard his producer—"

"Norma, I've had a long day and my ankle's hurting so I'm going to head inside."

"Oh, sure. Can I help you?"

"No, thank you." I throw a bag over my shoulder and adjust the crutches. "I can make it."

"Okay, then. Don't forget to watch JJ's story."

As the key turns in the lock, Norma's voice intensifies. "You can go to her Facebook page and vote on how you think he died."

Even after the door opens, she keeps going. "Poisoning by an angry listener has the most votes. In second place is—"

Inside, I offer an apology. "You wouldn't believe the day I had."

Not only would Oscar not believe it, he didn't care once he saw the shrimp pellets.

JJ's story leads the newscast, of course. It takes a solid two minutes of melodramatic reading before the full video plays. The black-and-white images are hazy, but you can make out a woman the receptionist described to police. Or maybe not. Anyone can toss on a shoulder-length wig. Wearing jeans and a dark shirt, and carrying what must be heart-shaped tins, the person comes through the main entrance and heads straight to the elevator. In the next shot, she approaches the front desk. After a short exchange where the receptionist barely acknowledges her, the woman leaves the cookies and walks out of frame. The last clip shows her getting off the elevator and going out the front door.

JJ's face fills the screen as she tells viewers detectives are searching for the "mystery woman." In the next shot, JJ is on the set sitting next to an anchor urging anyone with information to call Phoenix police.

"JJ, I understand your reports on Larry Lemmon have generated a record number of comments on the station's Facebook page."

"They sure have." She broadcasts a *Mona Lisa* smile. "That's where you can take our exclusive poll and watch the full video of the mystery woman. And because we are breaking stories and sharing new information before anyone else, we've created a special section on the station's website for all my special reports."

"Impressive work, JJ. Thank you."

My fingers slide along the side of my phone. Don't do it. I slap the phone against my palm. Checking JJ's page will only make it worse. My fingers drum the backside until a text shows up.

Call if you want to talk.

Thanks, Gina. I'm ok.

More than 700 people have voted in JJ's poll, and so far, 480 people "like" the video. I watch it again and again, four times in all, straining to spot something that flew by JJ or the police. Nothing stands out.

CHAPTER
24

After a restless sleep I climb out of bed without thinking. It's my first mistake of the day. My ankle's still sore but not as sore as my ego. Even Oscar is disgusted with me. I text Jim to call, adding 911. There's no way I'm slinking into the newsroom without something new. My phone rings as I pull into the station's garage.

"What do you want?" Jim asks.

"Good morning to you, too."

"Unless you're calling to apologize for hunting someone down at a funeral, I'm not interested."

Hunting? Defensive responses ricochet in my head. I did what I had to do. It's not like I ran after him, camera rolling, shouting questions. I bite my tongue and spit out an apology. Jim grunts before saying JJ didn't get the station's surveillance video from police.

"The original is high quality, not the crap she showed. We think someone with property management or security used their phone to record a copy. Probably shot it off a computer screen and sent it to her."

"It's out there now." The only parking space near the newsroom is next to David's Tesla. The license plate reads NEWSMAN. "How about sharing the good version with me?"

"No can do. We won't release the video unless absolutely necessary. I'm told detectives are close to identifying the woman and they want to talk to her."

I push the seat back and stretch my legs. "Who do they think it is?"

"Jolene, you know better than to ask."

"I just need to know if it's a woman named Rosie Rangel. She's been pushing hard to be interviewed. She has the same sort of hair as the woman in the video. Same size, too."

"I don't know who detectives think the woman is and I'm not going to bother them."

"Listen, Jim, I need something or I'm gonna have to do a stupid story about which dry cleaners is best at getting out spaghetti stains."

As he laughs, my hands ball into fists. "This is bullshit. I've played by the rules and all I've gotten is burned. I've been looking into your persons of interest, but it's slow going. I need a new angle."

"What you need is to be careful. If we get another complaint about you, we may end up doing more than writing a report. And no one has the time or resources to investigate any threats against you, so calm down."

"Jim, I'm under a lot of pressure."

"I hear you. And, if you'll recall, I've faced professional pressure of my own—especially after helping a reporter. I'm not going for a repeat. Give me another day and I'll get you the woman's name."

I don't have another day, which leads to my second mistake. I dangle the anonymous note in front of my managers. "Let's get this on the air. If the message is accurate—that I'm closer to Larry's killer than I know—reporting it could bring in vital tips."

"You sure?" Alex says. "Seems uh . . . I don't know . . . out of character for you."

"What's that supposed to mean?"

"It's an anonymous note. What's to report?"

"It was sent to me, right? And cops are investigating it. That's exclusive."

"Atta girl!" David says. "This is going to blow up on social media."

I hope it doesn't blow up in my face and ruin my relationship with Jim. I shove the thought to the back of my mind and demand it stay there.

The five o'clock producer says she's confused. "The ME's office has labeled it a homicide, but police are still calling it a death investigation. How do we position this?"

"By combining the key elements." My fingers tick off points. "Number one, cyanide killed Larry. Number two, cops want to find the woman who delivered the cookies, cookies that conceivably contained cyanide. And, number three, they're reviewing the anonymous note sent to me."

"I like it," Bob says. "Let's make sure we lead with the note and emphasize it's our exclusive."

"And don't forget the sexy audio clips," David says. "We should post the full exchanges on our website and use short clips throughout the day on different platforms. Tease to the newscasts and invite our friends to comment and share."

"Hold on," Bob says. "The note implies there is a killer, so we can't play the audio clips that came with it. We will not identify Phillip or Ignacio as murder suspects unless police do. However, you can show the note and mention there are persons of interest without specifically naming them."

Guess there's still a journalist buried inside my news director after all.

During the newscast Sexy makes me join Rick at the social

media center, which leads to my third mistake of the day, thanks to Rick going off-script.

"Now, Jolene, I understand in addition to the anonymous note, you received audio clips from Larry's shows. And they include heated exchanges. Who is Larry arguing with? And are police investigating the people involved?"

My body goes still, my head as empty as a mannequin's. Somehow, my mouth takes control.

"Well, Rick, as I reported, police have a list of persons of interest. It doesn't mean they're suspects, but they are people investigators will want to talk to. And police did pick up the anonymous note that indicated I'm closer to Larry's killer than I know. That note could become evidence."

"Evidence! Jolene, your reporting is creating a very spirited discussion among our friends." His finger scrolls down the screen. "Let's check our Facebook page. Mariana says, 'I hope police catch the killer soon.' Al says, 'Praying for justice.' And Casey says, 'How scary! Stay safe, everyone.'"

We get a lot of comments. And so do cops. At least, that's what I gather from the text Jim sends.

WTF? No time for this.

I'm unsure how to respond. Play it down? Plead forgiveness? Pay no mind? A minute later, I apologize, say I had to run something, and hope he thinks it was a management decision.

We had a deal.

I text him to call. He doesn't.

The highlight of the day is making it inside my apartment without encountering Norma. After feeding Oscar, I grab a fork, stab a potato multiple times, and throw it in the microwave. As I pull a bag of shredded cheddar from the fridge, the doorbell rings. So much for dodging my nosy neighbor. But there's no eggplant hair in the peephole. It's someone wearing a red shirt with their back to the door.

"Who is it?"

"Delivery for Ms. Garcia."

I don't recall ordering anything, but it wouldn't be the first time I forgot.

"Just a minute."

Holding a canister of pepper spray, I unlock the door and open it halfway. The body turns around, shiny green eyes agape.

"Hello, Jolene. You are looking lovely this evening."

My left hand clenches the door, prepared to slam it. "Hello, Oliver."

Keeping a hand behind his back, Oliver extends the other. "I'm delighted to see you again."

I plunge the pepper spray in my back pocket and offer my hand. His sticky fingers linger until I wiggle free.

"What can I do for you?"

"Oh, it is not what you can do for me, Jolene. It is what I can do for you."

People who overuse my name give me the willies. Toss in Norma's experience with this guy and he needs to go. My hand whisks behind me, fingers wrapping the pepper spray.

"Not to be rude, but I don't know you and I don't allow strangers inside my home."

"Oh, Jolene, we do not have to remain strangers."

Oliver's left arm charges at me and I jump back, landing on the bad ankle.

"Ow!"

"Forgive me, Jolene. I did not intend to frighten you."

He's holding a bouquet of red, pink, and white roses.

"These are for you. Not as beautiful as you, Jolene, but I hope that you will accept them as a token of my admiration."

Who the hell shows up at a stranger's house with roses? Is

this a Minnesota thing? Or another serial killer thing? What's the proper etiquette? I opt for risking rudeness over encouraging a potential stalker.

"Listen, I appreciate the gesture, but I'm not comfortable accepting these. I don't even know you."

"That can easily change, Jolene."

My serial killer radar starts screaming.

"I am a respectable man. As you are aware from the card I left, I admire you professionally and welcome the opportunity to also admire you personally."

"I don't think so."

"You can trust—"

"I have to go."

Oliver's teeth disappear as his mouth shifts into a hard line. "You are making a mistake, Jolene."

As the door slams, a snarl explodes from the other side. "Bitch."

Should've pepper-sprayed him when I had the chance. A rhythmic rustle in my ears keeps time with my heartbeat. I don't know if I'm more pissed at him or my scaredy-cat reaction. I triple-check the dead bolt and double-check the sliding glass door that leads to the courtyard. That's a generous description. It's a slab of concrete scarcely able to hold two chairs and a table. Twenty-four inches of gold gravel separate the concrete from a cement block wall. If anyone in the alley climbs over the wall, they'll be ten steps from getting inside. I attach the security bar to the sliding glass door and return to dinner.

When I open the microwave, my appetite evaporates. The potato resembles a shrunken head.

CHAPTER
25

A lengthy look through the peephole the next morning reveals no creep. But outside the door, my crutch lands on Oliver's calling card.

ROSES ARE RED,
VIOLETS ARE BLUE,
PLEASE ALLOW ME
TO ESCORT YOU.

Scattered petals line a path to my car. A passerby might assume they were lovingly sprinkled instead of hurled. To preempt any nosiness from Norma, I gather a bundle. A single red petal with crispy brown edges crept into the velvety bunch. I toss them on the floorboard in the back of the car. Despite my rolling down all the windows, a putrid odor persists. After parking, I flick the petals out and mentally prepare for the day.

Newsroom intern Pamela Worthy is ready for her undercover assignment. Based on her hair and makeup, she's mastered JJ's school of journalism.

"I really appreciate the opportunity. I won't let you down."

"I'm sure you won't. I know Nate showed you how to turn the recorder on and off. Do you have extra batteries?"

She nods and studies the purse I'm holding. A minuscule camera is planted inside a pen that's attached to the top. I set the purse on my desk.

"Okay, let's pretend this is the dry cleaner's counter. You want to move the purse to get different shots. Take your time and keep it steady. You can position it to get a wide shot of the register so it also catches what's going on in the back of the store. Then, when the employee takes the shirt, you can move the purse closer and turn it to follow the employee. If you're waiting in line, you can pan around like this." I swivel left and right. "Give it a try."

She takes possession like a running back heading downfield.

"Relax. Remember, you're just a customer conducting a transaction. Try not to get faces, but don't freak out if you do because we'll blur them in post-production. And remember the money shots. When you hand over the cash, do it in front of the camera and get the employee handing you the receipt. Any questions?"

"Don't we need permission to shoot video inside?"

"Not unless you see a sign prohibiting audio and video recording. Arizona is a one-party state, meaning only one person needs to give permission to record. In this case, it's you."

Her expression suggests I'm asking her to rob a bank.

"What's wrong?"

Pamela tugs a silver hoop earring. "I don't know. It's just . . . kinda weird to shoot video of someone at work when they don't know."

"I understand. But remember, we're not going to show anyone's face. The story is about the cleaning results, not the employees. We need the audio and video to prove where we dropped off the shirts and what we were told about getting the stain out."

"How good is the audio? Will it, like, pick up everything?"

"Depends on background noise. And where the camera is

positioned and who's speaking. It's more important to get the employees' audio, so try to keep the camera closest to them."

"What should I say to them?"

"Do what you would normally do. Show them you have a shirt with a stain. Ask if they can get it out. If they say yes, ask how much it'll cost. If they say no, ask why not. If they say they won't know until they try, then have them try. Got it?"

"I think so." Her sentence comes out like a question.

"Just remember before you get out of the car to check that you're recording. That's the most important thing." I hand her a piece of paper with ten locations. "No one expects you to hit all of these today. Do what you can and then get with Nate. He'll review the video and offer suggestions, if needed. Any questions?"

"Can I post to Instagram?"

"You're kidding, right?"

Her eyes drift up, as if the correct answer is floating above my head.

"Pamela, this is undercover work. I thought Nate explained that to you. We don't want to reveal what we're doing until we have all the shirts and information. You shouldn't even be talking about this assignment outside these walls. Do you understand?"

She nods. "Mm-hmm."

"Okay, you have my number if you need to text or call. Thanks for taking this on. You'll do great."

She swings the purse over her shoulder and sashays out the door. It wasn't that long ago that I was in her shoes. Of course, her heels are trendier than my flats. In the Midwest, people tend to gravitate toward sensible attire. Sometimes I contemplate what life would be like if I'd stayed in Omaha. Would I be the big fish in a small pond? No time to play "What if" though. I have persons of interest to track down.

But first, my gut tells me to deal with Jim. We've worked together too long to let our relationship die. I start texting an apology and delete. Been there, done that. I consider inviting him for coffee. Maybe buying lunch would be more meaningful— yes, this calls for kimchi. While I'm composing a text, another pops up. Nacho wants to know if I'm still interested in inter- viewing him. Only if I'm desperate at the end of the day. Re- ally desperate. But five minutes later, reality sets in and my tune changes. It's always better to have something than nothing. My dignity wobbles when I accept his offer to come to the station. It nosedives when Alex says Nate is unavailable to shoot the in- terview.

Staring at the whiteboard behind the assignment desk, I say, "There's no story next to Nate's name."

Alex tinkers with the scanner volume.

"Is he here?"

"He's, uh, 10–7."

"Out of service. What's that supposed to mean?"

"Don't shoot the messenger, okay?"

"What?"

"Nate said he needs a break from the Larry Lemmon case."

Hearing Nate doesn't want to work with me stings. Hearing Woman Hater will shoot the interview wounds. Hearing David's comment burns.

"Is this Nacho guy from the audio clips going to say anything sexy?"

"Don't expect a confession, David, but they did have a con- tentious relationship. We should get something worthwhile."

"Worthwhile is new for us, I guess. Not new for CNN. Try to get different sound than what they ran, okay?"

He walks away before I respond, which is best for both of us. When Nacho arrives, he uses the same lines he used on CNN.

"Larry and I disagreed, sometimes very strongly, but we al- ways respected each other's passion."

"C'mon, Nacho, I've listened to show clips. Are you telling me you liked Larry?"

"I didn't say that." He shifts forward, resting elbows on knees. "We respected each other's commitment to our causes. Of course, his causes were not in step with mine, or most of the country for that matter."

I've had my fill of politically correct responses and playing fair has gotten me nowhere.

"Why would someone like you, who claims to be committed to human rights and respect, choose to work with Larry? It didn't sound like he always displayed common courtesy."

Nacho sits up straight. "There were certainly times in the heat of the moment when one of us said something less than respectful, but we never took it personally."

"Really? Not even when he played the old Taco Bell commercial with the dog? Didn't you find it degrading? Or did you just accept it as the price you paid to get on a popular show?"

His hand thumps the table. "Larry's show was not that popular! The media should quit reinforcing inaccurate perceptions. He may have had a hard-core group of supporters, but they were a very small group, a puny minority in a country of more than three hundred million people. Most Americans understand that immigrants come here seeking opportunities for their families. They would do the same thing in their situation."

A low whir alerts me to the camera closing in on Nacho's face.

"Just because our side doesn't have an English-speaking talk show host spending four hours every day dehumanizing the other side doesn't make us less important. We matter." He shakes a fist. "And we will be heard! As Malcolm X said, 'We want freedom by any means necessary. We want justice by any means necessary. We want equality by any means necessary.' Larry refused to comprehend that. For him, immigration was entertainment. For us, it's always been about lives." He leans back. "I imagine Larry sees things different now. Wherever he is."

I'm not sure how to respond and go with, "Who do you think poisoned him?"

"No idea. There are plenty of wackos in the world." He smiles. "And they're not all talk show hosts."

"Have you seen the video of the woman delivering the cookies?"

"Yeah."

"Do you recognize her?"

"No."

"Are you sure?"

"Should I?"

"Have you closely examined the video?"

"What are you getting at?" A crease cuts across his eyebrows. "You accusing me of something?"

"Not at all. We expect police will scrutinize all the people Larry worked with. You know, standard procedure. Cops check relationships and alibis all the time."

"I've got nothing to worry about." Nacho opens his arms wide. "I hit the gym, had a breakfast meeting, then went to my daughter's school, where I volunteer to work one-on-one with students learning English. That's where I was when Larry died. It can all be verified."

"You're saying you didn't deliver cookies that morning, but what about the woman?"

"What about her? I don't know her. Maybe she's a deranged fan. Or a jilted lover."

I've had enough of Nacho and ask Hater to get cutaways, shots he can "cut away" to while editing. Nacho wants to know when the interview will air.

"It'll be up to the producers."

"The CNN piece brought us solid publicity. Traffic to our website spiked."

Yippee for you. Your interview's not going to help my professional standing. I want to talk to Darrell Arthur, but Sexy's not having it.

"You just finished the interview with Nacho. You need to put that together before you go chasing another angle. Get writing and we'll post a Facebook poll. How about this: Who do you think poisoned Larry Lemmon? We'll give them three choices: a fan, a colleague, or someone else."

"Pretty sure another station's already done that."

"So? They don't own Facebook and they're not the only ones who use it. We'll do the poll and show the results at our social media center. You can join Rick while he reads comments after your story airs."

No way do I want to chance another episode of Rick goes rogue. Rather than argue journalistic standards, I try return on investment. Efficiency equals savings. But first—flattery.

"You're right about the poll. For sure, it'll drive traffic."

With a nod, David dismisses me and returns to his computer.

"You know, it might be a better use of resources if I skip the social media center and catch Darrell after his shift ends. It'll save the station overtime pay. Besides, Rick is so polished, he doesn't need me getting in the way."

David's hands still, but he doesn't turn around. I'm going to have to go there.

"Think about the possibilities: a story doesn't get much sexier than an affair, workplace jealousy, and murder."

Now he turns. His eyes conduct a polygraph of my face.

"Excellent point, Jolene. Why don't you head out as soon as you finish writing? Your photog can meet you when he's done editing."

If there was a race for fastest newsroom exit, I would blow away the competition, even using crutches.

CHAPTER
26

Sitting in my car outside KFRK, I open an air freshener to counter Oliver's pungent roses. I clip it to the vent and listen to Darrell sign off.

"Together, we can make a better America for the next generation. May God bless you and your loved ones and continue to bless the United States of America."

It's the same smooth delivery used during his interview with JJ when he praised Larry's commitment to conservative principles.

"Thanks to Larry, the politicians in Washington took notice of our porous southern border. Many people like to claim they're patriotic, but Larry was a true patriot. A protector of individual rights against government overreach and a defender of our Founding Fathers' vision of religious freedom, liberty, and justice."

JJ had pressed the poison angle. "Do you have any idea why someone would want to hurt or kill him?"

But the oral surgeon wouldn't bite. Instead, he presented a smile that could make supermodels jealous.

"I'm not here to speculate," he said. "I'm here to share my memories of Larry and spread his teachings to those who did not have the fortune of knowing him or listening to his show."

Tributes to Larry are still being played on air, but the balloons, cards, and flags that flanked both sides of the entrance have disappeared. The only remnants are clumps of hard candle wax.

Considering some of the rhetoric on KFRK, it's surprising there's no secured parking area for staff. Jim told me guards patrol overnights and leave after the morning shows begin. I climb out of the car to better study the people coming and going and zero in on a woman with shoulder-length brown hair wearing a black dress and holding a phone. As I try to imagine her in jeans carrying heart-shaped tins, I catch Darrell out of the corner of my eye. He's a fast walker and there's no way I can catch up.

"Darrell, Dr. Arthur! Over here!"

When he recognizes my face, his reaction changes from curious to cross. If he's half the gentleman Kelly claims he is, there's no way he'll turn his back on someone using crutches.

"I'm Jolene with Channel 4 News."

"Yes, I know."

"You're a hard person to get ahold of. I've left several phone and email messages."

"As you might imagine, it's been an exceptionally busy time between my practice and the show."

"I can appreciate that. And I hope you can appreciate my job. Do you have a few minutes for coffee?"

"I do not."

He pushes up a sleeve, exposing a Rolex. Well, I don't know for certain it's a Rolex, but it gives off an expensive aura and that's the only brand that comes to mind.

"I need to get to an appointment, so please excuse me."

As he turns away, I blurt, "Do you know the police are looking at you?"

Where did that come from? That's not how I pictured this going.

Darrell swings back. "What are you talking about?"

"Not looking at you like a suspect. More like a person of interest."

"That's preposterous. The police have said nothing to me."

"They don't always announce the people they're investigating."

"Why in the world would they be interested in me?"

"Maybe they know about the child support for your teenage son."

Who is this sleazebag controlling my words?

"That is none of your business."

"I don't mean to pry but did Larry know? Was he blackmailing you to keep it quiet?"

Veins in Darrell's temples are storming to get out. "Is this what you call journalism? Digging into innocent people's lives?"

No, it's about trying to get answers when everyone refuses to give them, and everyone I work with hates me.

"As you know, police haven't ruled out anything," I say. "They're exploring people who had motives to harm Larry."

"Then do enlighten me. What would be my motive?"

Shrugging shoulders with crutches isn't particularly effective. Just like this conversation.

"Some might argue Larry's time slot is desirable."

"You think I would hurt someone for a job?" He shakes his head. "It's obvious you don't know me. You should be ashamed of yourself."

It does feel like slime is crawling over my skin. But what am I supposed to do? Sit back and let JJ, Network, and everyone else make me look incompetent? My reputation is on the line.

"Accusations like that won't make you any friends." Darrell turns away. "If I were you, I'd be careful."

I've heard that before, is what I want to say, but he's moving faster than disinformation on Facebook. When Darrell reaches his car, I reach for my phone and read a text from Jim asking me to call.

"First of all," he says. "You owe me an apology."

"I know, I'm sorry. Management wanted something new and I couldn't put them off any longer. We had to air the anonymous note."

He mumbles a four-letter word, the one my grandma said used to automatically lead to an R-rating for movies. "Do you know how many emails and phone calls we've received since you broadcast that asinine note?"

"No."

"Me either. I stopped counting at fifty. People claiming it was Larry's ex-wife who poisoned him or a jealous competitor, a politician. Even a stripper. What the hell were you thinking, Jolene?"

"I am so sorry. Really, I am. But you can't put the whole blame on me. JJ's station has a poll asking people to vote on who they think poisoned Larry."

I skip the part about our station's plan to do the same.

"You're all on my shit list right now. The only reason I'm talking to you is because I owe you for holding off on the shop-lifting lawmaker story."

Finally!

"After this, we're done."

"Yes, we're even."

"And we are done."

Done? Does his mean with this story? Or forever?

"Where are you?" Jim asks.

"Parking lot at KFRK."

"Alone?"

"Inside my car. No one's around. What do you have?"

A puff of air passes from his phone to mine. "You are annoying."

"It's called persistence, and that's what separates good reporters from average ones. Go ahead, please."

"I want us to be crystal clear. What I'm about to say did not come from me. You can't even say it came from a police source. Do you agree to those terms?"

"Yes."

"You know, I used to believe you. Then you aired that note."

"I can't apologize enough, but remember the note was addressed to me. You played no role, so you can't get into trouble."

Silence.

The air freshener has me feeling trapped inside a spinning clothes dryer. "Jim, you know how much I value our relationship. I promise to keep you out of whatever you tell me."

More silence. I toss the air freshener in the back.

"You still there?"

He sighs. "Okay, I'm going to trust you. This is the last time."

Enough with the last time talk, I want to say.

"I'll give you a copy—high-quality copy—of KFRK's security video."

"When?"

"When you agree to my terms."

"Considering JJ has already aired the video, that doesn't sound like much of a deal."

"You're pushing your luck."

"How much better is it than what JJ showed?"

"It's a clean copy, not a bootleg. Take it or leave it."

"I'll take it. You sending to my personal email?"

"No. It's on a thumb drive. I'll bring it to you."

"Want me to stay here?"

"Only if you want me to get fired. Let's meet at Forty-fourth Street, south of Thomas. Know where Costco is?"

"Yes."

"Park at the Petco next door."

"Why there?"

"My cat needs food. Then I can run into Costco for a hot dog. You still driving a blue Corolla?"

"Civic."

"Give me thirty minutes."

He takes thirty-six, but I'm not about to complain. Although Jim doesn't mention it, I suspect he's impressed with my parking selection far away from the entrance. I backed in, under a tree, so he could pull next to my window like in a spy movie. Jim drops a tissue in my palm. Hope it's not used.

"Open it, Sherlock."

I hate when he calls me Sherlock. But he pretty much hates me calling him at all, so I let it go. Thankfully, the tissue contains nothing more than a thumb drive.

"You're welcome."

Jim's SUV begins backing up.

"Wait—what can you tell me about the woman?"

"The deal was video only."

"I'll buy your hot dog. And a drink."

"You think her name's only worth a buck fifty?"

"I think I deserve a name to go with the video. Do I need to remind you the shoplifting story I held—at your request—had video *and* a name."

A feeble headshake means I win this round. Maybe he didn't mean it when he said we're done.

"We have a first name only."

"What is it?"

"You can't air it."

"I hear you. No name will be publicly reported."

"It's Susan."

"What else do you know about her?"

"That's it."

"Ah, that explains it."

"What?"

"The real reason for your offer. If we blitz video everywhere, you think someone will see it and give you her last name."

"Maybe." His fingers tap the steering wheel. "On the other hand, detectives could have it by now. They might even have interviewed her by the time you air the video."

"No, no. Don't let them. Please, let me have one night of glory."

"Is that what you call rubbing JJ's face in it?"

"Yes."

I squelch the urge to peel out of the parking lot. My restraint is not rewarded. The streets are as packed as Walmart on Christmas Eve. At every intersection, red lights heckle me. When I finally reach the station, I hole up in an edit bay like a Sundance Film Festival judge. The surveillance video quality is far superior to what JJ aired but not worthy of a grand jury prize. That honor would require close-ups. With cloudy features she could be any of a million women. I poke my head out of the sliding door and survey the row of edit bays. Help is exiting two doors down.

"Hey Nate, can you come here a sec?"

"No." He doesn't look at me. "On my way out."

Woman Hater's head juts out of the bay next to me. "I finished editing Nacho's interview. Want to see it?"

"I have something better that requires your expertise. Got a minute?"

He shuttles through the video. "Hard to make out her face. Want me to try sharpening it?"

"Does JJ Jackson want to marry rich?"

Woman Hater grins. "I'll take that as a yes." His fingers fly over the keyboard, erasing the walls, the floor, even the woman's body until only her head and shoulders fill the screen.

"Do you know her?" he asks.

"I don't think so." I lean in closer. "But there is something familiar about her."

"Maybe because you've been watching it over and over."

"Maybe."

Alex slides open the door. "We've got breaking news. William, I need you at a 2–11."

"What bank?"

"Grafton branch at Forty-third Avenue and Cactus Road. No one hurt, but cops are searching an apartment complex. Robber might be hiding there."

I resume staring at the woman who likely killed Larry Lemmon. Hair pushed behind one ear reveals a thin, tired face. No visible makeup. Full eyebrows. Average-size nose and mouth. I replay the original video, this time ignoring her face. Her gait is steady, yet uncertain, like she knows where she's going but isn't confident in what she's doing.

And then it hits me.

I comb through the video folders containing coverage of Larry's death and click on the oldest. I blow past cop cars, the ambulance, and the medical examiner's van before slowing to survey the people in the parking lot.

"Where are you?"

She's not in the group gathered near the front. She's not with the guy standing off to the side. She's not the woman alone on a phone.

She's not there.

But I swear she was. Closing my eyes, I replay the scene until a woman approaches JJ to ask what's going on. She shows up after JJ's Twitter video. That's it! David, I may owe you for harping on me to tweet.

I burn through photos on my phone, bypassing Larry's memorial service and the handmade condolences at KFRK, back to the day it started. And there she is. Watching the action by herself. As my fingers zoom in, I burst out of the chair. I've heard people describe adrenaline coursing through their veins and always thought it was an exaggeration. Until now. I need to snag undercover gear from the equipment locker without a manager's interference. David is lurking around the assignment desk. Bad for Alex, good for me. I gather my bag and crutches and hurry to an exit. No roadblocks in the hallway. I hustle to the locker room where Roger "Snail" Hale is checking his gear. And thwarting my success.

"Hi, Jolene."

"Hey, Roger. How you doing?"

"Oh, you know, same ole, same ole."

"I hear you. Hey, I just need to get back there real quick then I'll be out of your way."

"Sure. Just give me a minute."

No time for a Snail minute. "I'm in a hurry so you'll have to excuse me." I mash my body against a table littered with bags, batteries, and microphones. Roger and I avoid physical contact but a crutch squashes his foot.

"Ow! Watch it." He slides out of my way. "Geez, I was almost finished."

"Sorry, Roger. It's really important." I seize the recorder, purse, and extra batteries. "All done. Thanks."

"Hope it's a good story."

"It's got to be."

CHAPTER
27

By the time I arrive at the coffee shop across the street from KFRK, my thumbnail is ragged. Excitement and nervousness have been duking it out. Excitement is down for the count after being pummeled by nerves.

Behind the shop, I back into a parking space to watch people while I test the hidden camera. After hitting the record button, I zip the purse shut, sling it over my shoulder, and adjust the strap against the crutch. Halfway to the door, I stop for B-roll, discreetly moving to the left, back to center for five seconds, and then to the right. That should be enough video to set the scene. Near the entrance, a brown-haired woman with her back to me is talking on a phone. I prowl closer to eavesdrop.

"And I was like, whatevs, I don't need you, we're done. Good. Bye."

Sunglasses cover her face as she passes.

"Susan?"

No response. The only other women with darker hair are working behind the counter. I order a green tea. When I pay with cash, it takes the barista a minute to remember how to handle the transaction. If this visit turns ugly unexpectedly, I want no documentation linking me to the business. One employee is taller, the other is thinner. One hairstyle hangs below the chin, the other is a tight bun. Both appear more poised than the person in the video. During a lull, I explain I'm looking for a woman with shoulder-length brown hair named Susan.

"She comes and goes."

My heart does a backflip. "You know Susan?"

"Sure. But haven't seen her for maybe four or five days. Have you, Mia?"

"No." She notes a clock on the wall. "But when she shows up, it's around this time."

"Does she work nearby?"

"You could call it that. She panhandles."

"Do you know Susan's last name?"

Mia's eyes scrunch. "What do you want with her?"

"I'm a reporter working on the Larry Lemmon case. Just following up with people I saw the day he died. Susan was part of the crowd watching the police activity."

"It'd be interesting to get her take," Mia says. "He wasn't very kind to her. Neither was his friend."

"What do you mean?"

"Larry always complained about Susan but we didn't want to make her leave. She wasn't hurting anyone. And she was always polite."

Boisterous laughter breaks up our conversation as three customers roll in. As Mia presents the tea, the flaw in my plan becomes evident. I can't carry a hot drink using crutches. I thank her and bungle an excuse for changing my mind. I take my time returning to the car since I have no idea where I'm going. A visual sweep conjures no clues. Two office buildings, one parking garage, and no Susan. She could be anywhere.

"Psst!"

I notice the shopping cart first. A clear plastic bag packed with aluminum cans is tied to the side. Luggage emblazoned with

Mickey Mouse is stored below. An overstuffed duffel bag shares the basket with a tired blanket. At the front, where a child might sit, is a teddy bear. Positioned between its arms and legs is a sign written in the color of a well-done steak: "Hungry. Please help."

"Over here!"

A man with stringy blond hair and a scraggly beard stands by a dumpster holding a dollar store bag. Even though it's sunny and eighty-five degrees, he's dressed in layers.

"You looking for Susan?"

"How'd you know?"

He motions me closer. My eyes scour the lot. No people. A scream for help would have to be loud enough to penetrate buildings. I ease forward, keeping more than an arm's length of distance between us. Like the woman I encountered outside the convenience store, it's tough to tell his age.

"What can you tell me about Susan?"

"Hold up, hold up. Not so fast. You a cop?"

"No, I'm a reporter. My name is Jolene. And you are . . . ?"

"Garrett's the name." He rams his left hand through the plastic handles to extend his right hand.

Is he being polite or is this a ploy to grab me? I pretend not to notice his outstretched hand and reposition the crutches.

"Glad to meet you, Garrett. How did you know I'm looking for Susan?"

He brushes his hand against a dirty pant leg. "'Cause you ain't the only one. Cops were here yesterday harassing me." He straightens his jacket. "If they'd treated me better, I mighta helped 'em out."

"Do you know where Susan is?"

"Whatcha want with her?"

"To talk about Larry Lemmon. Do you know who he is?"

"Never heard of him." Garrett wipes a hand across his nose. "Where's he hang out?"

"Across the street. Used to. That's where he hosted a talk show. I saw Susan in the parking lot the day he died."

"So?"

"I'm trying to talk with people I saw that day. Any idea where I can find her?"

His head bobs up and down. "Susan's a nice lady."

I say nothing.

"You gonna get her in trouble?"

"Just want to talk to her."

Garrett swings the bag three times clockwise, and three times the opposite way. "If Susan's hungry she might be at St. Vincent's for lunch. Know where that's at?"

"Sunnyslope?"

"Yeah, Tenth Avenue, south of Hatcher. Look for the blue tent."

"And if she's not there?"

"If she's doin' okay with money, might wanna try Barbara's Brew. She gets away sittin' in them places better than me."

"Where is it?"

"Dunlap and Central."

"That's a crowded intersection. Do you know which corner?"

Garrett's eyelids droop as he draws a square with his finger and points at corners. "Some medical thing there, don't know what that is, there's Popeyes." His eyes open and fingers snap. "It's across from Popeyes."

"Anywhere else I should try?"

He scratches his beard and thinks a minute. "You know Burton Barr, the library on Central? Susan's a big reader."

And a killer.

"Thanks, Garrett."

"You find her, tell her I said hi." As Garrett's hand dives into the dumpster, mine digs into a pocket and pulls out a five-dollar bill.

"Hey Garrett, I'm not allowed to pay for information so would you consider this a gift? Not a payment."

"Sure." He crams it down a front pocket and shuffles to his cart.

I drive to an area of Phoenix known as Sunnyslope. A hundred years ago it became a haven for outsiders with tuberculosis. Doctors suggested they move to the desert, thinking the dry, clean air on the city's outskirts would improve their health. Some of the wealthy settlers opened businesses and a hospital. Others barely had more than the tents they slept in. Today, Sunnyslope is in the heart of Phoenix and still flowing with financial extremes—homes valued at more than a million dollars and people living on the streets.

It's almost twelve thirty by the time I spot the royal-blue awnings Garrett mentioned. They flank a single-story stucco building with window bars painted the same sandy color as the walls. A metal gate surrounds the property. If you somehow make it past the gate when you're not supposed to, a chain-link fence with razor wire circling the top should sever your plans. The narrow street is lined with people sitting and standing, alone and in groups. Men crouch on bicycles built for children, darting between parked cars. In front of a repair shop, I park my car between a battered truck and a sedan missing a front bumper. Turning on the recorder, I say a silent prayer to find Susan—just in case someone with power and time is willing to help me out. I approach a woman sprawled across a patch of weeds, head propped against a sleeping bag, feet splayed out.

"Excuse me."

Her eyes are open, but nobody's home. I manipulate crutches around broken glass bottles and try two guys leaning against a graffiti-covered block wall. Neither admit to knowing any Susans. My gaze lands on a group across the street from the center's gate. Three women and two men. Third time's the charm, I tell myself.

"Hello," I say with a smile. "Excuse me for interrupting. I'm trying to find someone and hope you can help."

Every face rotates toward one woman. The alpha of the group.

"Who you looking for?"

"A woman named Susan."

"Lots of Susans. Gotta do better than that."

"In her thirties or forties. She has brown hair." I pat a shoulder. "Maybe this long. Couple inches taller than me, not overweight, not skinny."

Alpha blows bad breath through wrinkled lips. "Doesn't sound like you know her. You 5-O?"

"No, I'm a reporter."

"La-di-da." She lunges forward, cold eyes challenging me. "What do you want with stuck-up Susan?"

Show no fear, I tell myself. She can help.

"Oh, you know Susan?"

"I know she thinks she's better than us."

"Do you know where I can find her?"

A shirtless man with an arm covered in tattoos says, "She ain't been around for a while." Alpha shoots him a warning, but he keeps talking. "Last I heard she was surfin'."

"Surfing?"

"You know, couch surfin'. Told me her sister's in San Diego. She always wanted to go there."

What better time than after committing murder?

"What else do you know about Susan?"

The man opens his mouth, but Alpha's raised hand cuts him off. "No, you answer my question: Why do you want to talk to her?"

"Has she ever mentioned a guy named Larry Lemmon?"

"Who's that?"

"A talk show host."

"Let me school you some, Miss Reporter." Alpha's arms flap. "Out here, we don't get a lotta TV."

"He's on the radio."

Tattoo guy hoots and Alpha lobs a scowl.

"We don't know no Larry Lemmon. But I know the law. And I know if you're a cop and I ask if you're a cop, you gotta tell me. You a cop?"

"No, I'm not. I swear. I'm a reporter covering Larry Lemmon's murder."

"What's she got to do with it? You think stuck-up Susan killed him?"

Why, yes, I do.

"Susan was in the parking lot the day he died. So were a bunch of other people. I've been talking with them and I'd like to talk to her."

A whistle catches Alpha's attention and she nods to the others. As they collect their belongings, a clatter bursts from the dining room. The six-foot-wide opening is disappearing. Fast. Just as I reach the gate, the lock slams into place.

"Hello! Can someone come here?"

From the sidewalk, a woman calls out, "Lunch's over, honey. Dinner's at four thirty."

Despite my pleas for attention—or maybe because of them— the gate stays shut. No one wants to hear from me. Except a pesky newsroom manager.

Where are you?

I ignore David's text and plod to my car.

Need u live @ 5 @ social media center.

"Not if I can help it." I flip my phone to silent mode.

Since Barbara's Brew is on the way to Burton Barr Central Library, it's my next stop. Garrett's directions lead to a confusing corner of commerce. A slew of stores forms a straight line with stalks of businesses sprouting throughout the block-long parking lot. It's like driving through a corn maze. I finally spot Barbara's next to a barber shop. Sitting alone, nursing a drink, is a woman with shoulder-length brown hair. Someone a neighbor would describe as "a nice person" after being shocked to learn she's a killer. But I won't be interviewing neighbors because I'm about to interview the killer herself.

"Excuse me, Susan?"

Her body lurches and liquid sloshes across the table. She flies up and the chair clanks to the floor.

"I'm sorry." I snatch napkins off the next table and sop up the mess. "Please, let me get you a fresh drink."

She eyes her cup. "It's okay. Still some left." She picks up the chair but doesn't sit. "Who are you?"

I adjust the purse so the camera captures her face. "My name is Jolene Garcia. I'm a reporter covering the Larry Lemmon case."

Susan backs away. "I don't know anything about that."

"I saw you outside the station the day Larry died."

"Wasn't me." Her hip clips the condiment counter.

"You asked another reporter what was going on."

"Can't help you." She turns away.

I will not let the biggest story of my career walk out the door. Not after everything it's taken to get here. Facing JJ's taunts. Watching Network's undeserved scoop. Enduring David's obnoxious comments. What happens next could erase all the frustration. What happens next could validate my work. What happens next could advance my career.

"Susan, I know it was you. And so do the police."

She stops mid-stride. "What are you talking about?"

My crutches flounder between tables as I angle to get in front of her. Here comes the money shot.

"Police have surveillance video of you delivering the cookies that killed Larry."

Her eyes fasten on the door.

No, Susan, don't run. I cushion my voice. "Did Larry do something to you?'

"What?"

"Why did you do it?"

"I didn't do anything."

"You delivered the cookies. Larry ate them and died."

"But I . . . I didn't make them!"

"Who did?"

Her lips tremble. "I didn't know they were poisoned."

"If you didn't make the cookies, where did you get them?"

Her palms press against her forehead. "Gotta get out of here."

And I gotta keep her talking. "Susan, if you didn't know the cookies were poisoned, it's not your fault. What happened?"

"A guy." Her words, barely audible, draw me closer. "He offered me twenty bucks to deliver them."

"What guy?"

Her eyes plead with me. "Just get out of my way."

"Listen to me, Susan. I know a cop who's involved in the case. He's a good guy. If you tell me what happened, I can explain it to him."

She looks away, a tear trapped in the corner of an eye.

"Who asked you to deliver the cookies?"

Her finger catches the tear.

"Susan, who was it?"

She whimpers.

"If you tell me, I can help."

"His friend."

"Whose friend?"

"Larry's."

"Susan, do you know his name?"

She whispers a response that can't be right.

"Who?"

"Ralph."

"The same Ralph who worked with him?"

She sniffs and nods. "Sometimes I'd see him at the coffee shop. Never gave me money. Until . . ."

"Until when?"

Her eyes flit to the floor and her feet rock. "He asked if I wanted to make easy money. Told him I'm not that kind of person. I thought he meant sex or drugs. He said it wasn't anything immoral or illegal, said he wanted to surprise his friend with his favorite cookies."

"And?"

"I said okay. He brought the cookies the next day, told me not to eat any, said he knew how many there were. Gave me a twenty-dollar bill and told me where to take them." Her voice cracks. "I never would have done it if I'd known."

Her torment radiates like summer heat off Phoenix pavements.

"Susan, you need to tell the police. Let me put you in touch with my friend."

"No. They won't believe me. You said there's video."

Video! I need to get some of Ralph before cops get to him.

"You know what, Susan? It probably would be best to hold off—just for a day though. Let me talk to my friend. Then, I'll tell you what he said and you can decide what you want to do. I'll call you."

"I don't have a phone anymore."

"Do you have access to one?"

"Maybe."

I hand her my card. "Call me tomorrow. And if you want, I'll put you in touch with my friend. He'll make sure you're treated right."

"How do you know he'll believe me?"

"He trusts me. And so can you."

With a smile that I hope conveys confidence, I say good-bye to Susan and hello, Emmy. All I need is five minutes with Ralph. No confrontation, keep it low-key, and maybe he'll say something incriminating. Even if he doesn't, I'll leave with exclusive video and break the news to Jim—with the understanding that I'll be the only reporter allowed to record video of Ralph's arrest. Take that, Network. Hope you're wearing waterproof mascara, JJ. What's that, Bob? You're going to take me off the dry-cleaning story so I can concentrate on legitimate reporting that'll bring national attention to our station? Superb choice.

I thumb through my call history until I find Ralph's number. After four rings, an automated voice tells me to leave a message. I hang up and call again. By the third ring, I sink faster than a brick in a bathtub. On the fourth ring, as I'm about to end the call, a stern voice picks up.

"Hey, Ralph. It's Jolene from Channel 4. Glad I caught you."

"I'm busy—that's why I have voice mail."

"I just got some new information from police I'd like to run by you."

"What kind of information?"

"The kind that's not public yet. Can we get together and talk about it?"

"I don't have time right now."

"I can come to you."

Silence.

"Ralph?"

"I'm almost home. If you want, you can meet me there."

He gives me an address in Laveen, an area southwest of downtown Phoenix. For decades, cotton fields and dairy farms dominated the landscape, but spotting cows is no longer the norm as people keep selling to developers. Shopping centers and housing subdivisions snake closer to residents more accustomed to solitude than traffic backups caused by In-N-Out Burger's drive through. I call the newsroom to tell Alex where I'm going.

"Stand by, got another 2–11."

"What?"

"Bank robbery. In progress."

Clunk. Alex dropped the phone on the desk. Sirens from the scanner almost overpower his directions to a crew. "What's your ETA?"

After sixty seconds of listening to Alex's second language, I hang up and call back. "Listen, I want to let you know I'm going to Ralph's house."

"10–4, Alf's house. Keep us posted."

Alex disconnects as I try to correct him, but his lack of enthusiasm can't dampen mine. As the downtown high-rises shrink in the rearview mirror, random fields of corn, tomatoes, and pumpkins rise through the windshield. Cow manure mixes with exhaust fumes from the Loop 202 South Mountain Freeway, also known as the Congressman Ed Pastor Freeway, named after the first Mexican-American from Arizona elected to Congress. Before the housing bust and Great Recession, Ralph bought a ranch house on a lot that's ten times the size of new construction. According to tax records, his property value has quadrupled. Developers gobbled up parcels around him and spit out cookie-cutter houses ten feet apart. Subdivisions stuffed with red barrel-tile roofs are divided by a swath of undeveloped land. The openness, along with the GPS navigation system, tells me I've arrived. So do signs along the property line. One warns, No Trespassing. Keep Out. And if that doesn't deter someone, there's an image of a handgun dripping with bloodred text, Protected by Armed Homeowner.

Armed homeowner signs gained popularity after a high-profile trial. A man arrived home to find a guy running out his back door. The homeowner shot the guy as he climbed a wall to get away. He died at the hospital. The guy had broken in and stolen cash and jewelry. Since he was running away, the prosecutor determined the homeowner was in no immediate danger and charged him with manslaughter. The homeowner's attorney used the "justification defense," claiming it was self-defense and lethal force was necessary.

"Even if you don't buy that argument—and I believe you should," the lawyer told jurors. "No law requires the homeowner to back off."

She urged the jury to send a message to criminals that Arizonans have every right to defend their property. Larry and Ralph discussed the case daily, and during the trial KFRK freaks sat in the courtroom. They wore shirts with sayings like, a man's home is his castle and an armed homeowner is a living homeowner. The judge threw one guy out for wearing a shirt that read, shoot first. ask questions later. After deliberating less than ninety minutes, the jury acquitted the homeowner. One seasoned court observer pointed out that deliberations conveniently lasted the duration of the court's lunch break and speculated that jurors could've wrapped up in thirty minutes if they hadn't wanted a free lunch.

The driveway leading to Ralph's house is a mix of dirt and gravel with ruts so deep I worry they'll consume my tires. A jackrabbit's ears protrude from a PRIVATE PROPERTY sign. He leaps at the sound of crunching rocks and zigzags away. The last sign produces a ripple of nausea: BEWARE OF DOGS.

Come on, you can do this.

Biting a thumbnail, I remind myself what's at stake: salvaging my reputation. I park behind two pickup trucks. One is dingy red with a faded LOCK HER UP! sticker on a dented tailgate. The other is shiny ebony, its body slogan free. I release the steering wheel and roll my shoulders, failing to dislodge the steel rod jammed between them. Slowly, I open the door. A machine gun blast of barks breaks out. My heart rockets to my throat as I slam it shut. Saliva evaporates. If the dogs get to me before I can call Jim, what will happen to my body? And my exclusive video?

I text Jim what I've learned and tell him to stand by for my call. Realizing he won't appreciate my request and to avoid an argument, I power off the phone and push the door open. The rat-a-tat-tat of woofs isn't winding down. Neither is my pulse.

You have to do this.

A sliver of common-sense creeps in. In case I need to dial 911 before I'm mauled, I turn the phone back on. And set it to silent mode—can't have rings or pings ruining Ralph's last words before his arrest. Deep breath in through my nose, long breath out my mouth. I stick the key fob in my front pocket, position the crutches, and straighten the purse so the camera's view is clear.

This is going to make up for all the stress and shame. The payoff is coming.

CHAPTER
29

Behind the house, Ralph is on his knees, gun in a hip holster. With his back to me, I can't figure out what he's doing until he stands. A scrawny dog shakes off soap as Ralph picks up a hose. Beyond them, a chain-link fence outlines a play area and agility course. Random patches of green are mixed with mostly dirt that serves as the canvas for a tunnel, teeterboard, and weave poles. I count five dogs—all humongous—roughhousing in the fenced area, and four—even more menacing—sprawled on the ground outside the fence. My fingers bond to the crutches' handles, preparing to use them as weapons.

When there's a break in the water flow, I call out a greeting. Ralph's hand bolts to the gun. My eyes veer from his firearm to the weapons behind him—two dogs surging toward me. Steadying my stance with one crutch, I punch the other toward the beasts, squeeze my eyes shut, and brace for impact.

"Nein! Bleib!"

I peek an eye open. Both dogs are twenty feet away, rooted in place.

"Good boys." Ralph pats their heads and gives me a look I can't interpret. "Didn't hear you sneaking up."

With wobbly legs, I try to square my shoulders, and I straighten the purse. "It's not sneaking if you know I'm coming, right?" My voice comes out high-pitched, like a frightened child.

"Should've announced yourself. Some of these dogs have been treated bad. They don't trust people." He pulls treats out of a pocket and rewards the aggressive guards. "Bullet and Trigger are real protective of me."

Bullet and Trigger?

"Thanks for calling them off." I force myself to take a step forward. "You speak German to them?"

"Just commands."

"I know nein means 'no' but what was the other command? Sounded like blibe?"

"Yes, bleib. Means 'stay.'"

"I'm glad they listen."

"Geh, boys. Go."

Without hesitation, one dog returns to his friends lounging on the ground. The other, obsessed with my presence, lets out a deep rumble. Ralph kneels next to him.

"Beruhigen." He repeats the word while rubbing the dog's ear.

Bullet's—or maybe Trigger's—wild eyes swerve from me to Ralph.

"Geh."

The dog lollops back to his pack and I suck in air.

"What did you say to him?"

"Beruhigen."

"Burr-WE-gun? What's it mean?"

"Calm down."

Ralph flings the hose away from the skinny dog. She shimmies and the desert floor drinks the moisture.

"Why German?"

"It's strong, forceful. And there's no confusion if they hear someone else giving commands in English. They only respond to German commands."

He tosses a treat. The damp dog wolfs it down and trots off to her friends.

"So, what brings you out here?"

Keep him comfortable, I remind myself. Then, get him to say something that'll be damning to air after his arrest.

"Guess who I just ran into? Darrell. If he gets the weekday slot, do you think you'll work with him?"

He pulls on his mustache. "Haven't given it much thought."

"Great ramada." I point to a picnic table and grill. "You have so much space. How many dogs?"

"Today? Twelve. Sometimes less, usually more. I've had up to twenty."

"Where do they all stay?"

Ralph nods toward a long structure opposite the ramada. "The kennel has beds and runs. The dogs have freedom here. Not like where they came from. Bastards would chain 'em to trees or keep 'em in cages all day and night. Once they get used to this place, most of them like to stay outdoors. A few will sleep inside the house. There's a doggie door so they can go in and out whenever they want."

"Sounds like a lot of work for one person. Did Larry ever help? I mean, I know he helped financially. Did he like to hang out here?"

His eyes tighten. "Larry was not one to clean up dog shit."

That's prizewinning sound but we can't air "shit," so let's try again.

"You know, his second wife kept the dogs after they broke up. Did he ever get another one?"

He thrusts a hand in a pocket. "I have work to do. Thought you had something to tell me."

"I do. Would you like to sit down and talk?"

"No, I need to feed these guys. Food's over there." He regards my foot. "Can you make it?"

"Sure."

Gravel replaces compact dirt and the path gets dicier. Crutches are designed for city cruising, not all-terrain traveling. But the larger peril spurts from my pores. Teetering past Bullet, Trigger, and their oversized friends, I pray the underarm cushions trap my sweat. Just passing through, boys, please don't get up.

"Need some help?" Ralph asks.

"No, thanks."

A spot-check reveals no canines calculating an attack. I follow Ralph into a large shed turned pet supply warehouse. He heads to the front where a sink and counter have been installed.

"Seems like you run a full-service clinic."

"Yeah, I stock up during sales." Standing on toes, he opens a cabinet and pulls out a bag. "But you didn't come here to watch me feed the dogs."

"Right." My body twists for a better camera angle. "You know cops are trying to track down the woman who delivered the cookies. Have you watched the security video?"

"You mean the blurry shit from that ding-a-ling JJ?" He turns back to the counter, grabs a knife and slices the bag. "Yeah, I saw it."

"Do you know the woman?"

"No."

"She's not familiar to you?"

If I hadn't been watching, I would've missed it—a micro hesitation.

"Told you I don't know who she is."

"Police are looking for her."

"Makes sense." He lines up bowls. "That's your big news?"

"It could get bigger pretty fast. Cops are close to talking to her."

"Yeah?" He palms a scoop from the counter. "How do you know?"

"I have a good source."

Ralph digs in the bag. "What else does your source say?" Food clatters into a bowl.

"I have the woman's name."

"Doesn't sound like much."

I clinch the purse strap, ready to record the most crucial video of my career. Will Ralph show surprise? Act confused? A dollop of sweat worms down my spine.

"Maybe if I told you her name?"

He waves the scoop at me. "Let's hear it."

Only if you turn around. I didn't come face-to-face with Bullet and Trigger to not see yours. Maybe silence will make him curious enough to turn around. Another plop of food. Maybe not. The sweat drops are multiplying.

"You still here?" He swings toward me, holding an empty scoop.

I prepare for the ultimate shot, tightening every muscle to counter my nerves. Ralph is facing the camera and when I say Susan's name, his obvious guilt will be recorded. I'll play along and act like I believe whatever he says—all the way to my car where I'll call Jim and plan for more exclusive video.

But he turns back before I can answer.

If I could kick myself I would. Get on with it. Any more stalling will make him suspicious.

"Her first name is Susan."

"I went to high school with a Susan. She got married and moved to Utah."

"Know any other Susans?"

"Not off the top of my head. I'm sure we had a Susan on our show over the years, but no one stands out."

This is not going the way I want. I thought her name would cause a reaction, maybe he'd make up a story about a disgruntled fan. Easy to believe, considering they sent Rosie Rangel a restraining order. I poke along a wall lined with shelves. They're loaded with boxes marked "balls," "Frisbees," and "toys." One smells like my grandma's Sunday breakfast.

"What's with the bacon box?"

"Dental hygiene. Mostly toys with bristles to fight plaque and tartar."

"You're a doggie dentist, too?"

He continues scooping. "I can treat a lot of stuff. Digestive issues, rashes, allergies."

Above the toy shelf, medications are arranged in alphabetical order. Albuterol for asthma relief. Benadryl for allergies. Cephalexin for bacterial infections. What I see next causes my heart to howl.

Cyanide.

Pins and needles pierce my chest. My feet beg to flee but a voice in my head sings, "Exclusive video." I aim the camera toward the shelf and silently count to three Mississippi. My eyes whip to the one-man assembly line. Scoop, pour, and repeat. I skim past piles of blankets, sail over stacks of food, and stop on containers with treats. Mostly plastic bowls, some glass ones. And one heart-shaped tin.

Do not screw this up.

Hands trembling, I nudge the camera closer and start counting. At two Mississippi, it hits me. No food crackling against bowls. I release the purse and meet Ralph's venomous stare.

"Oh, Jolene." He breaks into Dolly's song. "You disappoint me. I expected more from you."

I swallow hard. "Listen, Ralph." I try to force a smile, but my lips twitch in protest. "I know you're busy, so I'll just get out of your way and let you finish up."

He storms forward, plants arms across his chest, and stomps his feet wide apart. "But I'm offering you an exclusive, Jolene. Isn't that what you want?"

"I should go. My producer's expecting me."

"You can't leave without getting the facts right. What kind of reporter are you? Obviously, not a good one. You were focused on the wrong thing."

My backpedaling gains momentum.

"Don't you get it? It wasn't the tins."

"Listen, Ralph, I don't know anything other than what the cops are saying. They want Susan. She's the one who delivered the poison."

"No, she didn't. I did."

My feet freeze.

"It wasn't the cookies." His arms spread in triumph. "It was the coffee."

My internal voice pesters for steady video, but erratic breaths and quivering hands destroy any chance.

"You poisoned Larry's coffee?"

"Brilliant, huh?"

"Why?"

"Remember what I said at his service? People aren't always what they seem. That was Larry."

I wiggle a crutch behind me, struggling to find the door. It whacks a wall. "If I'm not back at the station any minute, they're going to call the cops. You don't want them to find me in trouble."

"What makes you think they'll find you?"

My fingertips brush the doorframe and I take off. Running is out of the question, so I go with a slide-hop combination, as far away from the sleeping dogs as possible.

"Bullet! Trigger! Hier!"

My slide loses steam as I look back to make sure *hier* doesn't mean, "Kill the reporter." The dogs run to Ralph's side.

"Jolene, did you know pit bulls are very loyal?"

My slide-hop combination revs up.

"How they behave really depends on the people who raise them. How do you think I've raised them, Jolene?"

Slide, hop. Slide, hop.

"Jolene, I asked you a question. How do you think I've raised my boys?"

Slide, hop. Slide, hop.

"All right, I'll tell you. My boys here have been trained to obey and protect."

Slide, hop. Slide hop.

"They're trained to latch onto their target, sink their teeth in, and not let go until I say so."

Slide. Stop.

I can't outrun Bullet or Trigger.

"Ralph, I'm really sorry I got in your way. I just want to leave and we can forget all about this."

"Oh, you'll be forgotten all right. But first, don't you want to know how you screwed up?"

"I screwed up by coming here."

"That's true. But you also fell into the lazy reporter trap. You accepted the first answer presented to you. The cookies. They also happened to be easiest to orchestrate. No one even considered the coffee I made for Larry every morning."

I pivot the purse so the camera points at him. At least they'll be able to promote exclusive video of my final moments. That's if they find the purse.

"Why'd you do it?"

"Larry was a despicable human being. Portrayed himself as an animal lover, but he hunted man's best friend."

"He what?"

"When the shelter got full, Larry always offered to take some of the dogs. Everyone thought he was so generous. Claimed he found them new homes. But the bastard killed them."

"How do you know?"

"He told me. Didn't mean to. He accidentally blind copied me on an email to his disgusting friends. Larry organized hunts on his property. He had fenced land, no one around for miles. They used horses and ATVs to chase the dogs as they ran for their lives." Tears coat his face as his arms wrap around Bullet and Trigger. "He killed them. Even Max. My best buddy."

"I'm so sorry."

Sorry and scared, and sliding toward an escape. Staying quiet while Ralph seeks comfort from his companions.

Slide, hop. Slide, hop. Slide, hop. My heart is banging so hard it may burst before I reach the side of the house. I pull the car key out of my pocket. Almost there.

"Where do you think you're going?"

The key falls from my fingers when I see what's in Ralph's hand: a gun pointed straight at me.

"Ralph, please," I stammer. "Larry was repulsive. I understand why you did it."

"I never wanted it to come to this. I tried to keep you away. Why do you think I sent you on the trail of Phillip and Nacho? They had motives."

"Please, I won't tell anyone. Just let me go."

"We don't always get what we want, Jolene." Ralph edges closer, Bullet and Trigger following at his heels. "Push too hard and look what it gets you. Everyone will be talking about how that reporter was trespassing where she didn't belong."

My crutch hits a rock, throwing off my balance and knocking me to the ground.

"Oh, they'll feel bad you died, ripped to pieces. But in the same breath they'll say, 'You know, it's not the dogs' fault. She was in the wrong. She trespassed on private property. Poor dogs were just protecting their home.'"

Pushing against the gravel, I heave myself up, pebbles clinging to sweaty palms. "Ralph, you don't want to do anything you'll regret."

He stops. So do the dogs. Ralph squats between them. "Should've let sleeping dogs lie, Jolene. I'm sorry, but this is all on you."

When I close my eyes, two questions appear: How excruciating will death be? And will the hidden camera video survive?

"Police! Drop your weapon!"

Ralph and I spin toward a line of officers advancing our way.

"Drop your weapon! Now!"

Neither of us moves.

Behind the brigade, Jim shouts, "It's over, Ralph. You're surrounded. Hands up now!"

But Ralph's not willing to quit. Neither are Bullet and Trigger. They follow his glare back to me.

"Fass! Fass!"

Bullet and Trigger charge at me. Shots ring out. I swing crutches to block my body and the rapid fire of barks gets closer.

"Nein! Bleib! Bleib!"

My eyes pop open to find Jim standing between me and Bullet and Trigger.

"Platz," he orders.

Both dogs lie down, craning their necks, searching for their pack leader. Ralph is down, too, a puddle of blood spreading across his chest. But he'll have to wait for help, no one's coming to his rescue until the dogs are secured. Two officers, each carrying a pole with a cable noose at the end, go after the animals outside the fence. After sliding nooses over their heads, they lead them to the kennel. The small dog that, moments earlier, had been enjoying a bath, runs into the shed. Her buddies behind the fence unleash a chant of protests. Bullet and Trigger expand their chests and push their legs.

"Platz!" Jim lowers his voice. "Platz!"

I drift closer.

"Stay back, Jolene. We'll use a catch pole to secure them."

Bullet—or maybe Trigger—begins moaning and shaking, confusion covering his face. I set my crutches aside and sit so we're eye level.

"No, Jolene."

"Hey, boys." My voice is soft but surprisingly firm. "Burr-WE-gun. It's okay. Burr-WE-gun."

Their shaking eases. Or maybe it's mine.

"Burr-WE-gun, Bullet. Burr-WE-gun, Trigger."

When the pole-carrying officers approach, their bodies tense. Bullet—or Trigger lashes out with a string of barks. The others join him.

Jim leads me away. "Come on. We need to talk."

Blinking back tears, I watch Bullet and Trigger trying desperately to bite the pole, but the cable nooses around their necks are too tight.

"Hey, don't hurt them."

"They'll be fine." Jim directs me to the ramada. "Better to use the poles than a Taser—or worse."

I set my purse on the picnic table, lean the crutches beside it, and prop my throbbing ankle along the bench. Wish I had X-ray vision to see through the paramedics and cops encircling Ralph.

"How bad is he?"

"You're welcome, Jolene. Glad we could be of service and save your life."

"Thank you. I didn't—"

"Think? You know, after twenty years as a cop, very little shocks me. But I gotta hand it to you, Jolene. I actually had to read your text twice because I thought, 'She can't be dumb enough to go visit Ralph alone.' And what do you know? Turns out, you were."

"Hey, I was doing my job. I'm not dumb."

His arms flail. "You call this smart?"

"Let's just call it off, please. Thank you for not waiting to hear from me."

"You can thank Susan. She was terrified we were going to arrest her for murder. She called us to set the record straight. And she said you told her not to call. Please tell me she was mistaken."

"Susan was nervous, didn't think you guys would believe her. All I said was if she waited a day, I would put her in touch with you. But that's nothing, Jim. I saw the cyanide. It's in the shed. And it wasn't in the cookies."

"What?"

"The cookies were a distraction. Ralph told me he poisoned the coffee. Did you check Larry's mug?"

Jim says nothing.

"See? You do need me. Want to know why he did it?"

"We have that covered, Sherlock. We found emails on Larry's computer."

Visions of an enormous dog surface. While the Facebook photos of Max rattled me, so did Ralph's tears over losing his best buddy. His pain nicked my heart.

"What about the other guys involved?"

"Detectives tracked Larry's movements the weeks before he died. When investigators talked to the two guys Larry hunted with, they gave slightly different stories, enough to raise suspicions. One of them cracked."

"Guilt can do that."

"Wasn't remorse. No one was adopting them, he said. Most had significant health problems and behavioral issues. The way he saw it, they were doing the dogs a favor. Saving them from a life of misery." Jim notes the scene behind us. "Others might say Ralph did the real favor."

"Uh, let's not forget he wanted to kill me."

His eyes return to mine. "And let's not forget who kept that from happening. Next time check with me first, okay?"

"Next time? No, no. There will not be another time I come face-to-face with a killer."

Jim flashes a skeptical look before insisting a paramedic examine me.

After checking my pulse and blood pressure, she announces I'm fine but recommends staying off the ankle. "At the very least, try to avoid situations where you might be forced to run for your life."

"Thanks, I'll keep that in mind. Am I free to go?"

"No, you're not," Jim says. "You need to talk to detectives."

"Sure, after I talk to my boss."

"No, first you talk to us."

"Hey, I'm not a suspect. Cut me some slack, Jim."

His look cuts me down. "After what you've done, you are in no position to negotiate. You will avoid talking to anyone until we have your statement. We don't need a defense attorney showing Channel 4's exclusive interview with 'Our very own Jolene Garcia just moments after gunfire rang out.'"

"Oh, shit!" I claw at the purse. "I need to get video of Ralph before the ambulance leaves!"

Jim takes hold of a crutch. "You are on private property and this is an active crime scene. You are not authorized to shoot video for public consumption."

"But the active crime part is over."

"Don't make me confiscate your camera."

I hold up my hands. "Okay, okay. Can I please give my station a heads-up? What if someone hears this call on the scanner? Or one of your guys tips off another station? Imagine what I would have to deal with."

"Imagine if I cared."

"Jim, please. Let me give them the basics so they can start planning and send a crew to meet me at police headquarters, okay?"

His hands scrub his face.

"We won't go on the air with my role until after I've talked to detectives. I promise."

"You've got five minutes. I'm serious, Jolene. Do not mess with me."

"Understood. One last request. Can I take a couple quick pics for our website? Promise not to use them until you say we can."

His mouth opens but no words come out—only a brash exhale before he pivots to the ambulance. A bloody bandage is wrapped around Ralph's shoulder. Most of what he's saying is garbled, but I make out "self-defense" and "trespassing." As I pull out my phone, an officer orders me to stop.

"I need to make a call. It's all good. Commander Miranda knows."

"Please wait, ma'am, while I check your story."

Story?

He presses a button on his shoulder mic. I can't hear Jim, but the cop recaps the conversation. "You're clear to use your phone, ma'am. I was asked to remind you of your agreement with Commander Miranda."

"I haven't forgotten. It's been like sixty seconds."

Stomping away is impossible with crutches. Calling the newsroom is maddening.

"Stand by," Alex says over a barrage of scanner traffic. "There's a 9–98 in Laveen. Doesn't sound like any officers are down, but someone was shot."

"Wait, I—"

He puts me on hold and I'm treated to our anchors' recorded banter.

"Hi, I'm Rick. And I'm Rachel. We're so excited to share details about how you can get involved in Channel 4 Eyewitness News."

When Rick starts gushing about the social media center, I hang up and call back. "Do not put me on hold! I'm at the officer-involved shooting!"

"You're at the 9–98? Are you okay?"

"I'm fine, but only have two minutes to talk. Get Bob on the line."

Bob is more excited than when he relives the Chicago Cubs beating Cleveland in the World Series. He's a lifelong Cubs fan—even wanted to name his son Wrigley. His wife wouldn't go for it, but the family cat is named after the famous field. We go back and forth on what we can and can't publicly report at this time. We agree the station will send a text saying Ralph's been taken into custody following a shooting on his property. Nate and Elena will meet me at police headquarters and, if the timing's right, I'll sneak in a Q&A with my colleagues before talking to detectives. They can put it together so it's ready to air as soon as my interview with the police is over.

When they figure out which hospital Ralph is going to, David says they'll send a crew. "Do you want to do a debrief in studio or live shot at the hospital?"

"Hospital. And if Ralph decides to talk, I get the interview."

CHAPTER
30

Jim wants an officer to drive me to police headquarters. Claims I shouldn't be behind the wheel after a traumatic experience. But he really wants to make sure I don't report anything before talking to detectives. I decline and he assigns an officer to follow me. Elena and Nate are waiting outside the entrance.

"Oh my gosh, Jolene, I'm so glad you're safe!"

As Elena embraces me, I look over her shoulder, trying to read Nate's eyes. We haven't worked together since I flipped off JJ at church.

"You had us worried," he says. "I hope you learned a lesson."

Of course I have—not going to follow a killer into a shed again.

"Ma'am, I'm under orders to escort you directly to detectives," the officer says.

I ask for five minutes, assuring her Jim would approve. When that doesn't work, I suggest she call him. When she steps inside the building, we crank out the fastest interview of our careers. Nate catches the officer heading our way and swings the camera in the opposite direction as the door opens.

"Ma'am, come with me, please. Commander Miranda prefers you talk with detectives first."

"Of course, Officer." I whisper a warning to Nate and Elena. "Nothing can air until I'm done."

"Hold on," Nate says. "What about your video? Didn't you take the hidden camera?"

"Yes!" I open the purse and hand the recorder to Nate. "I can't believe it slipped my mind. This video is almost worth my life."

His eyes broadcast concern.

"What's wrong?"

He pushes buttons. "When was the last time you checked this?"

"Nate, do not tell me the video's not there."

"Don't freak out," he says. "But it looks like the batteries are dead."

"No, no, no!"

"Calm down. It could've just happened. I'll pull the video while you're inside."

The officer clears her throat. "Ma'am, I need you to come with me."

"Nate, if it's not there . . ."

"Everything's going to work out. We'll see you soon."

The officer leads me through two sets of locked doors to a creaky elevator that takes its time reaching the second floor. We walk along a hallway with dim fluorescent lighting, into a room that practically requires sunglasses. I sit in a folding chair at the kind of table my grandma used to set up for card games with friends. I describe how I tracked down Susan, who tipped me off to Ralph. Forty minutes and numerous questions later, the detectives promise to stay in touch as the case progresses. Before getting in the elevator, I text Elena that it's okay to run our interview and reply to David that I'm on my way to the hospital.

I walk out the front door and into a proverbial media circus. Journalists from every Phoenix outlet hover in anticipation of a juicy story. Although police have not released details of my involvement, I play it safe by avoiding eye contact—until black leather boots come into view. JJ demands to know what I was doing inside. Without a word, I step around her.

Despite being under a no-parking sign, my windshield is ticket-free. First, my life is saved, and now my wallet. Maybe I should buy a lottery ticket. As I unlock the door, a *whish* on my phone signals my station's breaking news alert.

Find out how Channel 4 Reporter Jolene Garcia helped cops catch suspect in talk show host's murder.

There's a link with details and my interview with Elena and Nate. Glancing back, I catch JJ looking up from her phone. It's too far to make out her expression, but I flaunt a million-watt smile. No way can thigh-high boots beat me this time.

Driving to the hospital, Darrell keeps me company.

"If you're just joining us, we want to bring you up to speed on the latest developments in a tragic case that impacts all of us who work at KFRK and listen to KFRK."

He shuffles papers and reads from a lawyer-approved statement.

"Ralph Flemski, longtime friend and producer for Larry Lemmon, has been arrested in connection with Larry's death. Mr. Flemski was placed under arrest at a medical facility where he was taken after a shooting at his home earlier today. We are told Mr. Flemski suffered a wound to his shoulder and is expected to remain hospitalized overnight before being transferred to the Fourth Avenue jail tomorrow." Darrell takes a heavy breath before continuing without the legalese. "To say this is shocking would be an understatement. All of us at KFRK are devastated. We expect to learn more details from police in the next few hours and, of course, will bring them to you as soon as we get them."

The detectives told me Ralph fired his gun as he was struck in the shoulder. Rather than splintering my tissue and crushing my bones, the bullet shattered a window six feet from where I stood. In the future, escaping a dog mauling and gunfire will be a personal point of pride, but right now, confirming video of my harrowing experience takes priority. If I can find parking. My laps up and down the rows finally end when another driver blocks me. I chew a thumbnail and curse his rudeness for trying to muscle an SUV into a space that's plainly too small. On his third attempt, I call the newsroom.

Alex stuns me. Not a single police code crops up before he transfers me to David.

The SUV driver finally gives up and I take the spot.

"Hey Jolene, glad to know the cops let you go. We were afraid they might lock you up after that guy's trespassing complaint."

"Your comedic skills still stink, David. But keep hope alive."

"Okay, we're even."

"Nate didn't respond to my text about my video. What's going on?"

"You're not driving, are you? Station policy doesn't allow cell phone use when—"

"I'm parked. And using speakerphone. What about my video?"

"I need to tell you something and it's going to hurt."

"No, David." It feels like a live truck is ramming my gut. "No."

"I'm sorry. The batteries in the recorder died after you left the coffee shop."

I pound the steering wheel as my brain notes the obvious: my quest for the greatest video has been quashed. And it's all my fault.

"I forgot to turn off the recorder."

An astronomical error.

"Don't beat yourself up over it," David says. "We still have you talking to Susan. Good audio and video of her detailing how Ralph paid her to deliver the cookies."

"But I had dogs sicced on me! And gunfire! And video of cyanide!"

I thought I did.

"Jolene, listen to me. You have been through an extraordinary experience. I think you should step away for a bit."

"Are you bonkers? No way am I giving this up."

"I'm only suggesting a break. We have plenty of reporters and photographers to cover all the angles."

"Excuse me, can you please get the real executive producer on the line? Because the one I know would be ecstatic to have me on the story. No one else gets to interview the guy who tried to kill me, okay? That's nonnegotiable. After I talk to him, then you and I can talk."

The scene inside the hospital is less chaotic than outside the police station. All the local media outlets are here, along with freelancers serving as placeholders until the national outlets show up. The constant stream of sick people and worried families compels us to behave as civilized humans. Most of us speak at respectable levels as we camp out in the main lobby, crammed in a corner, waiting for the hospital's public relations representative.

My photographer, Mike Cadriel, asks if I think Ralph will talk.

"Hope so. And it better not be with JJ. He owes me."

"You're probably last on his list."

Chances are some networks will engage in checkbook journalism, offering to cover Ralph's "licensing fees." That's the language they use so they can claim they're not paying for an interview while still paying for an interview. They say the "undisclosed amount" is meant to cover the use of personal photos and videos provided by the interviewee. And if the person travels to New York or another location to do the interview, the network picks up the tab for the flight, hotel, meals, and "incidentals."

ABC News caught flak after it became public the network had paid two hundred thousand dollars to the family of two-year-old Caylee Anthony. The girl's skeletal remains were found inside a bag in a wooded area near the family's home in Florida. Experts testified an air sample test from her mother's car indicated the presence of a decomposing human body. Caylee's mother was acquitted of murder and, according to court documents, the network's money went to her legal defense.

A voice calls out, "There she is," and the pack of starving journalists reacts like a five-course meal is being served.

The hospital representative pockets a lipstick and phone. "Shall I wait for everyone to set up their cameras?"

"That depends," Mike says. "Are we getting any information?"

Her face says we should be content with any morsel.

"As you all know, federal law prevents us from releasing patient information without their consent. Unless the patient authorizes the release of such information in writing, we will have no updates on the patient's condition. We have shared your interview requests and the patient has declined. That's all I have. Would anyone like me to say that on camera?"

She leaves after getting no nibbles and someone says, "TMZ has hospital pics and video."

In the photos, Ralph is being pulled out of an ambulance and pushed inside the emergency department. The video's shot too far away to make out anything useful. What's more fascinating is the audio. TMZ reports it has dramatic comments Ralph made. Gina handles that part during her live shot.

"According to TMZ, a source recorded audio of the radio

producer yelling obscenities to police and hospital staff. While we haven't been able to independently verify, TMZ also claims to have audio of Ralph Flemski saying Larry Lemmon got what he deserved, and he hopes—quote—Mr. Holier Than Thou is rotting in hell—end quote."

The next day, everyone hears from Ralph during his initial court appearance. They generally take five minutes or less. A commissioner lays out the allegations, appoints an attorney if needed, establishes conditions for release, and sets the next court date. Usually, the commissioner will ask if the defendant understands, they say yes, and move on. But not Ralph.

"I understand this is a travesty of justice," he says. "I am a defender of life and that includes the most defenseless creatures."

"Mr. Flemski, I would advise you to avoid speaking before you've had an opportunity to meet with your lawyer."

He turns to play to the audience, steel cuffs keeping his hands together.

"I am not ashamed of my actions."

I'm in the third row, the closest we're allowed, antsy for his attention—and an exclusive interview. As long as police are nearby.

"The shame is on those who take advantage of the weak like Larry Lemmon did. He got what he deserved."

"Look at me, Mr. Flemski," the commissioner demands. "Any comments you have will be addressed to the court. That means me. Based on the allegations, I am setting bail at five hundred thousand dollars cash. Please step to the side where you will receive paperwork explaining the next steps."

"I'm not done, Your Honor."

"Yes, you are. Clerk, call the next case."

Ralph is directed to a desk and handed a pen. After scribbling on papers, he shuffles past me without a glance and without the fear often visible on faces of the accused. Wearing a black-and-white-striped jumpsuit, Ralph leaves the room defiant, his head held high.

Jeff "Network" Cooper was not among the national media to book return flights to Phoenix. Still, there were enough to encourage JJ to strap on her highest heels and roam through a collection of cords, cameras, and tripods. But flashing a smile and a Phoenix connection isn't enough to make meaningful business contacts. As soon as they learn JJ is not the reporter who was nearly killed, interest disappears faster than ice cream in July. Cleavage can't compete with deadlines.

CNN requests an exclusive interview, a live segment with me outside the jail talking to Anderson Cooper from their New York studio. There's really no such thing as exclusive at this point since I've already talked to my own station, but they brand it as a "cable news exclusive." I do it partly out of spite (you watching, JJ?) but also for ego. I've never been on national TV. Note to self: accept Nacho's apology for talking to CNN before us.

While waiting to be interviewed, I ponder whether a foster parent would recognize me after all these years. Would they even remember my name? I imagine my grandma's friends watching and calling their own grandchildren to gab about my success.

When the producer says, "Stand by," a voice in my head says, "Don't mess up." I feel detached, like I'm watching someone pretend to be me. Anderson thanks me for being on his show and before I can say, "You're welcome," he's on to the next story about a congressman caught sexting an intern. I unclip my mic, thank the photographer, and almost bump into Jim.

"Hi, I didn't know you were here."

"Hard to see with all those bright network lights shining on you, huh?"

"Hey!" My elbow goes for his ribs, but the crutches limit

my range. "Listen, I really want to thank you. For everything. I know I was a little annoying at times."

"At times?"

"Okay, I was probably a little annoying most of the time. I know I created extra stress and appreciate all you've done. I especially appreciate you saving my life."

"I didn't fire the shot that hit Ralph. I just called in the cavalry."

"I'd like to send a thank-you note to the officer with great aim. How about giving me his contact info?"

"Jolene, I don't doubt your sincerity but I question your motive. The officer is not interested in publicity."

"Hey, I just want to thank him—or is it a her?"

"It's a him and I promised his name wouldn't get out. Send me the note and I'll make sure he gets it."

"Deal. Seriously, without you, I'd be dead. I can never repay you."

"Come on, don't go all soft on me. You ready for the next scoop?"

"Always. What do you have?"

He tells me Larry's ex-wife, Kelly, is organizing an event to find homes for Bullet, Trigger, and ten other dogs. Shana, the program director at KFRK, plans to promote it with Darrell serving as emcee.

"What about the guys who hunted with Larry?"

"We're recommending animal cruelty charges and it'll be up to the county attorney how to proceed. Our paperwork should be sent over by early next week. I'll give you a heads-up, but with so much interest, there are bound to be leaks, so no exclusive guarantee."

"The exclusive experience of nearly being killed should last me a while."

"Good to hear."

"Any word on Susan? How's she doing?"

"Better than she was. The city's Human Services Department got her into temporary housing. She plans to enroll in a program that helps people find jobs and permanent housing."

"That's wonderful."

"Yeah, if only more cases had positive outcomes. Listen, I gotta get back to work. Take care."

"You, too. And Jim, when you're ready for kimchi and barbe-cue, name the time and place. My treat."

On the way to the parking garage, I'm forced to weave off the sidewalk to avoid a throng of reporters and photographers. I can't see the person being interviewed. But I hear her.

"Oh, that Larry, he always counted on me to help stir things up. Even gave me a nickname—'Run 'Em Out' Rangel. Larry and I were real close. Ralph, too. You know, looking back, I could tell there was some friction between them."

By the time I get to the station, the late news is about to start. Rachel's on the set, Rick's at the social media center, and Bob is glowing as he gallops—yes, gallops—across the newsroom.

"There's our star reporter!"

He bops my shoulder. "Have you seen our ratings, Jolene? It's like we're back in the nineties. People are watching local TV news again!"

Sexy joins in, "Don't forget social media. We're trending on Twitter, we've doubled our Facebook followers, and our unique page views on the website have tripled. Tripled, Jolene!"

"So, what you're saying is we just need a reporter to come close to death and everyone's happy?"

They both laugh—too enthusiastically for my taste. I was hoping for that awkward laugh when you realize you said or did something possibly inappropriate. They're like kids watch-ing cartoons. Pure, unbridled joy. But hey, everyone's been under stress, right?

"Jolene, you have more than earned time off," Bob says. "I don't want you coming in on Monday. Have a relaxing weekend. Heck, take Tuesday off too. When you get back, we can talk about special projects. Lou mentioned a story his wife saw while visiting family back East, an investigation into unsanitary earbuds. She was shocked at the lab results."

Another note to self: find a way to avoid excessive ear wax. But for now, it can wait. I spend the weekend reading and watching too many stories about Ralph. I'm suffocating in coverage when Cruella de Vil's twin appears at my door.

"How are you feeling? Tuffy and I have been worried."

"I'm doing okay, Norma. What happened to the plum hair?"

"Too fuddy-duddy." She runs a hand along the side of her head. "This is what they call ombré. It's French for blending. What do you think?"

I think something was lost in translation. The top half of her hair is black, the bottom white. There's no blending.

"You don't have to worry about your hair clashing with anything you wear. Black and white goes with everything."

"Oh, you're so sweet. I'm sticking with this for a while. My hairdresser says changing colors is damaging my locks." She fusses with Tuffy's polka-dot bow. "You know, everyone at the beauty salon has been talking about that horrible Ralph. And Larry. Some of the ladies think Larry got what he deserved." She kisses Tuffy's head. "On the other hand, maybe Ralph should have called police as soon as he learned what was going on. Or maybe he could've roughed Larry up before the call— that would've been more acceptable. What do you think?"

"I'm trying not to think about it anymore."

"Of course. I understand." She scratches Tuffy's ear. "I have other news. Remember Oliver?"

My chest tightens and I force a nod.

"He's leaving. Moving back home to Minnesota."

Relief gushes out of my body.

"He says people there are friendlier."

"Good for him. Thanks for stopping by, Norma. I'm wiped out. I'm going to lie down now."

"Let me know if you need anything." She waves Tuffy's paw. "We'll be around."

On Monday, my binge-watching transitions from news to Netflix. Vegging out helps my ankle heal but my mind is turning to mush. I call the station and, miraculously, Alex doesn't put me on hold. I tell him I'm ready to return to work.

"Yes! I win!"

"Win what?"

"The pool we had for how long you'd stay away," he says. "David had you coming back to work tomorrow, but I'm counting this call. If you come in this afternoon, I'll split the money with you."

"I'm not coming in until tomorrow. But if it helps you collect, tell David I'm doing research from home."

"You know, you really could spend the day doing research here. Bob gave orders to take it easy on you. No running around your first day back. And you get to work with Nate on the investigation."

"Wait a minute. You can't expect me to go from identifying a killer to questioning dry cleaners."

Alex laughs. "Not that investigation. That story's dead. Nine out of ten spaghetti stains came out."

That's reassuring for my salsa snacking.

"They're moving you from entrées to desserts. They want you to investigate whether cupcakes are indeed gluten-free."

All of a sudden, chasing people with out-of-state license plates doesn't sound bad. Doesn't sound great, but it's less embarrassing than investigating cupcakes.

"What about the car registration story? Remember all those

people supposedly scamming the system to avoid paying fees? David said it was 'sexy.'"

"Not as sexy as falsely advertising cupcakes as gluten-free."

"That leaves me until tomorrow morning to come up with a real story to distract them."

"I have faith in you."

It appears Oscar has renewed faith in our relationship. Pretty sure he smiled at me today. Guess that's what happens when he gets dinner on time for three straight nights.

"Want to watch *Wheel of Fortune*?"

Oscar swims to the back of his bowl.

"Your loss."

As Vanna taps letters from the studio in Culver City, California, my mind wanders to a two-bedroom house in Omaha. Grandma would be impressed with my cable news appearance. Wish I could talk to her. The closest I get is watching someone else's grandma make it to the bonus round.

She has no trouble guessing the puzzle.

_ _ RSTIN_ _ITH PRI _ E

Neither do I.

Bursting with pride.

CHAPTER
31

TWO MONTHS LATER

This is the second-most uncomfortable night of my television career. Last year's Rocky Mountain Emmy gala was number one because I left empty-handed—and with possible organ damage, thanks to the Dillard's clerk who promised shapewear would give me confidence. In all fairness, I was desperate for a boost. Same as tonight but this time any digestive or breathing issues will be solely my fault.

My dress is long and billowy, my stomach free of constraint. To complement the rhinestone embellishment, the store's website suggested wearing diamond drop earrings and metallic silver strappy heels. I got cubic zirconia and chunky heels. I will not be remembered for falling on my butt in front of hundreds of people at the Fairmont Scottsdale Princess resort. Make it thousands. A lavish event with media people guarantees phones will be as accessible as drinks.

"Check her out," Tony says.

Tony's the firefighter I texted the day Larry Lemmon died. He was no help then but he's come through tonight. Gina wanted to set me up with a friend of a friend but I can't fake small talk when my nerves are raging. Tony's okay with being a friend date.

"Is she real?" I ask.

A figure covered in gold makeup, wearing a gold dress and gold wings, is standing on gold carpet, holding a gold atom with gold-gloved hands.

"She's real," Tony says. "She's breathing."

As we move closer, the living statue lowers her arms and rolls her shoulders. A man dressed in a tuxedo steers her to the opposite side and announces photos with Emmy will be available for twenty minutes. Suits and gowns whiz by to form a line. After ten minutes, it's obvious the photo op will wrap before we'll get to say, "Cheese," so we hit the bar. Tony supports his hometown brewery by ordering Four Peaks Kilt Lifter while I support my uneasy stomach with a Sprite. We head to the patio where Elena and her husband, Manny, are celebrating their latest work-related date night.

"We're supposed to save two seats for Gina," she says. "Her new man tends to be on the tardy side."

"She's dating the Olympian who won gold medals in track and field, right?"

I give Tony a "How do you know?" look.

"Word gets around."

Firefighters gossip more than news people, which makes them useful sources but dubious dates. We claim a table in the middle of the ballroom, far off to the side. Tables near the stage are reserved for stations that pay extra. The more you buy, the closer you get. JJ is front and center.

When Gina and her date walk in, conversations cut out. Even in a room full of designer clothes, gorgeous hair, and impeccable makeup, Gina and the Olympian dazzle. Introductions are quick because the host is lobbing jokes and dinner service is under way.

"I could use a beer," Manny says. "Think anyone will notice if I hit the bar?"

"Stay put," Elena says. "You don't want to miss your category." From the table centerpiece, courtesy of Cerreta Candy, she picks a wrapped French mint. "Pretend this is a mojito."

Once upon a time, Manny tells us, guests could drink during the ceremony, but after too many slurred speeches and raucous behavior, the awards committee cut it off. Along with acceptance speeches, because egos often equal excessive words. But if you stay through the entire event—130 categories from news, sports, and weather reporting to editing, directing, and lighting—patience is rewarded with an open bar. Free drinks last until the budget runs dry—about an hour.

Between plates of chicken cordon bleu being removed and strawberry swirl cheesecake being served, Manny receives an Emmy for a public service announcement on suicide prevention. Gina's story on the state's desert tortoise adoption program doesn't win in the feature category and she's okay with it. Tony and the Olympian are debating the pros and cons of CrossFit while I pretend a kettlebell isn't thrashing around my stomach.

Elena pats my hand and chirps, "This is your category!"

Now, a medicine ball is wedged in my throat. Four reporters, including JJ and me, are nominated in the breaking news category. I tell myself I'm okay with anyone winning except JJ. But that's a lie. Maybe I didn't deserve an Emmy last year, but if I don't get one after the Larry Lemmon ordeal, then I never will. And that cannot happen.

The clink of dishes diminishes as Ted Woods, Phoenix's favorite meteorologist, announces the nominees. If there was an Emmy for most beloved TV personality, Ted would win. Ditto for most attractive forecaster. But not for most accurate, which is why I'm grinding a thumbnail in my palm. The Oscar mix-up for best picture plays in my head. What if Ted announces my name and I accept the Emmy only to have it taken away and given to JJ?

"Whoo-hoo!" Elena is shaking my shoulder. "You won!"

Did I really miss the magic words? Gina leads a standing ovation at our table so it must be true. Walking to the stage is a bizarre experience. There's an overwhelming smell of coffee and snippets of chitchat are amplified, but faces are a blur. I manage to climb three steps without tripping and someone hands me a statuette—it's unexpectedly cold—and a photographer's camera clicks before I'm led backstage to trade the blank Emmy for an engraved one.

ROCKY MOUNTAIN EMMY

BREAKING NEWS

CATCHING A KILLER

JOLENE GARCIA

I am a winner. My peers—judges from other markets—say so. Technically, the academy says you don't win an Emmy, you earn it. But have you ever heard a person or show described as Emmy Award–earning? No matter the verb, the second-most uncomfortable night of my career becomes the best.

The next morning, a peculiar feeling stirs me awake. I flip over in bed and face Emmy. Stroking her smooth figure and curved wings, it dawns on me: the feeling is joy. The validation so foreign it frightens me. And has me longing for more.

I consider leaving Emmy on the nightstand so she's the first thing I see every morning but decide I'd rather have her welcome me home. The gold glistens against my walnut-colored IKEA table. An acceptable centerpiece, considering it's less dining table and more work desk. I open my laptop to check the Rocky Mountain Emmys Facebook page. More than five hundred photos have been posted. I skip cocktail hour pics, which leaves four hundred. Two hundred photos later, there I am, holding Emmy as naturally as a microphone.

Since we're going to be living together, I search online to learn more about her. Television engineer Louis McManus used his wife as a model, adding wings to represent the muse of art and an atom to represent the electron of science. In 1948, academy members voted for McManus's prototype. Emmy comes from Immy, a nickname for the early image orthicon camera. One company makes all the statuettes by hand. Chicago-based R.S. Owens dips each cast figure in zinc, copper, nickel, and pure silver, and finishes with twenty-four-karat gold. I stop reading when I realize I know more about Emmy than my mother.

On the drive to work Monday, I turn on KFRK. A voice I don't recognize beats the drum of border security. Maybe Ralph was right, maybe Darrell is considered too moderate for a main weekday show. I spend the morning researching food-labeling rules and gluten-free cupcakes. Now I'm craving bread, and not the gluten-free kind.

"Congratulations, Emmy Award winner," Nate says. "Ready to visit some bakeries?"

"How about a burger first?"

"Want to give Ben's another try?"

"No way. Let's skip the attitude."

"Sounds like you need Chicago Hamburger Company. And it just so happens I'm in the mood for a hot dog, Chicago style."

Fifteen minutes later, the owner, Bob Pappanduros, greets us with a smile as warm as French fries.

"Well, if it isn't my wife's favorite reporter."

I almost turn around expecting JJ.

"I think he means you," Nate says.

"Sure do. My better half started following you on Twitter during that whole Larry Lemmon thing."

So, his wife is among my seven hundred new followers.

After placing orders, we slide into a booth with a view of Chicago campaign signs going back fifty years, along with actual street signs from Clark and Addison, the famous intersection at Wrigley Field. Bob's never been clear about how the signs made it seventeen hundred miles from the Windy City to the Valley of the Sun.

Nate raises a cup. "A toast to one of my favorite reporters."

"One of? I'm not your favorite?"

"Most days." He taps my cup. "Congratulations on getting a groundbreaking exclusive and living to report it."

"I'll happily drink a Pepsi to that."

Bob presents a loaded tray: cheddar burger and garlic fries for me, Vienna dog and cheese fries for Nate. Plus, onion rings and two vanilla milkshakes.

"We didn't order all this," I say.

"Consider it a small thank-you for exposing the truth," Bob says.

"We're not allowed—"

"Thank you very much," Nate says. "We appreciate your thoughtfulness."

When Bob's out of earshot, I say, "I don't think we should accept free food."

"Jolene, it's onion rings and shakes. Not a hundred-dollar bill."

"Don't you think it's unethical?"

"How? Is this a secret payment to get us to do a positive story about the place?" He waves a spoonful of ice cream. "You may choose to deny the owner of this fine establishment the pleasure of satisfied customers, but I will not." His taste summons a look of bliss and sound of rapture. "But hey, no pressure. Shake's not that good anyway."

"You know, the station's code of conduct says we can't accept anything valued at more than twenty-five dollars. These extras don't cost that much."

With a sparkle in his eye, Nate slides the onion rings next to my burger. A familiar sound causes my fingers to drop the golden batter.

900 @ city hall. Need you 2 go.
                    900?
Check welfare.

Nate squints at the text. "That's weak."

"Like you say, there's always time to eat." As my teeth sink into cheese, my eyes slide back to the phone.

Mayor's stuck in elevator.

Good grief.

No one else available.

This better be worth it.

ACKNOWLEDGMENTS

If you're like me and read the acknowledgments first, rest assured there are no spoilers. Only gratitude.

Thank you to Anne Hillerman, the Western Writers of America, and Minotaur Books for sponsoring the Tony Hillerman Prize, and to Joe Brosnan for seeing the potential.

This is my first adventure into the world of publishing and, thanks to my agent Jill Marsal's excellent navigation skills, it's been a smooth, enjoyable journey.

As a new author, I was uncertain what to expect from an editor. I hit the jackpot with Madeline Houpt. Maddie, I asked you to push me and you did. Thank you for listening, understanding, and caring about Jolene.

As I write this, there are publishing professionals I have not yet met—and some I may never meet—who are critical to this book. It pains me not to be able to acknowledge every person who helped make my dream come true. I'm happy to thank those I can, including Andrea Morales, Meryl Levavi, Benjamin Allen, Laurie Henderson, Gail Friedman, NaNá Stoelzle, M. A. Longbrake, and Noemi Martinez Turull. To the people behind the scenes responsible for printing, binding, and shipping orders, I wish I could thank you in person.

David Rotstein, you nailed the cover. Sara Beth Haring and Hector DeJean, thank you for spreading the word in creative and authentic ways. Special thanks to the Macmillan sales team and booksellers.

Before Minotaur Books, there was Kellye Garrett and Mia P. Manansala. Your encouragement kept me writing. Your talent and generosity keep me inspired. The writing community is better because of you.

Thank you, Steven Cooper, for reading a ridiculously early draft. Looking back, I can now appreciate how kind you were. Phillip Estes was kind too, but as my brother, he's semi-obligated.

Reading J. A. Jance's Ali Reynolds series planted the seed for my writing, while Hank Phillippi Ryan's Jane Ryland series helped it grow. Thank you both for writing books that have impressed and entertained me for years.

For people who choose to spend time plotting bad things, crime fiction writers are a caring bunch. I've been fortunate to encounter many writers who believe helping others helps us all. Special thanks to International Thriller Writers for supporting debut authors and to Sisters in Crime for continuous education and advocacy.

*Write*NOW!, sponsored by Sisters in Crime Desert Sleuths, was my first writer's conference and has become a favorite annual tradition. As a founding member of Sisters in Crime Grand Canyon Writers, I've had the privilege of learning from authors who share their expertise with us every month. Thank you to the board members and volunteers who invest their time and energy to advance both outstanding groups.

Few people advocate for locally owned businesses like Brandon Stout of Changing Hands Bookstore. Brandon, thank you for showing local authors love. And to Gayle Shanks, Bob Sommer, and Cindy Dach for your lifelong devotion to the community.

I've lost count of how many times I've said "Thank you" to

Barbara Peters, owner of The Poisoned Pen Bookstore. When she learned I had received the Hillerman Prize, Barbara immediately included it in The Pen's newsletter. Barbara, your support for debut authors is beyond measure. Patrick Millikin, Patrick King, John Charles, Larry Siegel, Susan Kelly, Bill Smith, and everyone at The Pen, thank you for making me feel welcome and spreading book joy. Paul, you are missed.

While *Off the Air* is a work of fiction, it contains many real Phoenix businesses, locations, and references. Derrik Rochwalik, thank you for ensuring Metrocenter Mall's most excellent farewell. Thanks, Mike Fornelli, for confirming Phoenix's first rainbow crosswalk by mere hours. It's at Seventh Avenue and Glenrosa. Thank you, Patty Talahongva, for sharing your experiences as a student at the former Phoenix Indian School and inviting people to learn more at the visitor center located at Third Street and Indian School Road.

John Glynn with the Fairmont Scottsdale Princess resort graciously provided Emmy party décor and menu details, while Lara Gates, who successfully guided the NATAS Rocky Mountain Southwest Chapter Emmy ceremonies for many years, shared inside information I think readers will relish.

Mentioning every reporter, photographer, producer, anchor, assignment editor, and news director who supported my work, left a lasting impression, or became a friend would take almost as many pages as the novel. Rather than risk forgetting someone, I offer a group appreciation. For everyone along my news path—whether we clashed, connected, or both—thank you for experiences that have influenced my writing.

Without Phoenix, this book would not exist. When I moved to Arizona, I never expected to stay past my three-year contract. That was more than twenty years ago. Phoenix is home and I can't imagine living anywhere else—except maybe during the summer.

Mark, thanks for never asking, "Is your book done yet?"

Bentley, my four-legged angel, you were the best writing partner ever.

I'm indebted to bookmobile drivers, librarians, and assistants who nurtured my love of reading. Your jobs, always important, have become much more complex. Thank you.

To anyone reading these words, my heartfelt gratitude. There are so many wonderful books and I truly appreciate you giving me a chance. I hope you enjoy going behind the scenes of local TV news.

CONTENT ADVISORY
(IN ALPHABETICAL ORDER)

This story contains references to abandonment, ageism, animal cruelty, child neglect, classism, homelessness, racism, sexism, sexual coercion, and substance abuse.